D0109734

PHOENIXVILLE RISING

RISING

A NOVEL

Robb Cadigan

Rodgers Forge Press

Copyright © 2013 by Robb Cadigan.

All rights reserved. No part of this publication may be reproduced, distributed, or transmitted in any form or by any means without the prior written permission of the publisher, except in the case of brief quotations in reviews and certain other noncommercial uses permitted by copyright law. For permission requests, contact the author at the website below.

Robb Cadigan/Rodgers Forge Press
www.robbcadigan.com

Cover design: Larry Geiger Design
Author Photograph: Kristin Potter Dempsey / KPD Photographics
Phoenixville Photographs: Caroline Joy Photography

Phoenix Steel Corporation logo and select archival photographs courtesy of Historical Society of the Phoenixville Area.

"Heroes" (David Bowie/Brian Eno)
© 1977 Jones/Tintoretto Entertainment Co. All rights reserved.
Publisher: Tintoretto Music (BMI) administered by RZO Music, Inc., Screen Gems-EMI Music, Inc. (BMI) o/b/o EMI Publishing Ltd., Careers - BMG Music Publishing (BMI).

Publisher's Note: This is a work of fiction. Names, characters, places, and incidents are a product of the author's imagination. Locales, events, and public names are sometimes used for atmospheric purposes. Any resemblance to actual people, living or dead, or to businesses, companies, or institutions is completely coincidental.

Phoenixville Rising / Robb Cadigan.
ISBN 13: 978-0615839776
ISBN 10: 0615839770

For My Family

"Though nothing will keep us together,
We could steal time, just for one day.
We could be heroes, for ever and ever.
What do you say?"

—David Bowie, "Heroes"

"Hey! You can't be back here."

I turn towards the voice. A cop, flashlight in his hand, coming at me. I think about running. Even at my age, even after all this time, my first instinct is to run.

"You're not supposed to be in here," he says, his voice louder as he gets closer.

I point my own flashlight at him. A dark uniform, brimmed cap. Borough police, maybe, or a security guard for hire. I sweep the beam to his belt—no holster, no gun. Rent-a-cop.

"Just out for a walk," I tell him. "Good night for a walk."

He stops and cups his hand over his eyes, shielding my light, blocking the mist that's been swirling since dusk. "Not really. No, it isn't."

He's right.

October in Phoenixville always arrives on a cold wind, beneath a sky heavy and gray, as lingering memories of summer slip into sepia tones. The trees here surrender their leaves all too easily and people are quick to close their windows tight against the weather. I remember Phoenixville just this way, a perpetual October.

"You have to leave," the guard says. "This is private property. There's a sign—"

"I didn't see a sign."

I start walking again, away from the guard, away from the hole in the fence I'd climbed through to get in here. The hole beneath the sign.

"Steel-mill property," he says, coming after me. "No one's allowed back here."

I wash the empty field with my light. Nothing there. Nothing but weeds and debris and gravel roads leading nowhere. But the shadows play tricks, as they do at this time of the evening, and phantoms appear and disappear in the mist. Buildings rise from the field and Furnace Boys rise from the dead, ghosts in the machines.

"I don't see any steel mill."

"Not now, no. Gone. But the land still belongs—"

The Furnace stood just there, along the creek. The rolling mill on the distant lot, together with the shed and train tracks and a small iron bridge. I thought there would be more here. Some foundations and broken structures, fragments from those days, now covered by graffiti and littered with beer cans. Hangouts and hideaways for kids up to no good. The way we were once up to no good.

I guess part of me expected to find you out here as well, making this same walk among the ruins, revisiting these same memories. After all, our roads were parallel lines there for a time. I know this sounds crazy, but sometimes, usually in the last embers of the day, I can hear your voice again. There, floating from the shadows. There, drifting on the ripples of French Creek. Maybe this is why I've come back to Phoenixville: to hear the voices one more time.

Or maybe it's because no matter how far away I ran, I realized I could never escape. Because October always comes back around and those days are reborn, brand new and screaming.

I swore I would never return, yet here I am. Living again in Phoenixville for almost nine months now. But this is my first time inside the millyard since those days when we were teenagers. The first time looking for old ghosts. My first October since coming back.

"Mill closed down years ago," the guy tells me. "A developer owns the land now, but they ain't done nothing with it yet.

Everybody says three more years, three more years, but I've been hearing that since I got here and I got here a long time ago."

"The more things change ..." I say, almost to myself.

He puts the beam in my face again, then drops it away. "Do I know you?"

"I'm just out for a walk."

"You got kids up at the school?"

"Nah."

"From church, maybe?"

"Not really a religious man," I say, shaking my head.

He frowns as he tries to figure out what I'm doing here, trespassing. I don't look like trouble. Middle-aged, well-dressed, a banker or a lawyer. Not the kind of trouble he's paid to watch out for. Definitely not a Furnace Boy, all grown up, one of the few who made it out alive.

"Look, I won't be much longer," I tell him. The library is just a five-minute walk from here. And a thirty-year journey. Thirty years since I last set foot in that building, thirty Octobers since I last saw you. "Just give me a few more minutes."

The guard considers this, but doesn't want to go along. "You can't be in here ..."

I forgive him. He doesn't understand where we are, he doesn't know we walk on sacred ground. I raise my light one more time, letting it dance off the fog and the silhouettes of Bridge Street. My best friend died not far from here, a soldier in the field, when we were all young enough that the promise of our town was still unbroken.

Phoenixville was born in a fire. A Pennsylvania steel town not all that different from the others, at least on the surface. But you taught me to see the history beneath the currents, flowing through wars and tragedies, victories and romances and death. I get that now: we are shaped not only by our individual pasts, but by all the lives lived before and beside us. Their stories are carved into the walls around us and the pavement beneath our feet, if only we would stop to notice. This millyard, the library, every narrow street of this small town. Just like the iron and steel, I have been forged by all of this.

"It's all right, you're just doing your job," I tell the guard.

The man wipes his hand over his face. He wasn't hired to deal with me. Vagrants and delinquents, those he can handle. Not me.

"Sorry, guy, you gotta go. Now."

I've lived another lifetime since my days here, but come every October, it is as though I never left Phoenixville. My memory is triggered by the simplest acts, the smallest moments. An old sweater pulled from the back of a closet at the first chill of autumn. The stale smell of a house not visited for years. A melody, a voice, a dream in the night. The arsenal of memory. It all comes back, no matter how much we might try to let it go.

No, I'm not a religious man, but I do believe in resurrection.

"Look, you can't be back here."

I find myself too tired to argue. Besides, it's almost time to see you again. And so I turn away from this man who guards an empty field in a town still working its way back from the dead and I start walking, back the way I came.

Phoenixville was born in a fire.

And I rose from its ashes.

ONE

1980

"What's the matter, Boo, ain't you never lit no match before?"

"Shut up."

"Go on then."

"You wanna do it?"

"Chickenshit."

"How d'we know they'll even be here?"

"They'll be here."

"Yeah, but how do we know?"

"Fine, I'll light the damn thing. Jesus."

Sometimes I wonder if that is in fact how it all started. Maybe it was some point earlier, or maybe a little later. But when I really think about it, as I do most days and nights, I always come back to the matches.

We were the best of friends—two teenagers, still too young to drive—stalling for time in the emerging shadows of the old northside cemetery. We'd left our bikes back at the fence and half-walked, half-crawled out to the hilltop overlooking the small valley. We crouched behind an obelisk, tall and pale, capped by a chipped Celtic cross. Against a bruise of blue-black clouds smeared low over the town, the October sun was setting early, already weary.

I snatched the matchbook from Boo's hand and struck the flint like a pro.

"That's how you do it, see?" I held the burning match in front of me until the flame licked my fingers and I had to let go. "Nothing to it."

"Not so loud," Boo said, his voice a strained whisper, his eyes darting down to the lower cemetery field overgrown with weeds and studded with crumbling tombstones.

I laughed, but not too loud. "Nobody's gonna hear nothing. You just stay quiet, all right? You're the one we gotta worry about."

We both knew one of Boo's coughing fits would be enough to shoot the whole plan to hell. Like a car's backfire, the explosive hacking staccato could come with no warning. In the middle of class, during a movie, whenever, you could count on the phlegm-filled interruption, so violent you'd swear it was going to crack the poor guy's sternum. I always thought Boo's coughs could wake the dead. Still, I felt a momentary pang of guilt when Boo looked away, his eyes downcast.

"We set it up right, didn't we?" I asked, pointing at the knapsack Boo wore tight over his scrawny shoulders. "I mean, you didn't forget how—"

Boo bristled. "You think I'm gonna forget ..."

He wouldn't forget. This was Boo's plan, after all. It was always Boo's plan.

"Just making sure."

Boo was a runt of a kid, even smaller than I was, with baby-fine strawberry-blonde hair and goofy freckles and the perpetual cough of his illness. He was so skinny he was almost translucent. A road atlas of blue veins covered his body, which everyone made fun of when we all went swimming at the YMCA. Our friend Harley said it was like some grotesque version of the Pennsylvania Turnpike running right along Boo's back, his bony spine like the Appalachian Mountains. Boo talked all the time about lifting weights or bulking up on milk and eggs, but best anyone could tell, his daily regimen revolved exclusively around the junk he could swipe off the shelves at the 7-11. He ate non-stop, but it made no difference. Maybe Boo was just one of those guys born to be small, so everybody else could feel huge.

"Hey, Boo?"

"Yeah?"

I glanced over at him, then looked away. "Nothing."

"What?"

"You ever think about leavin'?"

"Leavin'? What, Phoenixville?"

"Uh-huh," I answered. "You ever think about just getting the hell out of here?"

"Running away?"

"Yeah, I guess so."

Boo picked at a blade of grass and twirled it between thin fingers. His nails were gnawed to the quick. "You goin' somewhere, Sketch?"

"Nah," I said right away. "I'm just sayin'. I mean, sometimes it feels like this town's all done, you know? Like everything that's ever gonna happen here has already happened."

Boo grunted. "Where you gonna go?"

"Never mind. I'm just talking, is all."

"No, no," Boo said, "every time you bring this up, I never know what the hell you're talking about. You gonna drop out of school, join the circus, what?"

"Forget it. That's what I'm talking about." I looked down into the valley again, played with the clasp on my backpack plopped next to me in the grass. I felt Boo's eyes on me, waited for it. Waited.

Finally, he pointed at my backpack and changed the subject. "What you got?"

"Not much," I said, exhaling. "Slow week, really. A tape deck out of a Ford LTD and an FM converter from a Trans Am that left his windows down."

"Windows down, dumb shit." Boo laughed and shook his head, then stopped. "Wait, that's it? Two pieces. Deacon ain't gonna be too happy with two pieces."

I shrugged. "How 'bout you then?"

He opened his own bag and gave me a glimpse of metal and wires inside. "An Alpine, two Realistics, and a Jensen, baby."

"Alpine. Nice." Alpine was always a treasure find. "Realistic is crap though."

"Plus, a CB radio out of a pickup left overnight at the bowling alley."

"A CB? Deacon doesn't want no CB!"

"Never know. He just turns 'round and sells it anyway. Somebody'll buy it. Besides, that ain't everything."

After one more look around the graveyard, Boo reached into the darkness of his backpack and pulled out a cloth. Or something wrapped in a cloth. I knew what it was before he unfolded it, but I held my breath and watched him do it anyway, hoping I would be wrong.

"What the hell, Boo—"

"From my garage hopping the other night—"

He just held the revolver there in front of him on the cloth, like it was priceless, like he was afraid to touch it. I sure as hell wasn't going to touch it.

"You can't steal a gun! Are you insane? People report those things."

"They report car stereos, too," Boo said.

"Yeah, but the cops don't waste their time looking for cheap-ass tape decks. A stolen gun they'll look for. Christ."

"You always think you know every—"

"I know, Boo. We shouldn't be messing with no guns, serious. No way."

"It's not like I can put it back," Boo said, closing the cloth and returning it to his backpack, slowly, like it was a carton of eggs. "I ain't gonna put it back."

"Shit." I didn't know what else to say.

"Whatever."

A goddamn gun.

"C'mon, let's just do this."

Still eyeing me, Boo reached into the grass between us and extracted the end of a fuse. The wire led around the obelisk and out to a spiderweb of connections stretched in a lazy arc along the edge of the valley. The strand was punctuated at perfect intervals by an array of miniature missiles, perched with care in old bottles propped against gray headstones. Beautiful rockets and whistlers we'd copped off a pyro from Boo's social-studies class. A baker's dozen. That's what the pyro had said. The guy didn't even ask what the fireworks were for, he just took our money and grinned knowingly. Partners in crime.

"What's your hurry?" Boo asked.

"I told you already," I answered, "I just can't stay long."

Boo grunted again, as he chanced another look around the obelisk. "Tara?"

"What?"

"You doin' somethin' with Tara?"

"C'mon—"

"I didn't think you even liked her."

I made a big show of tearing off another match. "I just got homework is all—"

"Shhh—" Boo held up his palm. "They're here."

The Northside Slags owned the cemetery. It had been that way since forever. The Slags owned the cemetery and the Furnace Boys ruled the old millyard. Everybody knew it, everybody liked it that way. Night after night, the rivals retreated to separate corners, where even the cops left us alone, and all was right with the world.

I leaned over Boo, who was breathing a little too quickly, and took a good, long look down into the field. Sure enough, a cluster of shadows slithered from the trees along the old entrance road. Orange glows of cigarettes bobbed like serpent eyes in front of the silhouettes. The Slags entered the valley two by two, laughing and poking each other and carrying on. Their voices, muted and indistinguishable, floated over the cemetery field like ghosts. I counted thirteen in all, another baker's dozen, and allowed myself a brief smile at the coincidence, even as I hunkered down beside Boo behind the stone. I still wasn't sure we'd chosen a spot far enough away from the Slags.

"Shit, they're here already," Boo said, his voice hushed.

"D'you think they weren't going to show?"

Boo started to respond, then caught himself, but it was too late. His eyes went wide as his whisper gave way to a brief riot of coughing, which he only just managed to stifle with the crook of his arm.

"Damn, Boo," I said, slapping him softly on the back, "shut up, would ya?"

We'd been through this before and we both knew Boo's fit could end right away or last all night. So we waited. The laughter and the muttering of the Slags consumed the cemetery. Finally, as abruptly as it had arrived, Boo's coughing subsided, his breathing resumed a steady rhythm, and I exhaled with relief.

"C'mon," I said, "let's go."

Boo didn't move. "I don't know..."

"You don't know?"

"I don't know. I mean, what the hell are we doing this for, anyways? Maybe this is stupid, us doing it by ourselves and all."

"This was your idea!"

"Yeah, but—"

"'Yeah, but.' Jesus, Boo, c'mon..."

"You ever think what might hap—"

"Deacon," I said. "We're doing this for Deacon."

Boo stopped, considered this, then a slow smile crept across his face. "Can you imagine how much he's gonna love this? When we tell him what we done, Deacon's gonna laugh his ass off. We'll be in for good, right? Furnace Boys, you and me, Sketch. In for good."

I smiled too, then patted his arm and moved around the obelisk without another word. I knew Boo would follow. Soon, we both were crawling on our bellies from monument to monument, soldiers through the weeds, until we reached the large mausoleum perched closest to the ridge. Just below us, the voices of the Slags were suddenly loud and distinct. They talked about girls and cars and nothing at all. I hardly heard them.

"Whoa, check this out," Boo whispered, pointing at a nearby tombstone, crumbling and weathered green. "Civil War."

Boo was one of those history kids, just loved everything about it. He was always talking about where we lived, with Valley Forge right around the corner and the Liberty Bell a field trip away. He ate it up, talked about it all the time.

"Civil War?"

He nodded, pointed at the dates in the stone. "Born 1845, died in 1864. Nineteen years old. Oh yeah, definitely a Union soldier. Homegrown."

Mostly, he loved the war stuff: soldiers and weapons and battlefields, all that. Me, I couldn't have cared less. But whenever Boo talked about it, I listened anyway. I guess it was fun to see him so excited about something.

"Pretty cool," I said.

"Right here in our town, man. Crazy."

I knew he would go on forever, stalling, so I took a step around the edge of the mausoleum. Without turning, I held out my hand behind me. Nothing came. I looked back through the shadows at Boo, who had the fusewire clenched like a bayonet between his teeth. Glaring, I thrust out my hand again. This time, Boo gave me the fuse.

I hoped he couldn't see my hands shake as I tore the match from the book and struck the flint. I touched the match to the wick, then dropped the wire to the ground and crouched again next to Boo, who was bouncing with what could have been either glee or fear.

As the fuse rushed around the mausoleum, its sizzle died away and for a moment I thought the flame had gone out. Then, with thirteen glorious whooshes, the rockets launched across the valley and the sky was suddenly pock-marked with small comets moving at breakneck speed. The rockets' arcs were low and precarious, weaving like drunken bats, until they burst into explosions of sound and spark that sent a united boom over the field.

It has always been some small frustration that I never knew just what the Slags did when the fireworks went off. I imagined they scattered like wild, pissing themselves and screaming like little girls. Or maybe they figured out right away just where the fuse had been lit and came running up the hill in search of their attackers.

Me and Boo, we didn't wait to find out. Victorious and laughing with abandon, we grabbed our backpacks and raced to our bikes waiting at the opposite edge of the cemetery. I reached mine first and was away before Boo even pulled his old Schwinn from the ground.

"See you later on," Boo called out. "See you at the Furnace."

The distance spread between us as I pumped my pedals hard and crested the hill by the forgotten playground. I hunched low over the handlebars and picked up speed as I raced for home. Wind in my hair and cold against my face. I didn't even glance up as I slipped beneath the rusted-out railroad bridge, where my graffiti tag from two summers before still gleamed in neon green. I only stared straight ahead, the abandoned carcass of Phoenix Iron & Steel opening up before me.

I thought I heard Boo's voice far behind, but I didn't look back. Instead, with a quick wave, I took the first turn after the creek and disappeared into the dusk, as another darkness drifted like slow ash over the tired buildings and narrow streets of the town called Phoenixville.

TWO

"Is he here yet?"

I dismounted my Mongoose and leaned the bike against the shed. Nobody looked up from the card game, so I asked again, louder this time.

"Is Deacon here?"

The twins and Harley finally shook their heads. Boo mumbled something, but his mouth was full of cheese puffs, the evidence smeared in orange fluorescence over his lips, and I had no idea what he said. Before I could ask, Tara appeared from the shadows, her head down as she kicked a rusted Yuengling beer can over the dirt.

"Hey," I said, offering a quick smile.

"Hey."

More nights than not, I was the last of our crowd to arrive at the Furnace. Sometimes it was because of homework or some chore my mother wanted me to do, but usually it was just because I couldn't get myself going for the Furnace as much anymore. Knowing Tara would be there made it a little easier. Tara was about the only thing there for me.

"Deacon didn't show yet," Harley said, as he tossed three cards into the dirt and waited for the twins to show their hands. "Maybe something happened."

I considered this, then shook my head. "Nothing happened."

Mickey flipped his cards into the pot and sat back as Markie collected his pennies and nickels. "How you know?"

15

"'Cause nothing ever happens here." I picked up a stone and sent it soaring toward the chain-link fence. The stone somehow found the NO TRESPASSING sign in the dark and a metallic echo rang through the millyard.

"Aw, you whining again, Sketch?" Harley asked. "You thinking about leaving us or something?"

I shot a dagger at Boo, who stared down at his Converse hi-tops with great concentration. "What makes you say that?"

"Everybody wants to be someplace else," Harley answered.

I snorted. "You think so, Socrates?"

"Who?" Mickey asked.

"Only thing is," Harley said, "someplace else always turns out to be just like here, you know?"

I picked up another stone, but this one I juggled a few times in my palm before absently slipping it into my pocket.

"Where've you been?" Boo asked. "I thought you were following me over."

"I told you I was gonna be late, you spaz. Had to stop back home to grab some stuff. Homework and shit."

Boo took this in. "You look like crap."

Self-conscious in front of Tara, I pushed the hair from my face and tried to shrug off the remark. "I ain't getting much sleep lately. And then school today was worse than normal. An assembly right after lunch? I could hardly keep my eyes open."

Boo cast a suspicious glance at Tara. "What, you stay out all night again?"

I shook my head. "Nah, couldn't sleep."

"Uh-huh," Boo said. "Well, you really do look like crap."

"Jesus, just didn't sleep is all."

"Gotta put away the porn after midnight, man," Harley said. "Give the boy a rest now and then."

Everyone laughed, including Tara, as I muttered, "Bite me."

Maybe figuring he'd made me look bad or something, Harley shifted the subject. "Hey, how 'bout those Phillies?"

The rest of us gave him blank looks.

"World Champions, baby," Harley said. "Didn't you see it? There's gonna be a parade tomorrow down on Broad Street."

"We get off school for it?" Markie asked.

"Nah."

"Then who gives a shit?"

Back and forth, back and forth. The back and forth was what we did, every night. We'd been hanging out at the Furnace for two years, weekends and school nights, rain or shine, because that was the way it had been ever since the steel mill closed. The way it had always been. But this was all getting old, at least for me. It was already too cold and standing under a disintegrating roof that did nothing against the wind was no longer my idea of a good time. We had to make do with the shed because only the juniors and seniors got the Furnace itself, where the darkness of the old foundry was a small price to pay for walls and places to sit and a few degrees of warmth.

This reinforcement of status also provided a lookout service for the older teens inside the Furnace. We younger guys watched for cops or the occasional high-strung parent and announced any such arrival at the top of our lungs through the main door of the Furnace. Years ago, when the mill first closed, rent-a-cops watched over the place at night, but someone decided there wasn't anything worth protecting there anymore. If kids wanted to use the place to hang out, what harm was there? Better there at the mill than having us underfoot at the diner or Tomney's Drugstore or jamming up lanes at the bowling alley.

"It's too freakin' cold for this tonight," said Harley, who complained about the temperature even more than I did. Right now, Harley was shivering like an old lady in the leather-sleeved letterman's jacket he earned last year as a freshman on the football team. Before he got kicked off for his disaster of a report card.

"Yeah," Markie agreed, "but what else we gonna do? Go hang in Boo's basement and watch reruns on that crappy little black and white?"

Boo talked through another mouthful of chips. "How about we go up to the Y, sneak a peek into the girls' locker rooms again?"

I quickly checked Tara, who showed no reaction, then shook my head. "Nah, that was stupid."

"Ring and runs?" one of the twins suggested.

"What are you," Boo scoffed, "ten years old?"

Harley let out a heavy sigh. "Man, I miss summer. Catching rays, baseball, water ice. Come on now, bring back those chicks in the little bitty bikinis with their baby oil and all that good stuff." Then, with mock sheepishness, he added, "Sorry, Tar."

Tara shrugged it off the way she shrugged off everything. She was no bigger than Boo, but somehow didn't seem even half as fragile. Her eyes, a little sad at the edges, were quick to find a smile whenever one was warranted. Her hair was a constant parade of styles and colors and, as far as I could tell, her only conceit. She'd already had three hairstyles in the two months since school started and this week she had it cut short, with a defiant streak of violet down the right side. The look had something to do with that new music she brought with her when she moved to Phoenixville from New York last summer, but I had to admit I didn't quite get it all. I pretended to like the music, of course, but Tara no doubt saw through the charade. I hadn't bought a 45 since the Woolworth's closed (and I hated venturing into Record & Tape Traders, which reeked of enough pot and incense to make anyone nauseous). Still, Tara's taste in music was another thing that made this new girl different and Phoenixville sure as hell could use a good shot of different.

As Tara trembled in the denim jacket she always wore, the one studded with *Rocky Horror* pins and New Wave buttons and an *Empire Strikes Back* patch, I thought about getting closer to her, maybe putting my arm around her, but our relationship was so new I didn't have a clue what I was supposed to do. There, in front of the guys and all. Besides, it wasn't like she was complaining about the cold. Tara never complained. She was so laid back that everyone usually forgot she was even there. Everyone but me.

"It's no big thing," Tara told Harley, "I'm cold, too."

"Anyway, we're leaving soon," I said, immediately regretting it.

"What the hell?" Boo said. "You just got here."

I shrugged, an insincere apology. "We got plans."

"We?"

"Me and Tara."

Everybody exchanged looks, not trying to hide what they were thinking. Whatever. At that point, I didn't really care.

"We're going out to Wishing Manor," Tara said.

"Wishing Manor?" Boo repeated, like his heart just cracked.

I was ready for him, I knew what he would be like. After all, we'd found the place together, me and Boo, and ever since that day he acted like we owned the old house or something.

"Whatcha two gonna do up there, Sketch?" Harley asked, leering like only Harley could leer.

"Shut up."

"Yeah, shut up," Markie said, mimicking my whine perfectly. Bastard.

"I've never been up there," Tara said. "So Sketch said he'd take me up to check it out."

"I'll bet he did," Boo muttered. I stared him down and he stopped talking, even though he obviously had something more to say. He stopped talking and he did what he always did: he started coughing, sputtering out a series of noises and convulsions that should have won him a goddamn Academy Award.

"Are you OK?" Tara asked, moving to him.

"You don't always have to mother him, he's fine," I said, waving her off. "He's faking."

"I don't think so. Look at him."

"Look at him? That's all he wants us to do! Trust me, that ain't his real cough."

Tara placed her hand on Boo's back anyway and he met it with another impressive battery of coughs. I swear he winked at me as Tara ran her hand between his shoulder blades, but I let it go. Wasn't worth it.

"You OK?" Tara asked him.

Boo nodded, then coughed some more, for good measure. Tara patted his back again. I just rolled my eyes.

Boo saw her first. That's what he always said. When Tara first arrived at school, Boo was sitting in the Principal's Office for some usual bullshit and she walked in with her mom. And Tara smiled at him. Or talked to him. Or gave him her phone number. Who knows? His story was never the same. In any case, he saw her before I did, so he didn't take it too well when Tara showed up in my math class and started helping me with homework. Soon enough, we were talking about hanging out and next thing you know, bam, next thing you know. I was never sure if Boo was angrier at Tara or me or just ticked at us both, but no matter, it was obvious that Boo sure wasn't happy with the way things went.

"You ain't gonna have time to get out to Wishing Manor," Boo said. "It's a school night."

"We're not staying long," I told him.

"Yeah, no more than fifteen minutes," Harley said.

I stopped. So over all this. Boo stopped too, but he kept staring at me, like he had something more he wanted to say. I looked away from him, my eyes landing on the backpack at his feet. The one with the gun inside.

Everyone else had grown tired of the drama and went back to the card game. Markie launched into one of his note-perfect Steve Martin "Let's Get Small" monologues and soon we were all happily distracted, so distracted we almost didn't notice the car creeping slowly outside the chain-link fence. And just like that, Boo wasn't thinking about me and Tara no more and I wasn't thinking about some stolen gun. All attention was on that slow-moving car. Boo prided himself on his lookout abilities, always bragging about some kind of internal radar, but we all knew he was just anxious to get in good with the

Furnace Boys and looked for any chance he could get to put his face in front of them. Especially Deacon.

Boo's brother hung with Deacon back in the early days of the Furnace Boys, before everything turned dark, before my brother Rusty pulled the James Dean and went and died before his time. Rusty and Boo's brother, Billy T, were fast friends, bound by a taste for risk and the stupidity of youth. Deacon was a few years younger than the rest, but things weren't as segregated back then and the younger kids like Deacon could hang in the Furnace without getting their asses handed to them. So Deacon was with them that night, the night before high-school graduation, when Rusty and Billy T led their gang to Black Rock for the pre-dawn ritual of booze and skinny dipping.

Deacon said no one saw it happen and no one ever contradicted that. He insisted all he knew was that the boys were scattered all over the dam, sliding into the water, showing off for the girls, everybody stripped and wet and buzzed with graduation and cheap beer and apple wine. Rusty must have hit the water with hardly a splash, because no one noticed he was missing for some time. Billy T went in after him, then everyone did, but Rusty struck the wall on his way down and was gone before he hit the water.

Billy T was the one who told my mother and me. He showed up at our front door as the dawn bled over his shoulder and a tired cop stood next to him on the porch with all the empathy of a statue. Billy T was never the same. Less than a week after the funeral, he left town for Wildwood and never once came back to Phoenixville. The rest of those original Furnace Boys scattered too, even as they rose to legendary status in town, the last of a breed and all that. Some to marriages or jobs in other towns, some miraculously to community college or even a state school, and some to their own individual tragedies. In many ways, Deacon was the sole survivor, a banner he wore with distinction, for anyone who cared to remember those days.

"You going, Boo?" Markie asked.

Outside the fence, the car headlights turned off.

"Think so," Boo said, with hesitation, his eyes not moving from the chain link. He knew a false alarm was only slightly better than no alarm at all.

The car door closed.

Harley sniffed in through his nostrils like a bull and twisted his neck to work out some kink. Tara slid down from her perch on a wood crate beside me and stepped back a little into the shadows of the shed. I squinted at the gate across the lot, thinking yet again of escape.

THREE

Two figures, too dark and distant to be identified, moved along the fence, looking for an opening.

"Someone we know?" Harley, ready for anything.

"Maybe." Boo, like he knew what he was talking about.

"Could be a cop." Mickey, as if no one had thought of that.

I looked over at Boo. Slags didn't often travel by car, and usually only in big groups, but you never knew.

"Boo?"

"Shh," Boo said, his voice tight, like he was stifling a cough, "let's see. Another minute."

There was a penalty for a botched lookout job, always different and never pretty.

"Why don't you get closer?" Tara suggested.

"Why don't you?" Boo answered.

"'Cause it's not my ass if it's a cop."

I snorted, but said nothing. Boo had my attention, the way he was holding his knapsack now, the way he was fingering its clasp. There was no way he was going to pull out that gun. I told myself this. No way.

When the gate rattled and the gap widened enough for the figures to slide under the chain, albeit not without some difficulty, everybody relaxed.

Deacon, with his main thug, Bigfoot Thompson. One enormous guy, the other even bigger.

"He does like to make an entrance," I said.

Deacon was impressively fat. With a wine-cask chest and beefy arms, his body still held the vestiges of a school football career gone by, but his current girth was ample evidence that television and betting halls were the closest he got to sports nowadays. Still, there was no one in town, definitely no one who hung at the Furnace, who wanted to challenge Deacon's agility. When he squeezed that body under the padlock and through the gap in the fence, it looked like some kind of magic trick. His gait hampered by battered knees, Deacon moved slower than a young man should. That past summer, he had shaved his head, which Harley said made Deacon look like a perversely terrifying version of Curly from the Three Stooges. He wore the same coat he always wore, the tattered camouflage jacket of a Poconos deer hunter. As far as anyone knew, Deacon was no deer hunter.

We all stayed quiet, just watching the two Furnace Boys walk across their millyard, heading for their hangout. They never even looked at us.

"Good thing you didn't say nothing," Harley said.

Boo shrugged. "I knew it was them."

"When d'they get a car?" I asked.

Nobody answered. Because something shocking was happening: Bigfoot had come out of the Furnace and was heading straight for us. Boo let go of the backpack and let it drop back to the ground.

"Nerds," Bigfoot said.

Boo scrambled to the front, wiggling with all the enthusiasm of a Chihuahua welcoming home its master.

"Hey, man, what's going on?"

"There's too many of you crying, brother, brother, brother."

"Uh-huh," Boo answered, clearly not understanding, but covering with a particularly dramatic coughing fit into his cupped hands.

"Deacon got a new ride there?" I asked, pointing back toward the shadow car outside the fence.

"That's my new ride, boy." Bigfoot grinned. "You like?"

"Yeah," Boo said, getting involved, like he always did, "oh, yeah. That's a sick ride, right there. I bet it's got everything—tinted windows, top-notch stereo, mag wheels, the works, right? Must have cost you, too, huh? Damn, that is *sweet*. A new car. Damn."

Boo's neediness was pitiful but harmless and although I cringed through it all, I just let him do his little lap-dog act undisturbed. Tara, on the other hand, who already was no fan of the Furnace Boys, muttered something. The utterance, indiscernible as it was, was enough to make Bigfoot turn.

"What's that, babe?" Bigfoot said, a smile smeared thick as maple syrup across his face. "You say something?"

No one else spoke, but all eyes shifted to Tara. The twins got up from their card game and stepped to the side, like cowboys in a saloon. Tara's hand found mine behind my back and gripped it tight, but no one could see.

Tara drew a breath, held it for a long minute, then slowly exhaled.

"I didn't say anything."

"Not like I go anywhere? Is that what you said?" The Furnace Boy just kept staring at Tara, sizing her up.

As Tara swallowed, I thought I recognized a flash of nervousness on her face, but it vanished quickly. I considered inserting myself, protecting my girl and all that, forging my own myth. But before I could do anything, Tara spoke again.

"Yeah," she answered. Then, perhaps to solidify her suicide, she repeated, "I said, what d'you need a car for when you guys never go anywhere."

Tara's voice sounded like it was in a vacuum, like a phone call overseas. Every other sound in the millyard had slipped away and for one excruciating minute it seemed like the rest of the world had gone dead.

Then, Bigfoot smiled broader still and placed a hand on Tara's shoulder. I wanted to kill him, but I let him do it. "I might go somewhere someday, though. Hear? I might someday."

More quiet. Then, the welcome interruption of another coughing fit from Boo broke the subsequent silence and served its purpose in separating Bigfoot and Tara from their stalemate. Over the years, I had become adept at translating Boo's coughs, the way a parent can decipher a baby's cries, and there was no question this last fit was manufactured, as much to calm the moment as it was to shift the attention back to Boo. I shot him a look and he returned it with one of artful innocence.

Chuckling, the Furnace Boy touched a palm to Tara's cheek and she flinched. The rest of us were frozen. At last, Bigfoot stepped away and looked at me.

"So, Sketch."

"Yeah?"

"You got a minute, little man?"

This was it. I was going to bear the brunt of Tara's misguided bravado. Maybe that would be the chivalrous thing to do. But why was it up to me to be chivalrous? What was Tara even doing there anyway? One morning in math class, she had asked what kids around town did for fun and then she just showed up at the millyard the next night. Nobody gave it much thought, people came and went all the time. Tara was just another Phoenixville punk in her own little rebellion against the twin forces of boredom and uptight parents. I figured she would go away soon enough, when she saw there was nothing at the millyard for her either. I let go of her hand.

"She didn't mean nothin'," I said.

"It ain't about that."

"What, then?" I asked. "You picking up the stuff tonight?"

Usually Payroll was the one who took our backpacks, emptied out the loot, gave Boo and me our cash.

"Deacon wants to see you. Inside."

Inside? Jesus. I had never been inside the Furnace before. None of us had.

"I don't know ..."

Another shattering of coughs, this series genuine, came from behind me. I ignored Boo this time and instead looked to Tara, whose blue eyes were large in the shadows, and searched for the right answer. I wanted to go inside, if only to report back, if only to look brave to the others, to Tara.

I had been favored by Deacon over the years, out of respect for Rusty no doubt, and maybe I served as some connection to those glory days. I knew it would be wrong to decline the invitation, that Deacon would see it as some kind of personal affront. Why shouldn't I go in? This was after all the reason we hung out at the millyard, a rite of passage, a stepping stone to the sanctuary of the Furnace. Still, I couldn't for the life of me imagine what Deacon could possibly want to talk about with me. From the darkness, Tara's eyes offered a message, but I couldn't read it. I avoided Boo, I already knew what Boo thought.

"Let's go," Bigfoot said. "Deacon wants to see you. There's no thinking, there's nothing else you need to know."

All the attention made me uncomfortable and I shifted under its weight. I knew the others were placing themselves into my shoes, their own answers forming, along with their jealousies and trepidations.

"What time is it?" I asked no one, anyone.

"Nine thirty," Tara answered, her voice so soft.

"What time you need to be home, Tar?"

There was the briefest of gaps then, the hesitation of a lie forming, but no one called it out. Instead, they all waited. When Tara finally answered, it was with all the assurance of someone accustomed to telling stories.

"Half hour ago."

"Uh-huh," I said. Then, to Bigfoot, "I promised Tara I'd walk her home. The girls, you know, they don't like walking alone at night no more and I told her I'd do it, I'd walk her. That's what I told her. So, why don't I just give you my backpack and ... you know—"

Bigfoot just stood there, no other response necessary.

"Damn, Sketch, somebody else can walk her home." Boo's voice was a little kid's whine. He was nearly foaming at the mouth, his body wracked from the illness and the cold October air and the eagerness. "It's Deacon, man, it's the Furnace."

He said this right out loud, with no attempt to take me aside. Bigfoot gave no indication that he'd heard Boo, although it was clear he had. I did nothing, except silently wait for time to pass.

"You come on, too, Boo," Bigfoot said. Then, no longer waiting for an answer, he turned his back on us and headed for the Furnace. Boo looked wide-eyed at me and mouthed "come on," then hopped down off the ledge, scooped up his pack, and followed the Furnace Boy. He turned once and waved for me to follow.

"Go," Tara said.

I just looked at her. "What was that? What were you doing, mouthing off like that?"

"Furnace Boys aren't nobody to be afraid of ..."

She was new. That's what I told myself. Tara was new.

"I'm not afraid—"

Tara reached over and squeezed my hand again. "Just go."

"I'll get her home, Sketch," Harley said. "Don't worry about it."

"We're going up to Wishing Manor ..."

"I'll wait," Tara said, smiling a reassuring smile. "Go."

I tried to smile too, but it didn't go so well. Then I grabbed one of my knapsacks from the handlebars of my Mongoose and followed Boo toward the looming darkness of the Furnace.

FOUR

With its multi-level roof and brick walls caked in soot, the old foundry building for Phoenix Iron & Steel—or what was left of it—stood at the corner of the millyard, just beside the creek. Its lone remaining smokestack reached into a starless night like a telescope still looking for angels who would never come.

The Furnace only received its nickname in the later years when the plant was closing and the work was being farmed out to the automated mill in Delaware. In reality, it was one of several "furnaces" on the site, although the tasks of the foundry's particular fires were specialized. Within its three enormous blast furnaces, which ran 'round the clock when the mill was at full capacity, iron was melted and molded to create the machine castings needed by the rest of the plant. Its roaring fires gave off billowing plumes of smoke, clouds so thick the children of Phoenixville swore they could climb right up onto them and come sledding back down on their Flexible Flyers. The noise of the place, the ceaseless clanging and banging, the blacksmiths striking at their anvils, the rush of the bellows, the percussion of the fire itself, this music played out at all hours, day and night, the soundtrack of a town building its history. Visitors would ask in awe how anyone could ever sleep in this town, or engage in conversation, or even think at all, but it was just background to those who lived there, as imperceptible as the steady rushing rhythm of French Creek itself.

"Sounds like you two flamers been up to no good," Bigfoot said when we reached the Furnace door.

Boo and I said nothing, because we didn't know if we were supposed to speak.

"The cemetery?" Bigfoot prompted. "Heard you started a little fire over there."

"Word travels fast," I said. I never found out how the Furnace Boys had learned about our prank so quickly.

Boo grinned. "You shoulda been there, man. Those Slags were cryin' like bitches."

"Mm-huh, aw-right. But the thing is, sometimes you'd best be careful with those little battles," Bigfoot said, "or next thing you know you got yourself a war. And I'm damn sure neither of you is built for no war."

He said nothing else, but simply opened the door and ushered us inside. Immediately, we plunged into a darkness as thick as soot and Bigfoot Thompson transformed into a mere shadow, a silhouette only just within reach. Boo and I stayed close, following Bigfoot's labored breathing as he guided us up a nearly invisible flight of metal stairs that shook with every footstep. When Boo adjusted his backpack slung over his skinny shoulder as we climbed, I did the same. My meager haul suddenly weighed a ton. At last, we reached the large open area of the second floor, where the darkness was dotted with the random glows of candles and cigarettes. A gauzy wash of light from the autumn moon and the lampposts along Bridge and Main spilled through broken windows. The floors were littered with fast-food wrappers and other debris and the whole place smelled like creosote and stale beer.

And right there, in the middle of it all, was Deacon himself, seated like a king in a black-vinyl recliner that had seen better days. How he got a recliner up there was anyone's guess and I found myself momentarily marveling at the sheer industriousness of the feat.

"Ah, the youngsters," Deacon said, his voice an oil slick over sandpaper. "Come in, boys, come in."

We inched forward. Too nervous to meet Deacon's eyes, I took a minute to look around.

Everybody was there. Payroll and Romeo, two goons who had been beside Deacon for as long as I could remember. Peanut Reynolds. Big Hal and Little Hal. Penny, Fat Tony, and Jimmy Twelve Hops. Those two inbred-looking guys from the bowling alley, the ones Boo always made fun of when they couldn't hear him. And there was a handful of girls, mostly just smoking and yakking, although one seemed to be checking me out as soon as I stepped into the room. I was too nervous to pay her much attention.

Deacon introduced us all, everyone but the girls, as though it was important to him that we all knew each other. I knew most of the Furnace Boys already. A couple of them went back to my brother's days, and a few I even talked to now and then when I saw them in town. The nicknames were so firmly ingrained I was hard pressed to remember their real names, if I ever knew them at all, and the origins of the names were just as murky. Romeo was the self-proclaimed ladies' man. Payroll was Deacon's money man, even though Deacon was the only one who ever seemed to have any cash. Jimmy Twelve Hops got his name when they were all kids skipping rocks on French Creek. Big and Little Hal were really brothers and, as far as I knew, neither was actually named Hal.

As Deacon finished the introductions, Boo started hacking up a storm, on account of the cigarette smoke (or maybe just the small fact that he was standing inside the goddamn Furnace). I pounded him on the back and, with a look of mild concern, Deacon waited for Boo to recover. When he finally did, Romeo was laughing at us.

"What'd these two do now, Deacon?"

Before Deacon answered, Payroll stepped in front of Romeo and held out his hand for our backpacks. We all watched silently as Payroll examined the stolen goods inside. My breath caught. But he never pulled out the gun. One by one, he extracted Boo's car stereos, examining each with an expert's eye. When he pulled out the CB radio from my bag, he snorted and showed it to Deacon with a bemused smile, then dropped it back into the bag without a word. When he was finished the appraisal, Payroll gave us a nod and handed the backpacks over to Little Hal.

I gave Boo a look.

The gun?

He answered me with a quick head shake. Which told me nothing.

"Those are our bags," Boo said, watching them disappear.

"Don't worry, little man, you'll get them back. Just like always," Deacon told him. "We're gonna have a quick conversation first, that's all. Let's talk in my office."

I knew the fireworks had been a stupid idea. Boo was full of stupid ideas. I imagined Deacon knew that already. I was hoping I wouldn't have to tell him.

Heads bowed, Boo and I followed Deacon to a small room in the back corner of the loft. The old supervisor's space, set off by glass-partition walls. Two of the panels were broken in half, but big shards of glass still clung to the frame. Inside, there was a dusty card table and four chairs. Deacon took a seat behind the table and motioned for us to sit. We did as we were told.

"So, here's the thing—"

"It was crazy, Deacon, you should have seen it!" Boo blurted out.

"What was?"

"The fireworks."

Deacon just stared at him.

"At the cemetery?" Boo said.

Deacon sat back, exhaled, loud and slow. "I don't know what the hell you're talking about, boy."

I jumped in before Boo could say anything more. "Why are we here?"

Deacon didn't respond to me right away. He just kept staring at Boo, like he wasn't used to being derailed. Probably because he wasn't. Deacon drew in a sharp breath, then cracked the knuckles of his beefy hands. He leaned his chair back onto its hind legs and I was sure the flimsy thing wouldn't hold him much longer.

"I wanted to see you," Deacon finally said, "because there's something I gotta go over with you. Something I should say. 'Cause of your brothers and all."

I had no idea. Not one guess.

"OK," I said into the pause that followed.

"I know you two, I know you been thinking about being Furnace Boys. I understand that, I get it. I mean, that's how it works and all. Or used to."

Boo stiffened in the seat next to me. I waited for the coughing fit. But nothing came.

"Thing is, me and the boys, we're going in what you might call a different direction," Deacon continued. His tone was calm and measured, even soft, in a way. "Things in this town, they're changing. You must see that. Of course. Everybody sees that."

I glanced over at Boo, who wasn't moving or making even one sound. He looked like he'd stopped breathing.

"Phoenixville's not the same place," I said. "You know, after the steel mill died—"

Deacon leaned back again, relaxed, and propped his feet onto a trunk that was shoved up against the office wall, one of those Army footlockers, battle green and covered with dust. It may have been my imagination, but Deacon seemed pleased I'd spoken, like he was happy for the help.

"Exactly right. This mill moved out and the whole town went to shit. Now there's no more order. We got battles breaking out right in the streets, boarded up windows on Bridge Street, the Slags taking up our business with that shit they're selling. Ain't right. Just ain't right."

"I don't understand," Boo said. He sounded like he'd just gotten younger by ten years. He was shrinking before my eyes into his brother's old corduroy coat, five sizes too big for him.

Deacon looked over at us like he'd forgotten we were there.

"Your particular skills, we don't need them anymore. Look, look, you are two of the best little thieves we've ever had. My most consistent performers, for sure. But the thing is, the future of this town ain't in car stereos no more."

Boo squirmed in his chair. "I still don't—"

Deacon sighed again. "You ain't gonna be Furnace Boys. We're changing it up, we're moving with the times and all. That's it, that's what I wanted to tell you. I figured you should hear it from me, out of respect, you know?"

Boo looked like he was going to cry. Right there, just break out into big old sobs. Jesus Christ.

"I get it," I said, even though I didn't. Not completely.

Deacon again seemed pleased by my reaction. Like he'd been braced for something else. But it wasn't like I was going to argue the point, definitely not with him.

I wasn't so sure about Boo. I figured the best thing to do would be to get the hell out of there, both of us, before anything else was said, before the world changed any more than it just had. I stood, tugging on the shoulder of Boo's coat.

"We should go," I said. "Tara's out there—"

"Tara? What, you got yourself a piece out there?" Deacon grinned that slippery grin. "Good for you, son. Good for you. Every man needs—"

"Listen, Deacon," Boo interrupted, "before you decide for sure..."

My hand fell away from Boo, the rest of me froze. I knew what was coming. I knew and suddenly I felt as though the world was closing in around us from all that darkness. Tired, exhausted, I just wanted to get back to Tara, to head out to Wishing Manor before it was too late. That was all I wanted.

All Boo wanted was to be a Furnace Boy.

"I already decided, boy," Deacon said.

"But before you make it, you know, official," Boo said. "I got something to show you."

I couldn't stop him. I couldn't move. Boo was already reaching into his jacket, pulling out the gun wrapped in that oiled cloth. He held the object out in front of him, handing it to Deacon like an offering. My throat tightened as I watched the big man unfold the cloth. One corner, two. Until the gun glistened there in the moonlight, a white stripe shimmering along its barrel. That little room had a heartbeat then, low and steady, but rising.

Finally, Deacon looked up at Boo.

"Where d'you get this?"

"Garage hopping on the northside."

"Slag territory."

"I guess."

"Mmm-huh."

Deacon placed his palm around the grip, the weight of it looking easy in his huge hand. He held the gun up in front of his face, studying it close, like it was a relic, something he'd never seen before. I seriously doubted that. The moonlight, that old moonlight, just watched it all like a silent spy.

"Lemme ask you something there, little man."

And the heartbeat pounded away.

Deacon leaned forward, right at us, close enough I could smell his after shave. Old Spice or something. "You think you can get more of these?"

I took a step back, almost to the door. I couldn't look at the gun, I couldn't look at Boo.

"Of course," Boo said. "No problem, Deacon, no problem."

I stared at my shoes.

"You sure?" Deacon asked.

"Boo, I don't—"

Boo ignored me. "No big deal at all. Easy peasy. What do you like, what are you looking for? I'll get it for you, Deacon. Anything you want."

Deacon placed the gun onto the card table between us and folded his arms over that barrel chest.

"This just might change some things," Deacon said.

Boo looked up at me, his eyes proud and beaming. I looked back at the gun.

"What do you mean?" I heard myself ask, my words sinking away into the heartbeat, now steady and loud.

Deacon looked like he was deciding whether to answer me. He just sat there, until the moonlight faded behind a cloud and he was cloaked in a new shadow.

"I mean this right here is a whole lot better than some CB radio," he said.

Slowly, carefully even, Deacon folded the cloth back over the gun and let it sit there on the table. All three of us just kept staring at the damn thing.

Finally, Deacon pulled himself to his feet. Boo stood up too.

"Looks like you boys bought yourselves a little more time," Deacon said, as he opened the office door and let it fall against the partition. "Listen, here's what we'll do: you two bring me some more of this here, say, by tomorrow night and I give you a little taste of the action, you got me? Hell, I'll throw a party for you right here in the Furnace."

"Will you make us Furnace Boys?" Boo asked.

Deacon just grinned. "You go on home now. We're done here."

As we stepped out of the office, Deacon added, "I'm handing you a gift, boys. The rest is up to you."

FIVE

"A gun?" Tara asked. "What are you talking about, 'a gun'?"

"Just what I said."

"But where did he get a gun?"

"He stole it."

"But ... why?"

We sat together on Wishing Rock, a black mass of granite that jutted out over the muddy cliff on the north bank of French Creek. Rising up from the weeds, the rock stuck out like the bow of a ship or a hand reaching toward the town. From up there, the Furnace and the mill all around it looked like nothing more than one of those train gardens people built in their basements. Small and meaningless.

"It's what he does," I told her. "We steal things."

"We?"

"Look, it's not that complicated. Boo and I have been lifting things since forever. I don't know why. Boredom, fun, whatever. No big deal. It's just always been something to do. But OK, this, this is different. I get that. I mean, until now, we were just talking about Bubble Yum and comic books and stuff. Nothing serious. Not really."

Tara was quiet for a long while. "What about the backpacks?"

"What about them?"

"What was in your backpacks?"

I pointed to the satchel I'd placed next to the rock. Tara shook her head.

"Not that one," she said. "You know what I mean. The one you took into the Furnace with—"

"Radios. Car radios."

More silence as she absorbed this. "So, not Bubble Yum and comic books."

I sighed, leaned away from her. "I guess."

"What the hell, Sketch?"

"For Deacon. The Furnace Boys. It's how it works, the whole system. Me and Boo, we boost what we can and then, when we got enough, we deliver our haul to Deacon. He gives us a little cash and we go on our way. That's all. Beats a real job."

"Like Oliver Twist," Tara muttered.

"Huh?"

"Deacon is your Fagin. He sends his little boys out into the world and you do whatever he wants. That's sick."

I didn't know what she was talking about with the Fagin stuff. "My brother did it, Boo's too. It's how they became Furnace Boys. They all did it—"

"I don't care who else was doing it!"

Her voice carried out into the landscape in front of us, rising over the rooftops and then falling away.

"So? I don't give a shit. You're not my mother."

Tara said nothing to this. She could have said a million things, yelled and screamed and carried on the way girls do. But she said nothing. That made it worse.

She just kept staring out at the town below. Few cars were on the streets, few lights burned in the windows. After ten o'clock, this town was nothing but deserted.

People said it used to be a real town way back when, but I didn't remember that. For me, the place had been dying since the day I was born. Just another on that long list of Pennsylvania steel towns that had given up the ghost. Now there were no jobs, no prospects, and all that was left was a town full of dead people who didn't even know they were dead. Like zombies out of some horror movie. But not me. I already knew I was dying too, I could feel it eating away my insides, and I sure as hell wasn't sticking around for that. Soon enough, I was going to put plenty of miles between me and this place—goodbye Phoenixville, hello Anywhere Else.

"Look, Tara, I'm sorry. I've wanted to tell you, really. Thought about it a bunch of times. But it never seemed all that important. You know, it's all been harmless stuff, nickel and dime … "

"Until now."

"Yeah, I guess."

"I had no idea."

I shrugged. "Now you do."

When I'd first found the rock, I hadn't wanted to come anywhere near it. Too close to the cliff's edge, too dangerous. But on that late afternoon a few months before, when I'd finally worked up the courage to climb out onto the rock and I let my feet dangle over its side, I was rewarded with the best view in Chester County.

For all its distress and neglect, Phoenixville remained a remarkable panorama of rooftops and smokestacks and faded billboards, nestled with stubborn dignity among the Pennsylvania hills. I could see it all from there. The church steeples and clock towers dotting the town, the vaudeville theater, the hospital on the hill, the bank and the school and of course the abandoned mill. In the distance, Valley Forge Mountain rose up to the south with its evergreens and its patriotic myths. To the north was the billowing steam of the new nuclear power plant—far away, but close enough. It was all there from the rock: something to see.

"You can't go through with it," Tara said. "You can't get involved in guns, Sketch. I don't care what Deacon wants you to do. You can't."

I turned toward her. The full moon was dim and hazy behind a bank of clouds and Tara seemed almost a ghost, an illusion. I touched my hand to her cheek, to make sure she was there. Really there.

"C'mon, don't be mad at me."

She softened, but only a little.

"I'm serious, Sketch, you can't."

"I know." I didn't want to talk about this anymore. I just wanted to be with her, to kiss her. "It's just ..."

"What? There's nothing you could say that would convince—"

"Boo. It's Boo."

"So what?"

"Forget it."

Me and Boo, we found this place. This was ours.

Despite the number of times I'd been out there, the cliff still made me nervous, its overgrown grass and tangle of weeds my only protection from a fatal plunge over the side. The French Creek below, as dark and murky as the town it bisected, had been running low of late and its exposed teeth of sharp rocks only added to the water's menace. But it was the old house looming large behind us that unsettled me the most. Back there, in the dark. The place had been abandoned for years and in all my visits I had never once seen another soul out there. Still, I kept my distance, never venturing through the trees to inspect the house up close.

I had heard the stories.

I first noticed the house when I was a kid, riding in the backseat of my mother's boat of a car, my brother Rusty riding shotgun the way he always did. It must have been winter, maybe Christmastime, because the trees were bare and my mom was driving over the bridge that led to our cousins' place. I still remember staring out the car window at the huge rising cliff, its surface jagged and raw, as if the fingers of God himself had just scraped out the creekbed and left the crude yet indelible evidence of his handiwork.

"What's that?" I asked my mother.

"What's what?"

"That big house up there." I pointed at the cliff, just to be sure she knew what I meant. "Who lives there?"

"That's Wishing Manor."

I frowned. "They call a house a name?"

"They've called it that since I was a little girl, and no one lives there. Not for a very long time."

"Ooh, don't go up there," Rusty said, turning around with an ugly sneer. "That place is haunted. Ghosts and goblins and all kinds of monsters living up there. The kind that'll rip out your guts—"

"Shut up."

"Rusty, that's enough," our mom said. Then, glancing at me in the rear-view mirror, she added, "Something very sad happened there, that's all. A long time ago."

"What?"

My mother paused a good long while, as the car slipped over the bridge and the house disappeared from view.

"I don't remember," she finally answered. But I knew she did.

From the time I got my bike and the freedom it offered, I was determined to find the path to that place. But it was more difficult than I ever imagined, as though the house, abandoned and forgotten, had been permanently cut off from the rest of the world. Whenever we could, Boo and I probed the edges of the borough, looking for some way to slip back onto the property, but the maze was impossible to decipher and even after weeks of searching, all we ever managed to do was get lost, more than a few times. Then, one day, when we were just about ready to give up the search, I found it—the hidden dirt road that whispered to me even as I rode right past it. I circled back, then—almost on a whim—plunged into the brush, venturing slowly and with growing skepticism, until the thicket finally cleared and I found the place.

"I didn't bring you out here for this," I told Tara.

She placed her hand in mine. "I know why you brought me out here."

"Can we stop talking about Boo and Furnace Boys and all that shit, just for a little?"

"Sketch ..."

I kissed her, wet and tentative. I'd only kissed a few girls by then, but none was Tara. I placed my hand at her side, beneath her jeans jacket. We kissed some more. My hand slipped under her sweater and moved north. She stopped me, holding my wrist. I pretended not to notice and she kissed me again and I let her.

After a time, we took a break.

"I brought you out here because I wanted to show you something," I said.

"I'll bet."

"No, for real."

I retrieved the satchel from the ground and pulled out the notebook I'd been carrying everywhere for months. It was a nice one, with big spiral rings and paper thick enough that my inks wouldn't bleed through. I'd paid for the thing myself, even though Boo had offered to lift it for me when we'd seen it in the office-supply store in town. I had some money that day, a ten I'd swiped from the wallet I found in the kitchen when my mother had one of her dates spend the night. It wasn't like the guy would miss it. Not as much as I would regret not taking it, anyway. So I'd slipped it into my own pocket, nothing to it.

"I wanted you to see this," I said, handing Tara the sketchbook. "It's time you see it."

I ignited a small flashlight and held it as Tara opened the notebook on her lap. She turned the pages slowly, through the dozens of patient pencil studies of church spires and the foundry's roof and the tall flagpole atop the post office. I felt some measure of pride as Tara scanned the drawings, lingering on some, going back to others, never saying a word. They were good renderings, careful and exact. No one told me otherwise. In fact, no one said anything at all, because I kept the book to myself. This way, my work was always perfection, and I was an artist. Not another teenager lost in the crowd, or a bike rat slipping through town, or the bastard son of a nurse and some random welder. There on my rock, with my pencils and that view, I was myself. Alone. And I did alone just fine.

I had always kept myself company, blessed or cursed as I was with one of those imaginations that hummed along like a kitchen appliance, always on, sometimes quiet in the background, sometimes whirring into action with the loud grinding of a well-used motor. One little trigger and I was a million miles away, so far within myself that the world could be in catastrophe and I wouldn't even notice. Up at Wishing Manor, I didn't live the puny little daydreams of other kids. Up there, my dreams were full-blown, Technicolor, million-dollar productions. It was a kind of meditation, this gift I used in secret.

My sketchbook was nearly filled with my intricate drawings of the town. Perfect pictures, entirely true to life, with one important distinction: in a town that seemed to be falling apart around me, the architecture and landscapes in my book were complete. Where I saw destruction, I drew renovation. A battered roof became whole again. Broken windows were restored. Storefronts were no longer empty, but stocked with goods to be admired by well-heeled customers. Through my pencil, the death of Phoenixville became a resurrection, a gleaming town, intact and brand-new. This was how I saw the role of the artist: to right what was wrong, to make whole what was incomplete. It was a kind of superhero skill, I thought, this ability to bring back the dead. But I knew this gift was something more than that. I truly believed that my drawings would be my ticket out of that town. Just as a basketball or a garage band or a science project would do it for others, my drawings would provide my escape.

"They're amazing," Tara said, as she closed the book. "Amazing."

"I don't know ..."

"Aw, c'mon, you know. You must know! You have a talent, a real gift," Tara said. "Well, today is just full of surprises."

She laid her head on my shoulder, her hair soft against my cheek. Vanilla and honeysuckle and the last hours of the day. We sat like that for a long while. Quiet.

"It is kind of beautiful, you know?" Tara said. "This town."

"From up here. Yeah, I guess."

"Why do you draw it all like that?" she asked. "Everything looks so ... new."

"You don't like it?"

"I didn't say that. Not at all. I was just wondering. Is that how you see the world? How you see Phoenixville? I thought you'd given up on this place."

"It ain't what it used to be."

"Was it ever?"

I held her there, her head resting on me, my arm around her shoulder. I wanted to kiss her again. To stop thinking about all this. About Furnace Boys and guns and this goddamn town.

"You know how it is when you know it's gonna rain?" I said, after a time. "Not a little drizzle or nothing, but one of those freak thunderstorms, when the sky turns all black and the wind starts gusting like wild? You know when it's coming, you can feel it in your bones. Well, that's how I feel about this place and, the thing is, it's like I'm the only one who feels it. I look around and I don't see nobody else, you know? Everyone else in this town, they're just finished. Wiped out. They're all just spent and they don't feel nothing anymore. And now those clouds are all forming right there above us and no one is even bothering to look. Something is going to happen. Something bad."

Tara raised her head and looked at me. The moonlight had emerged again from behind its cloud and caught her eyes just right. I turned back toward the Furnace, no longer so small below us.

"Maybe it's not their fault they can't see the storm, Sketch." She gestured out across the millyard and toward the Chester County hills far beyond. "Maybe you can only see it from up here."

She kissed me again. She tasted like cherry bubble gum. I hadn't noticed it before. I kissed her back, hard, and this time I kept my hands where they were. I think she liked that.

"We should go," she said, when we finally came up for air. "It's gotta be so late. My parents—"

"Yeah, all right."

I took the sketchbook from her lap and slid it back into my satchel. We both slid down from Wishing Rock.

As we pulled our bikes from the ground, Tara placed her hand on my arm.

"You have to tell him, Sketch. That's all. You have to tell Boo that you're not going to steal any more guns and he shouldn't either. We're not talking about Pepsi and Pop Rocks here. For God's sake, Sketch. Guns."

"I know!" I said, too quickly, too loud.

"Then you know I'm right."

"I'm not an idiot."

"So don't be."

I turned away, but Tara pulled me back. Then, she stepped against me, pressing her body against mine. One more kiss, this one different from the rest. I held her tight, her lips on my neck, then at my ear.

"Him or me, Sketch," she whispered. "Your call."

"Welcome, sir. Nice to have you here this evening."

The old woman in the library doorway smiles as she hands me a tri-folded brochure and directs me to the stairs.

"Thank you," I say. "It's nice to be here."

I actually mean it.

The Carnegie Room is almost full, so my seating options are limited to the back few rows. Which is just fine with me. I take a seat on a folding chair on the aisle and try to avoid eye contact with anyone. The woman next to me is knitting a scarf or some kind of sweater from a fat ball of yarn at her feet. I resist the urge to tell her that the colors don't go together. The rest of the room is full of the eager and the curious and the bored, people looking for something to do on a chilly Tuesday evening, people looking for connection. People looking for you, the hometown girl made good.

I don't see you. A quick scan of the room, but no, I don't see you.

I pretend to study the brochure for the twentieth time. Reading through your profile, the summaries of your novels, the impressive quotes from critics. I own all of your books, although I confess that I haven't read them. You may remember that I was never much of a reader. But this new book, the novel you're here to promote, this one I will read.

A man with a pleasant face and a tweed jacket steps to the podium and clears his throat. The microphone gives a jolt of feedback.

50

"Good evening, everyone. Good evening. We are so excited that all of you are joining us here tonight. We have wanted to welcome this author back to Phoenixville for quite some time and we're glad this weekend's homecoming event provides the perfect opportunity for a long-awaited reunion. Judging by the size of this crowd, you are just as enthusiastic as we are to have her here. In fact, you may be happy to know this is the largest book-signing event Phoenixville Public Library has ever hosted. That's right, ever. Yes, please, give yourselves a hand."

Robust applause all around. You have your hometown fans, to be sure. I realize a little too late that I'm not clapping. Still preoccupied, trying to find you in the crowd. Nervous that you will see me first.

"Tara Hart needs no introduction, but I will provide one anyway," the man says, eliciting some polite laughter. *"Born in Oklahoma—"*

I didn't know this. I never knew this.

"—Ms. Hart spent her youth in four different towns before she turned twenty-one. Lucky for all of us, one of those towns was Phoenixville, Pennsylvania."

Yes, lucky for us.

"Ms. Hart has been quoted as saying that her time in Phoenixville was the most formative of her early years. It was here that she discovered her love of history and the written word—perhaps in books borrowed from this very library—and began to explore her talent for creating stories of her own. Each of Ms. Hart's novels has been a NEW YORK TIMES bestseller and two have already been turned into successful television movies. Wonderful, just wonderful. But tonight, we are particularly pleased to hear about Ms. Hart's latest novel,

which is the first of her works to deal specifically with Phoenixville. Yes, how about that! THE FURNACE BOY pays homage to our town and the people who made it the great place it is today. And tonight, thanks to a special arrangement Tara has made for us with her publisher, you will be the first readers in the country to get your hands on this remarkable new novel."

The man adjusts his glasses on the bridge of his nose and peers down at his notes. "In a starred review, PUBLISHERS WEEKLY recently named THE FURNACE BOY to its list of Winter Must-Reads. The reviewer described the novel as 'a poignant historical romance with all the charms of Hart's other novels, but with a new richness born from the glowing embers of a Pennsylvania steel town.' Quite nice, yes?"

Enthusiastic nods from the crowd. Anticipation building. The woman beside me actually puts down her knitting needles.

"Well, enough of my jabbering. You didn't come out on a rainy evening to listen to me. Ladies and gentlemen, it is my distinct pleasure to welcome home to Phoenixville: the talented writer we are proud to call our own, Tara Hart."

And suddenly there you are, rising from a chair in the front row, taking your place behind the podium. The effect is immediately jarring, the photographs I've studied for so long on your book covers now suddenly come to life. You are older, of course, with hair now streaked with gray and wire-framed glasses you didn't need way back then. And beautiful, still beautiful, just as I expected.

"Thank you for that kind introduction, Vincent," you say, your voice a warm caramel, "and thank you all for coming out on a school night. I'm so pleased to see you here."

Your eyes flit around the room, never quite landing. A woman accustomed to public speaking. I slouch a little lower in my chair.

"It has indeed been much too long between visits to this borough. As Vincent said, I have lived in many different places in my life, but as I think you'll be able to tell from my new book, I have always considered Phoenixville my hometown. So I am especially pleased to be back here tonight, to be able to spend some time talking with all of you, and hearing how the town is doing now."

Then, for a moment, our eyes meet. At least, I think they do. It's hard to tell from the back row, hard to tell if that is recognition on your face or simply uncertainty. I break the connection as quickly as I can, returning again to the brochure now damp and crinkled in my hands.

"Driving along Route 29 this afternoon on my way into town, I must say I found myself wondering just what I would find here. In its earliest days, Phoenixville was a proud and prosperous milltown, as you well know. But that Phoenixville, the one I write about in THE FURNACE BOY, no longer exists. Still, when I arrived today, I was so happy to see Bridge Street is now bustling with activity and new restaurants, the stores and sidewalks are so full, and I knew that the Phoenixville of my own youth is also long gone. How interesting: two opposing but important points on Phoenixville's timeline—the boomtown of the 1800s and the declining borough I remember from my teenage years—have both disappeared.

"Or have they?

"And that is what I want to talk about tonight, the very reason I wrote THE FURNACE BOY. Our past never leaves us, never. It is always there for us to see, if we look hard enough."

The rest of the audience seems captivated, eating out of your hand, but I feel as though you are talking only to me.

"If you'll indulge me"—some false modesty here, I suspect, but you pull it off—"I'd like to read the opening chapter of the new novel. Then we'll open up the floor to questions, about this or any of my books. And finally, as I understand it, The Friends of the Library have provided some refreshments downstairs in the community room and I'll be available to sign books and say hello."

You begin to read and, as the rain drums harder against the tall windows of the library and your voice guides us back to another time, your story and my own come together once more.

THE FURNACE BOY

THE BOY FROM THE ROOF

As the final coat of paint was brushed onto the trim of the highest dormer window and the Negro man, quivering with nerves, made his way slowly down the wooden ladder, Rebecca Wilton watched it all from her favorite spot, a large rock at the eastern edge of her father's new property. In the heat of the day, with the commotion of construction loud and constant, Rebecca found the perch overlooking the creek a quiet sanctuary, a place to read her books and dream her dreams. A place to watch her new house as it rose day by day, brick by brick from the ground.

The house was something from her storybooks, more magnificent than a cathedral or the new mill itself, and seemed to Rebecca as wondrous as Arthur's Camelot. Yet, if the decision were hers to make, Rebecca Wilton would not be moving into this house. She considered such ostentation unseemly, especially in the troubled times in which the nation now found itself, and Rebecca was rarely given to displays that might call attention to her family's good fortunes. The permanence the house provided brought Rebecca the most concern. She could not escape the feeling that with this move her roots in this town would be decidedly and irrevocably in place. It was not that she wallowed in misgivings about her own hometown, but at seventeen, Rebecca believed she had not yet seen nearly enough of the world, a belief only affirmed by her recent summer sojourn to Paris and Florence. Such were her thoughts as she sat on the rock by the cliff, at once marveling at the workmanship which built this house and dreading the sight of her books and trunks being carried through the doors of Wilton Manor.

The name was her father's choice, over Rebecca's protests and less literal alternatives. Like the iron born endlessly from his factories, the name Elijah Wilton gave this new house was functional and plain, devoid of any unnecessary flourish. When the crew began using the name in conversation, Elijah considered it nothing more than a name, yet his daughter heard it only as missed opportunity. For Rebecca considered the place something else entirely, a place to start and not to stay, a place to give birth to her thousand flights of fancy. So, Rebecca Wilton gave her new home another name, Wishing Manor, if only for herself.

Father stood now on the great stone patio, talking over some final details with the old Polish foreman and his small crew, Irish and Italians and Negroes. Elijah was the tallest among them, his large hands moving in a constant blur of confident gestures, and the other men nodded in quick deference to every point he made. Occasionally, Father indicated a particular spot on the house, a window sill or a piece of quarry stone, and the head of each man turned, but it was too far for Rebecca to discern exactly what it was they were discussing. Still, the points seemed minor and, Elijah's famous fastidiousness notwithstanding, everyone seemed more than pleased with the work as it neared completion.

Some of the crew were hands on loan from the mill, able-bodied and energetic young men primarily, no doubt thrilled by the exchange of the fire of the furnaces for the lesser warmth of the summer sun. As the sun now hid more frequently behind the clouds of the coming autumn, Rebecca knew these workers were thinking with some remorse of the job's end and their imminent return to the iron mill. The summer had been long and scorching here on the hill, the crew working on the building from early morning to dusk, waking Rebecca and her father with their raised voices and weary groans and frequent bursts of laughter shared over some coarse joke the young woman strained always unsuccessfully to hear. Given to ill temper in the early-morning hours, Father always made a show of complaining about the racket when he awoke, but it seemed pointless to Rebecca. It had been his decision, after all, to live in the small, hastily fashioned cottage in the shadow of their proper house as it was being built. Noise was to be expected. In any case, noise at all hours of the day or night was certainly commonplace in a town making its living from the forges.

Rebecca first noticed the young man with the thin waist and the broad shoulders on the first day he almost died.

Sure-footed and remarkably daring, he walked the edge of the highest roof, carefully inspecting the slate shingles and pointing out damage to two younger workers who followed tentatively behind, fastened together by a short length of rope and their obvious fear. Closing her book and tucking it beneath her arm, Rebecca found her attention drawn again and again to this lithe figure silhouetted like a weathervane against the sky. The manner in which he directed the boys behind him, his posture as he walked the roof, all bespoke comfort with authority and Rebecca began to think of him as a supervisor of sorts, though he appeared at most her own age and therefore still too young for a position of any real importance on the site. Yet he moved without hesitation, bending to examine the shingles and the detailing of the new iron rail at the edge and the masonry trim at the corners. His acrobatics demanded attention and when the boy climbed with no visible effort the steep angle of the roof over what would become Rebecca's new bedroom, she was watching him. She did so as surreptitiously as she could, adjusting the brim of her wide straw hat to hide her eyes, but her gaze never wavered.

The boy negotiated the sharpest slope of the roof as though he wore gum on his very soles and, as Rebecca and his own two apprentices watched, he climbed easily to the roof's peak and wrapped his arm around the brick chimney there. Then, removing a sharp tool from the back pocket of his trousers, he bent beside the chimney and poked at its mortar. He was mesmerizing, a carnival magician's trick, and Rebecca found herself unable to turn away from him. She slipped from the rock and stood in the shadows of a wide juniper, so she might watch him less overtly.

She was pleased she did so, because at that very moment, the boy stood again and, staring into the sun, drew his long-sleeved shirt over his head. In one graceful motion, the shirt was then cast over the side of the roof, where it fluttered to the ground like a graying feather in the breeze. His bare torso was lean and taut, a body built from work, and he possessed a certain ease in this shirtless state. He was to be admired and Rebecca was at once guilty and blessed of this, which was the very reason she was watching when the boy began his remarkable fall toward the roof's waiting edge.

A pail of slates, dropped from the hand of an apprentice, was the cause, drawing attention as it crashed against the roof and then fell to the ground with the clatter of a thousand horses' hooves. Momentarily startled, Rebecca's young man lost his footing and chased the pail, his bare skin burning against the hot slate. All time froze as, gathering her crinolines, Rebecca sprinted from beneath the trees, her book falling into a high thicket of black-eyed Susans. She could not watch and she could not turn away and when the boy swung out over the edge, his legs shooting over the short rail like broken branches in a storm, Rebecca thought for a moment the small iron rail would stop his fall. But the rail was no higher than a boot, a mere ornament, and it would not hold. Rebecca knew this. It would not hold.

The boy flew over the side like a shift of snow. As the seconds slowed to a near halt, it seemed to Rebecca as if he were frozen there, hovering out over the edge for a moment, a flag unfurled. Then, the boy twisted in the air, an ungraceful pirouette, and, miracle of miracles, he caught hold of the rail behind him with an outstretched hand. His body wrenched downward, slamming against the clapboard with a sickening noise, but his grip was solder and he remained at the roof's edge, hanging there like a chimpanzee from a jungle limb. The rail, fashioned only the week prior in the furnaces of the mill, held fast.

The world accelerated. Men poured around the house from all directions, rushing to the spot on the patio directly beneath the dangling boy. The Polish foreman yelled in his language and four men came running with two long ladders tied together, the very ladder the boy had used at the other end of the house to first ascend. Desperate to help, more men than were necessary grabbed hold of this ladder and raised it to the eaves, just beside the young daredevil. With his free hand, as though he had performed this trick a hundred times, he took hold of the ladder and pulled himself upon it. Once there, he paused for quite some time to steady himself or catch his breath and, only after being so assured, released his grip on the iron cresting above him. A few steps away on the roof, the apprentices, close enough to grab the boy's arm, watched this all unfold and did nothing but stand together with mouths agape.

The boy descended the ladder slowly and carefully, dropping at last into the waiting arms of his fellows. There was a boisterous release as the men grabbed at him, laughing and clapping and swatting him with their hats. Only when Rebecca stepped into their midst did the clamoring stop and the men part enough to let her pass. She relinquished the folds of her dress, which she had been unconsciously clenching, and took the boy's hands in hers in an unexpected gesture. Rebecca showed no concern that such a gesture might seem inappropriate; she needed to touch this boy, to confirm his safety for herself, with her own hands. In a reaction unanticipated, the boy grimaced at her touch, a pained expression that flashed across his face like lightning and dissipated just as quickly.

"Good morning, Miss," the boy said, smiling a radiant smile.

"Good morning," Rebecca responded, her own voice bringing her awake. She dropped her hands to her side and struggled to keep her gaze from the boy's bare chest.

Still smiling, the boy touched his fingers to an imaginary brim and said, "A pleasure to make your acquaintance, Miss Wilton."

His voice held the unmistakable lilt of Ireland, but his enunciation was oddly crisp, uncommon to boys from the mill. His face was angular and strong, unmarked by the whiskers so in fashion with anyone who did not work near open fires all day long. But it was the boy's eyes that apprehended Rebecca so, bright eyes green as the Atlantic. The kind of eyes that might make one forget about leaving this town for world adventures. Eyes that just might make a person put down roots.

Letting go, Rebecca fell into them without another word.

SIX

I was out.

I wasn't going to steal some gun. Not for Deacon, not for my best friend, not for anyone.

Now I only had to convince Boo.

I was a sight, juggling a Koffee Kake in one hand and doing what must have been sixty miles an hour down the hill by the diner. Big fun, as Boo always said, great big fun. With every block, I struggled to avoid the slick autumn leaves, shattered like bottles over the pavement. A faded "REAGAN FOR PRESIDENT" lawn sign floated in a puddle by the curb. A town elder in torn coveralls, sharing a morning bottle in a brown bag with another man on the stoop of a deserted rowhouse, yelled at me to slow down when I nearly ran over the old guy's toes, but I hardly heard. I was flying.

I almost lost it near Buchanan, taking the corner too fast and fishtailing like crazy, but I kept it together along the west end of Bridge Street and slipped down the alley behind the old movie theater where they filmed that Steve McQueen blob movie. Almost there. Down Nailer's Row and past the weather-beaten houses that had never quite recovered from the storms three autumns before. Finally, a turn on Main and back onto Bridge Street. I barely noticed the skeleton frames of forgotten businesses there, the boarded-up windows of the old Woolworth's on the corner, the empty Laundromat, and abandoned antique shop with junk still stacked high in the front window. I skidded to a stop in front of the corner store, leaving a nice black smear on the sidewalk, and chained my Mongoose to a lamppost.

Inside Tomney's, all the world smelled like fresh coffee and fried breakfasts. At the counter, on red vinyl stools lined up like neat little mushrooms, not one of the dozen or so customers looked like he had anyplace to go. They were slumped over their folded sports pages and want ads, remnants of scrambled eggs and sausage links on their plates, as they prepared for their make-do jobs or another lost day looking for work. Occasionally they lifted their heads to argue with one another or to add two more cents to conversations that had been going on there for years. When they spoke, they did so in raised voices, so they might be heard over the AM radio dissecting the Phillies' World Series win at full volume.

The town population was shrinking, but it was a gradual ebb. There had been little change in the years immediately following the steel mill closing as most families stayed in Phoenixville, hopeful that a white knight would ride in to save the factory from destruction, or paralyzed by the realization that no such savior was on the horizon. But soon, residents departed like campfire ashes swept by an advancing breeze, first for the suburbs, then to other towns and counties altogether. Local politicians and business owners tried desperately to stem the tide, promising miraculous turn-arounds that were always just a few years away. Occasionally, new stores and restaurants opened to fuel the hopeful rumors of a pending resurrection, only to shutter their doors after mere months. From time to time, a young couple, the kind with money and a taste for nonconformity, blew into town, buying up one of the old Victorians on Main Street or opening some shop on Bridge, only to abandon their grand schemes when faced with the obvious reality. A resurrection was not coming to Phoenixville, even at fifteen I knew this, and the customers planted at Tomney's counter, this core cast of the town from long before the mill went silent, knew it too.

The frayed expressions at the counter told you as much. There sat the woman who worked at the deli, no longer offering the free slices of cheese like she had when I used to go there with my mother each week. Beside her, shoveling a platter of pancakes and syrup-soaked scrapple into his mouth, was the man from the movie theater, who always forgot to tear the tickets in half and seemed continually distracted by his own film running in his head. There too was the groundskeeper up at Roberts Baptist, who once chased Boo and me with unexpected speed when he caught us trying to steal the baby Jesus from the Nativity display two Christmases before. (It had been Boo's idea to steal the thing, with the intention of placing the Christ figure on a bench in front of the synagogue.)

Looking at their faces, melancholy and resigned, it was difficult to believe the town once operated with a common optimism. When the mill closed down, something more than jobs was lost; a sense of confidence or spirit disappeared as well. Until the town, like the steel-mill buildings themselves, was merely a shell of its former self. Places like Tomney's became a kind of purgatory, where the dying waited for the end over plates of scrambled eggs and cups of coffee and the rest waited for a new path that would never appear.

Sometimes it seemed the only person unaffected by all this change was Jacob Tomney himself, who ruled his counter with a perpetual optimism and quiet efficiency, a demeanor owing less to his discretion than the loss of much of his hearing over his eighty-four years. The man was a Phoenixville legend, presiding there since before Pearl Harbor, serving up meals from a chalkboard menu that hadn't seen much change in all that time. Thin and pale, Tomney's movements had slowed greatly in recent years, a result of the early hours he kept and the arthritis insinuating itself into his joints. The difficulty forced Tomney to take on more help, and though he occasionally took out his frustrations with his health on the boys who stocked his shelves, he always greeted an arriving customer with a warm smile whenever the front door opened.

That morning, I managed to slip into the store unnoticed, the cowbell on the front-door handle notwithstanding, and immediately headed for the back corner when I spied Boo unpacking a carton of greeting cards into a revolving rack. Boo had been working as a stockboy at Tomney's since the previous summer, which I considered some kind of miracle.

Try as I might, I still couldn't picture Boo and Tomney co-existing, especially in a little store like that—Boo had a habit of driving even the most patient person mad and Tomney never seemed like the kind of guy who would put up with too much bullshit—but so far, so good. Any other store and Boo would be robbing the place blind, but I convinced him that an inside job at a store with a handful of employees might just narrow the obvious pool of suspects a little too much. This place we left alone.

"You going to school today," I asked, kicking the box, "or you plan on just hanging out here?"

Momentarily startled and instantly coughing, Boo looked past my shoulder at the Coca-Cola clock over the coffee maker. "Shit, that what time it is already?"

"Time flies when you're bringing home minimum wage."

"More than you got going on."

I shrugged. "Ain't in no hurry to join the working class."

As Boo closed the carton and carried it back to the stock room, Tomney shuffled around the end of his counter and surprised me with a friendly swat on my shoulder.

"Here for the new comics, boy?"

"Nah," I muttered, pointing after Boo, "just getting this guy for school."

Tomney rested his hands into the waistband of his Sansabelt slacks and fixed me with a look. "School going all right?"

I knew it was probably easier just to answer, loud and plain, and be done with it. Boo always said Tomney was never going to let go of something once he got hold of it, so it was better just to tell the old guy what he wanted to hear.

"School's all right," I answered.

But of course that still wasn't enough for Tomney.

"All right, hm? What're you working on?"

"Nothing," I told him, although I knew this answer would do little to end the conversation. So, in an inspired spurt of conciliation, I added, "Just some geography. That's pretty good."

"Geography?"

"I like maps, I guess."

To my immense relief, Tomney seemed satisfied with this answer. The man took a rag from his back pocket and turned to wipe at some nonexistent smudge on the already sparkling Formica countertop. Then, someone at the other end of the counter raised an empty coffee mug and Tomney was gone.

"You ready?" Boo asked, when he appeared from the back room with his backpack pulled tight over his scrawny shoulders.

"Yeah."

Before we were two steps past the end of the counter, Tomney's voice called out to us.

"Hey, boys. D'you buy your tickets yet?"

"Son of a bitch," Boo said under his breath.

"What?" I called back, stalling.

"For the Duck Race on Saturday," Tomney said, several smiling heads turning from their breakfasts to watch the familiar tussle. "Tickets are going fast this year. Good prizes, you know. We're talking big money."

Tomney was serving his umpteenth term as president of the local Kiwanis chapter, which ran the Duck Race fundraiser at the annual homecoming celebration. For the month leading up to the event, Tomney and his fellow Kiwanians peppered everyone in town with chances to "adopt" one of the rubber ducks to be dumped off High Bridge into French Creek. The ticket numbers which matched the numbers on the first few ducks to cross the finish line beneath Low Bridge won cash and some prizes donated by the usual-suspect businesses in town. Everybody only cared about the cash.

"How much?" Boo said, though he probably had heard the answer a hundred times already.

"More than you'll make working here," Tomney said, winking at his customers. "*Big* money."

I made a show of turning my jeans pockets inside out. "I'm tapped out this morning. Maybe tomorrow."

Boo offered his own apologetic shrug as we headed for the exit. The counter resumed its breakfast, Tomney resumed his cleaning, and the morning resumed its slow march into the day. Boo's hand was on the front door when I suddenly jumped.

"Shit!" I blurted out, throwing a hand to my chest as a large figure emerged from a dark corner doorway and then moved past.

For as long as I could remember, Gargoyle had haunted Tomney's store, performing odd tasks like sweeping the sidewalk and lugging the metal syrup canisters to reload the soda dispenser. He never spoke, always moving like he was walking underwater, in his own little world. My brother had given Gargoyle his nickname, on account of the way the guy would just sit up on a favorite corner stool and hover over the counter, not doing anything. No newspaper, no magazine, nothing. Rocking like a metronome to his own internal soundtrack, Gargoyle would just stare down at the little flecks of color in the Formica. It was enough to scare away any kids thinking about shoplifting for the first time, though the man's brain was probably no more developed than theirs.

Gargoyle still intimidated the hell out of me. He was a burly man, with oversized head and hands. All flesh and acne and perspiration, he looked stuck in a perpetual adolescence. His clothes, the same greasy workshirt and ill-fitting pants he always wore, looked like they'd been retrieved from the Goodwill boxes two decades before. His face was doughy and ageless and he smelled like, well, like nothing I could identify. And the way he moved, all groggy and confused, was enough to give anyone pause about getting too close. It was like approaching a caged grizzly at the zoo when you weren't quite confident he had been pumped with enough sedatives.

With a loud laugh, Boo pushed open the front door, the cowbell rang, and we fell out onto the sidewalk.

"Gargoyle still living upstairs?" I asked as we unlocked our bikes from the lamppost in front of the store.

Boo shook his head and ripped off a bite of a red Twizzler he had retrieved from his coat pocket. "Nah, I don't think so. He just cleans up the old man's apartment every once in a while. I'm pretty sure he's living up at that place for the mentals." Boo smirked. "Still creeps you out, huh? Yeah, I know. But Tomney likes having him around, especially ever since that robbery last year. Scares off the shoplifters and the winos. You want a guard dog, that freak show is better than a German Shepherd." Boo let out a popcorn burst of a cough, spewing red bits of licorice into the air. "Don't let him bother you. I never seen him hurt nobody."

"He doesn't bother me," I said, straddling my bike. "He just surprised me coming out of that doorway is all."

Boo wiped his mouth with his sleeve and then winked.

"Right."

"Screw you," I said. "C'mon, I don't want to be late."

"Late? Listen to you," Boo said, laughing, "all the sudden you're a damn honor student."

SEVEN

The ride to the high school was not even two miles and Boo and I made it with time to spare before homeroom began. We chained our bikes to the rack and took our usual seat by the front entrance as a bus unloaded a flock of country kids. Across the street, a few burnouts huddled on Cancer Corner, smoking their last cigarettes before the start of the school day. Two Eagles fans in matching Jaworski jerseys tossed a football back and forth in the middle of the intersection. There was no sign of Tara anywhere.

My disappointment must have been obvious.

"Did you take her out there last night?" Boo asked.

"Who?"

"Shut up. Who."

I didn't bother. "Yeah. Told you I was going to."

"Wishing Manor?"

"The rock."

Boo got quiet. I glanced over at him and was surprised to see the hint of a smug smile. I couldn't take that too long.

"What?" I asked.

All innocent, Boo kept watching a group of girls he had no chance of even talking to and tried his best to look nonchalant.

"Nothing."

"Whatever."

"I just hope she made it worth your time, that's all."

I didn't like him talking like that, not about Tara. But I let it go. We had bigger things to fight about.

"Where the hell are you going to get more guns, Boo?"

He had to know it was coming, but he still didn't seem ready for it. He fidgeted next to me, scratched at his face, played with the laces on his hi-tops.

"There's places."

Another bus unloaded. Most of the students ignored us, or at best offered a quick nod, but Boo watched each of them with suspicion. When he spoke again, he used a ridiculous conspiratorial whisper, so faint I had to keep leaning forward to hear.

"Besides, I'm not stealing more guns." But before I could feel any sense of relief, he added, "I got a better idea."

Nothing good ever came from Boo's "better ideas."

"I'm not doing it, Boo."

"What are you talking about?"

"I'm not doing it," I said. "I ain't stealing no gun. I ain't stealing anything else."

"You haven't even heard my idea."

"Don't have to. I ain't doing it."

In response, Boo let loose an impressive string of coughs. Frantically, he extracted his inhaler from his jeans and took a hit. Boo appeared more fragile this morning, if that was even possible, with his body buried in that damned old coat. His eyes were deep-set, the rings underneath so dark they looked like shiners. His skin was crazy pale. In an attempt to look casual, Boo slumped back against the brick wall, but he succeeded only at appearing a couple breaths away from collapse.

"Just listen," he said.

"Boo—"

"Two words," Boo said, holding up two fingers as he kept staring at me. "E.J. Wilton."

I was too tired to debate whether this was in fact three words. Instead, I sat in silence, smothering another yawn.

"You know him, don't you?" Boo asked.

"Sure, yeah," I answered. "The guy who started the town. Our founder or whatever. What about him?"

"Damn, don't you pay attention to nothing going on around here anymore?" Boo said, folding his arms over his chest. "You know that celebration on Saturday—homecoming? OK, so guess who's coming back for the festivities?"

"E.J. Wilton," I answered, searching for the thread. I couldn't imagine where Boo was going with this.

"Hey, Sherlock," Boo told me, quite serious, "Wilton is dead."

"No shit, Boo."

"Yeah, the guy is dead, but the library's got the next best thing," Boo said. "They got some long-lost Wilton relative coming back to dedicate this exhibit. See, the family donated a bunch of antiques and shit for the celebration—"

"An exhibit."

"No, no, listen to me," Boo said, growing impatient, "the library's got an exhibit all about this guy, Wilton, his whole family. I seen it the other day."

"What were you doing in a library?"

"Returning some war books. What? I read."

"All right."

"Anyway, they got papers Wilton wrote, and clothes he wore, and books—all that, a ton of stuff. Valuable stuff, antique and rare and valuable. In the library. Right out in the open."

And there it was. The connection, still unclear, but it was there. So now, although I still saw only a hazy picture, I was not just a little concerned. If Boo was serious about some plan, a plan involving an exhibit honoring Phoenixville's most prominent forefather, then I knew very little good could possibly come of that. I should turn and run in the other direction, no question.

"OK, so the library has this exhibit," I repeated, slowly.

"Right," Boo said. "And in this exhibit, there's a necklace ..."

The picture became a little clearer.

"A *valuable* necklace ..."

Clearer still.

"A necklace they call the Black Diamond."

"Black Diamond," I repeated.

"And you and me, Sketch, we're going to steal it."

Boo suddenly laughed, clapping his hands together. This outburst was, of course, followed by another steady stream of coughs and wheezing. In the distraction, I scrambled for some foothold.

When Boo finally quieted down, I said, "You can't just walk in and steal a necklace."

He smirked, all confidence. Somehow. "'Course we can. We're Butch and Sundance, man. This is nothing, I'm telling you. This'll be just like boosting Milky Ways." Boo snapped his fingers. "Nothing to it."

"But what the hell d'you wanna steal a necklace for?"

"Do you have any idea what a necklace like that is worth, Sketch? What someone would pay? I give that to Deacon and all he has to do is sell it off somewhere and hell, he could buy himself a whole truckload of guns."

"You're a moron, Boo. Seriously."

He looked hurt again, but I didn't care anymore.

"It'll be cake, I'm telling you," Boo said, not sounding quite as confident as before. "Those idiots are practically handing it to us. See, they keep the jewelry in a glass case right out in the open, just like I said. It's a simple smash-and-grab. Stupid-ass library, they're practically *begging* us to take it."

"I don't know," I said, trying to think. "I heard that place is haunted."

"Haunted? Shiiit."

"Seriously, some kind of ghost in there," I said. My brother used to tell me the stories late at night, scaring the crap out of me with tales of headless librarians and flying books. "That's what I heard."

"Ghost," Boo said, laughing.

I tried another approach. "Besides, don't they have a guard or something? If that necklace—"

"Black Diamond."

"If it's as valuable as you say, they can't just leave it sitting there like that—"

Boo made a dismissive sound and waved his hand at me.

"—without someone watching over it. Boo, I'm telling you right now, this is some stupid shit. How d'you even know that necklace is worth anything at all? It's just some old jewelry, maybe it don't mean anything. If the library doesn't even put a guard on it, doesn't that tell you something right there?"

"Yeah, it tells me they don't know what they got," Boo answered. "We're in Phoenixville, man. Ain't nobody gonna think big enough to do something like this. Well, almost nobody. No, they don't have no guard. They don't expect this. Believe me, they probably don't even know what an old necklace like that is really worth."

"Boo, they know," I said.

"Sketch, listen to me. This is it," Boo said. "We do this and Deacon *has* to make us Furnace Boys. He has to."

"Who gives a shit about the Furnace Boys? Who gives a shit about Deacon? Deacon is insane."

Boo laughed, like I'd made some joke. "Bull."

"No bull," I said. "To hell with Deacon."

"Doubt you'd be saying that if he was sitting here next to us."

"The Furnace Boys, too—"

"Hold up," Boo suddenly said, raising his palm at me. "Chalkboard coming."

As Boo sat up a little straighter, I turned to find Ms. Crowe heading our way.

Crowe was my homeroom advisor and taught me English Lit. Or tried to. Tall and still kind of thin despite her pregnancy, she walked with the self-conscious waddle of a woman unaccustomed to her new belly. She was my favorite teacher in the school, by a long shot. Not that I would ever let her know that, of course.

"Mister Walker," Crowe said as she reached the front entrance.

"Hey," I mumbled.

Then, glancing at Boo, Crowe nodded. "Franklin."

Boo thrust his chin forward in half-hearted greeting.

"About time to head in," Crowe told us.

"Uh-huh."

The teacher nodded and started to negotiate the stairs, her hand firmly on the railing. Then, she turned back and asked, "Will I see any of your art at the celebration this weekend, Mister Walker?"

"Doubt it, no," I told her.

It drove me crazy, the way Crowe was always bringing up my artwork. Apparently, I'd pissed off the art teacher when I rejected his request to draw some dumb school-play posters and the old guy got so frustrated that he had confided in Ms. Crowe. Crowe, in turn, asked to see more of my drawings, which I denied having. Still, the few assignments I had to complete in art class confirmed Crowe's suspicions. Now, like every other adult out there, the woman just never let it go.

"I see." Crowe frowned with disappointment and rubbed her hand over her belly. I couldn't help but notice her breasts looked bigger today, but I did my best to make sure she didn't catch me looking. "Tell me, that information you asked for, did you give it to your mother?"

I gave her my best blank stare, but I knew I was busted.

"The packet I gave you last week?" Crowe prompted.

I closed my eyes and wished the woman would just go inside. "Yeah," I answered. She probably was going to accept the lie, or at least let it float by, until I inexplicably blew it by adding, "I think so."

Crowe sighed and considered me for an exhausting moment. I couldn't look her in the eyes. "Stop by my classroom at the end of the day and I'll have another packet for you to take home. Or should I mail it to her?"

"No," I answered, "I'll give it to her ... um, you know, again."

Crowe's eyes narrowed.

"Really," I insisted.

This time, the woman left the lie dormant, nodded her head at us, then pulled herself ungracefully up the front steps and disappeared into the building.

"What the hell was that about?" Boo asked.

"No big deal. Just some test stuff I screwed up."

"Oh, been there."

"It's nothing."

Boo kept staring after Crowe, who was long gone. He stroked his puny chin with bony fingers, bright red, as though they had just been slapped.

"Nice rack."

"C'mon, Boo, she's preggers."

"What, you tellin' me you don't have a thing for her?"

"Dream on."

Boo shoved my shoulder. "Thought so."

We sat in silence for a while, watching the school wake up, the rest of the students arriving, the teachers herding them in. I was glad to have this time with Boo—we usually didn't see much of each other at school. Boo was a grade behind, because he was held back when he missed so much time during one of his hospital stays back in third grade. The kid had been playing catch up ever since.

"We can be heroes."

Boo said this so quietly that at first I wasn't sure I'd heard him right. When I looked over at him, Boo was just staring at me, intent.

"You and me, Sketch. We can be heroes, right here. We steal the necklace tonight, hand it over to Deacon, and—boom, just like that—Furnace Boys. The first guys to make Furnace Boy before junior year."

"Boo ..."

"Before our brothers, even."

Although the morning started off clear, the sky had taken on an ugly gray pallor, far too dark for this hour of the day.

The trees in the neighborhood across the street swayed with the breeze, their leaves overturned like skirts blown open. I zipped my coat to my throat and knocked my shoes against the steps.

"How would you even do it?" I heard myself ask.

Boo scanned the sidewalk again, let a group of kids walk by, then leaned into me. He still smelled like Twizzlers. "I got it all figured out. Remember how we snuck into that concert up at the college last year, the one where that girl puked all over the parking lot? How we just went in early, before any ticket takers showed up? We do it just like that. We go in the library after dinner, find a place to hide when they close up, then we do our thing and walk right out the door."

"You'll set off the alarm on the way out."

Boo looked skeptical. Then he shook his head. "Alarms are for stopping you from breaking in and I ain't breaking in. I'm already in. That's the beauty of it."

For as long as we'd known each other, since kindergarten, Boo and I had shared everything. But I knew he would have to do this job alone. It wasn't because I thought I was somehow better than Boo, but because, like a leaf caught in the current, I felt myself being pulled away little by little from my own life now. I also knew Boo would screw this up, there wasn't a doubt in my mind about that, and I knew I would never convince him of the sheer stupidity of this scheme. Now I stared at Boo, this little punk of a kid who just yesterday was crying over not getting picked for kickball, and said the only thing I could think to say.

"You're out of your damn mind."

Boo chuckled a bit before he needed to stifle the sound to prevent it from transforming into another vicious coughing fit. When he talked, it sounded like a smoker who hadn't yet exhaled. "I'm out of my mind? What's that make you? Deacon wants you, too—don't forget that. Why do you think that is, Sketch? Because there was a time not so long ago when you would do this in a heartbeat." Boo shook his head. "I don't know what's happening to you."

"Whatever."

"Yeah, whatever. That's all you ever say now," Boo said. "Lemme ask you one thing, all right? Is this because of Tara?"

"Is what because of—"

"Come off it! You know what I'm saying. Why are you going chickenshit all the sudden? 'Cause of her? Some girl?"

Boo looked so tiny, broken, like a discarded toy. One of the things I always admired about Boo, one of the traits the kid had always displayed, was that he just didn't know how small he was. Fragile was about the last word Boo would use to describe himself. Sure, he was ill, but lots of people were sick. And Boo had been sick so long, coughing that cough everywhere he went, that everyone forgot about it all. No, despite his affliction, his slight stature, and the nervous expression he always seemed to wear, Boo didn't see himself as small or ill or fragile. In fact, in his own mind, Boo was blessed with superhero nerves, balls of steel. This bravado made his nickname all the more comical, but Boo long ago convinced himself that the nickname was an ironic badge of honor. Maybe he knew his life would be more difficult than others around him, maybe the illness gave him a devil-may-care attitude about some things, but there was no doubt that Boo would make the most of his time here. And in that, I always believed, there was something to admire.

"I can't do it, Boo. I won't do it," I said. "Something's gonna go wrong—"

"How come you're so sure about that?" Boo was practically shouting now, his whispers of conspiracy shot to hell. "You're the one who usually pulls off this shit, and don't tell me different. Come on, Sketch, all the pranks you've done. It's us here, it's Boo you're talking to, remember? What makes you so sure something's gonna go wrong?"

I pretended to be fascinated by the words chiseled into the cornerstone behind us: PHOENIXVILLE AREA HIGH SCHOOL. Someone had crossed out "AREA" and scratched the word "ALWAYS" above it. I ran my finger over the white etching.

"What makes me so sure? Because it's you, Boo."

My words opened a gate into a long pause. I listened to the whine of the wind and waited.

"Go to hell."

"I just mean you're not a thief," I said. "Not like this. It's a compliment."

Boo pulled himself tall, as tall as he got. "Maybe I *am* a thief."

I released the letters into the stone again and watched them sink away. "This ain't baseball cards and Snickers bars. This is different, Boo, this is … real."

"Real as it gets," Boo agreed, with emphasis.

"I can't do it."

"You have to."

"I just can't."

"Gentlemen!"

The vice principal's voice, a baritone that didn't match his slight frame, called from the doorway. When we looked his way, the little man with a constantly surly expression pointed to his watch in an exaggerated motion.

"Showtime," I muttered.

Then, before I could go inside, Boo grabbed my arm and held me back. "This is how it happens, Sketch, this is how it starts."

"How it starts?"

"No more waiting for your life to begin," Boo said, entirely convinced, "don't you see? We're the next generation. Deacon is stepping away—you know he's into all kinds of shit now and it ain't kid stuff no more. It's only a matter of time before he leaves the Furnace. Anybody can tell that and nobody's stepping up. Bigfoot? Payroll? Them guys are nothing but muscle, man, they ain't Deacon. Don't think Deacon doesn't realize that, neither. He said as much last night. I'm tellin' you, he's watching out for us. This is our test, our—you know—our rite of passage. A gift, just like he said, and he's giving it to us right on a goddamn silver platter, if we want it. And I want it. Otherwise, what do I got?" Boo's eyes were tired, imploring, searching me for some evidence of agreement or, at a minimum, understanding. Finding none, he repeated, "What do I got?"

I watched an amber leaf skitter over the pavement at my feet. I poked it with the toe of my sneakers. "This is what you want to be?"

"It's who we are, Sketch."

The wind scooped the leaf from the ground and carried it away.

"It's not who I am," I answered.

We walked silently back into the school building, parting at the first corridor. I didn't turn to watch Boo go, but I couldn't avoid the squeaking of his sneakers as it faded down the hall. I knew this plan would change everything between us, and that fact alone broke my heart. As Boo disappeared from view, I found myself thinking of the fence around the steel mill and its futile efforts to contain the past. Now I had to do the same thing: protect what I had with Boo, protect my own past, or surrender it to a tomorrow I knew I didn't want.

Unfortunately, I didn't have a clue how I might do that. Not in the least.

I HAVE THOUGHT OF YOU OFTEN

Though she rarely went a day without thinking of him, Rebecca did not expect to see the boy from the roof ever again. After all, Phoenixville was already a large town and growing still and Rebecca infrequently ventured beyond the borders of her new home, except for the weekly ride to church and an occasional visit to Baron Brothers' Dry Goods on Bridge Street. In the deepest hours of the evening, however, when her books were set aside and Rebecca lost herself in that ether just before dreams, the thoughts of the tow-headed boys from church or the handsome piano teacher with his impeccable fashions were consistently shunted aside by the vision of the shirtless boy standing atop the roof, the same roof now over her head.

His name was Shane Ryan Hughes. Before his temporary assignment as a crew steward at the manor construction, Shane served as a blacksmith apprentice in the foundry at Phoenix Iron Works, the job to which he returned at the summer's end. His work there was long and exhausting, consisting primarily of shoveling coal, tending the fires, and keeping the forges clean. The position came with the benefit of room and board at the home of the blacksmith, an enormous Hungarian named Lovas. Lovas and his family lived on Nailer's Row, a stone's throw from the foundry's doors, though its proximity meant little to Shane as he spent most of his hours at the furnaces and rarely made it back to his small room on the third floor of the house on Mill Street. On the days when Shane worked around the clock, Lovas brought meals from home, pepperpot and crackermeal, packed for the boy out of concern by the blacksmith's wife.

Rebecca learned none of this for much of the early autumn, until she came down from Wilton Manor for the annual Harvest Festival. Organized by the Women of the Three Sisters, the trio of prominent churches at the intersection of Prospect and Ascension, the festival was held in late-October at the park in the center of town. The festival was the social event of the year, bringing together the entire town for a long day of drink and feast from the surrounding farmlands, a wonderful celebration of the grand abundance brought to Phoenixville by the toil of its community and the prosperous mill by the Schuylkill River. In recognition and as reward, Elijah Wilton even closed the mill for half the day, the only occasion other than Christmas so celebrated, so that his workers could attend the festival at its peak.

The Phoenixville Harvest Festival of 1860 was already well underway when Rebecca made her way into town with her constant companion, her governess, at her side. Determined the presence of this stern little woman would not spoil her mood, Rebecca spent the ride staring silently out the carriage opening, as the governess loudly complained the girl was lost in another of her frequent flights of imagination.

The road that led from the Wilton estate down to the high bridge over French Creek was bursting with fall foliage and autumn wildflowers and the air was rich with their fragrance. The carriage path itself remained muddy from the recent rains and more than once the wheels stuck in the deep ruts before the stallion could pull them forward. As usual, the bridge, among the tallest in Chester County, brought the governess to her nerves and the old woman's voice pitched higher as the boards rumbled beneath the carriage tires. Smiling to herself, Rebecca listened silently as the woman prattled on about nothing at all, until they reached the bridge's end and the whole of Phoenixville spilled out before them.

The town began with a nail factory, founded by Rebecca's grandfather, Nathaniel Wilton. As its fires roared with promise, the factory attracted an influx of hard-working immigrants and the growing town tasted its first prosperity. The Wiltons became known for fair wages and honest work, along with a certain bent toward local philanthropy, and the town grew rapidly around the factory. Optimism was fleeting, however. When the nail factory caught fire not ten years after it opened and burned to the ground, most families feared the town would die along with it. As an exodus began and the town grew more depleted with each passing day, no one seemed to notice Nathaniel walking the grounds of the old factory with his only son, Elijah. Not long after, from the ashes of the nail factory arose a new mill and a new name for a town now reborn.

With its location at the confluence of French Creek and the Schuylkill River, the ore of nearby mines, and the burgeoning railroads in close proximity, the Phoenix Iron Works was well positioned for the economy of industry sweeping the nation. The mill provided the rails and machine parts for much of the new train system crossing the country. It fashioned beams and tools for construction in states as far away as California and Maine. But true success came when Elijah himself invented the Wilton Column, a uniquely rolled support reinforced by riveted flanges. The column was the strongest of its kind and ideally suited, not to mention perfectly timed, for the country's emerging bridges and tall buildings. As its usefulness became widely known, orders soon poured in from governments as distant as Canada, Brazil, and Australia. Indeed, until the rebellion and the production of a weapon that changed that war, the Wilton Column was the invention on which Elijah built his company. Soon, the mill and its surrounding community were flourishing beyond immigrant dreams.

When the carriage finally reached the center of the town her family built, Rebecca did not even wait for the driver before she opened the door herself and bounded from the carriage into the park, eager to lose her chaperone in the crowd. The celebration, splendid in all its colors and swirling music, was in full swing. Townspeople from all walks were everywhere, filling the park and spilling out into the surrounding clay streets. Families sat together on blankets spread upon the ground, feeding each other slices of pies and cakes and buttermilk biscuits. With the loud voices of friendly buskers, vendors enticed the crowd with carts loaded with peanuts and salted pretzels. Beneath the statue of Rebecca's late grandfather, a small band of men argued over an article in a newspaper only a few of them could read. Rebecca watched it all and smiled. There was no question, this was most certainly her favorite day of the year.

"Rebecca!"

High voices rang out over the crowd and Rebecca spied a few of her friends, daughters of eminent town leaders all, and she hurried across the park to catch up on the latest news and gossip. Her path interrupted two boys playing mumblety-peg and she nearly got her dress clipped in the process. One of the boys made to say something to her, but then, apparently recognizing Rebecca, smothered his comments and drew his knife from the ground without a word as she passed.

Rebecca's friends beamed as she approached and fussed over her gown as if they had never seen it before. Their own dresses were imported and drenched in the new colors of the season, but Rebecca wore one of her mother's favorite dresses, a style therefore as out of fashion as it was sentimental. There were times, when the wind blew just so, that Rebecca swore she could still sense her mother in the silk. She did not share these thoughts with her friends, however, and the conversation returned to boys and hairstyles and respective miserable governesses. But Rebecca soon found her own attention distracted, not least by a rowdy gang of furnace boys, wrestling like squirrels nearby, vying for the girls' attention and making general fools of themselves. Rebecca was both relieved and disheartened to see that her boy from the roof was not among them. Unfortunately, she saw no sign of him anywhere else.

The rest of the day unfolded with much laughter and celebration, with great carrying on from all quarters, and when the first pink hints of sundown crept along the horizon, the end of the party appeared nowhere in sight. After checking in twice in the hour with her governess, who seemed uncharacteristically relaxed, Rebecca found herself alone at the edge of the celebration, discovering a comfortable spot under the branches of a wide magnolia. She watched the performance of the musicians beneath the new bandshell and before too long, despite the loud music and the ruckus of the dancers around her, grew quiet. Leaning back against the tree trunk, Rebecca closed her eyes and absorbed yet another rendition of "Camptown Races."

"If I should never hear this song again," a voice said, "then I shall be a happier man."

Drawing a startled breath, Rebecca opened her eyes and discovered her rooftop acrobat stepping out from behind the magnolia. He was dressed in new trousers of black wool and fine suspenders over a shirt of clean cotton and, although the near permanent ash about his face betrayed his occupation, Rebecca considered him handsome indeed. In fact, she was surprised to discover her memory had not been doing him justice over these past few weeks. Rebecca allowed herself to take him in only for a moment, before she looked away into the crowd, afraid for blushing embarrassment if she held those green eyes for too long.

"This song?" Rebecca said, after sifting through a dozen alternative responses. "But this is among my favorites. Why, I believe I could listen to this song all the day."

As if on cue, the musicians jolted forward into an additional verse of improvisation, the melody swirling with renewed enthusiasm.

"And so we shall, it seems," the boy said, laughing.

They stood together beneath the magnolia, each of them pretending to listen to the music, but hearing not a note. For her part, Rebecca was in territory entirely unfamiliar. She had spoken to boys, of course, endured their perspiring visits in her father's parlor, smiled at their childish jokes, and silently ignored their convulsions and awkward questions. To her mind, these boys, from families much like her own, were all children, bumbling clowns. Clowns with wealth and lineage, perhaps, but clowns nonetheless, and more concerned with the appearance of standing beside the right girl than with actually engaging her in conversation.

And Rebecca was the right girl. The daughter of Elijah Wilton! Could anyone imagine a more desirable catch?

Not that she was accustomed to such attention. Even now, Rebecca felt the eyes upon her, adhering like cobwebs in her hair. Such judgments, such gossip. She smiled at her friends, watching her from their huddle beneath a similar tree across the park. Whispers, light as coal smoke. A furnace boy, talking with Elijah Wilton's daughter? The girls returned her smile, yet made no pretense of diverting their attention. What did Rebecca care? Storybooks and romance were far more important to her than the opinions of others. Though there was one opinion she still coveted, a fact of which she was reminded when she spied her father making his way toward her from across the park. With stern expression, Elijah quickened his pace and Rebecca's world grew suddenly dark and narrow, as though she were slipping into one of the county's covered bridges.

Frozen, Rebecca tried desperately to conjure some defense, if not for herself then for the boy beside her, and avoided her father's glare. She did not see the crowd part before him, nor their smiles and greetings politely if hurriedly acknowledged as he passed. She did not see the frown on his face or the urgency in his stride.

Nor did she see his expression shift when he came within a few paces of the couple beneath the tree.

"Why, young Mister Hughes," Elijah declared. To Rebecca's ears, her father's words were as improbable as a sonnet coming from his lips and for a moment she could not be certain she was not daydreaming again. Then, as if attuned to his daughter's disbelief, Elijah repeated the name. "Mister Hughes, I trust you are enjoying yourself in Phoenixville today."

"Yes, sir," young Mister Hughes replied. "'Tis a fine time, indeed, sir."

Elijah looked at Rebecca, but she saw no question for her in his eyes. Only a smile.

"And you have met my daughter, I see."

The boy also smiled, glancing at Rebecca in conspiracy from the corner of his eye. "Yes, I have, sir. Twice now, it appears. Although I am not certain we have ever had a proper introduction."

"No?" Elijah asked, stepping back a pace and tucking both thumbs into the small pockets of his waistcoat. "Then, allow me, by all means. Allow me." Turning his attention to Rebecca, Elijah gestured toward the boy at her side and announced, "Miss Rebecca Augusta Wilton, may I present Mister Shane Ryan Hughes, eldest son of the Hughes family of Bryn Mawr."

The words poured forth like drenching rain off a broken gutter and Rebecca could only let them flow past, uncertain whether she absorbed even a drop.

"But, I ..." Rebecca sputtered. This was all she could manage to say.

"Yes, angel?" her father prompted.

Rebecca barely saw Elijah's arched eyebrow. She was staring too hard at Shane now, trying to determine if she had been played the fool by either or both of these men. Shane simply smiled, his eyes twinkling with the slightest hint of mischief. Or something else entirely.

"I did not know," Rebecca finally said. "I did not know you and Mister Hughes were acquainted, Father."

"Yes, well," Elijah answered, "I should like to say I know all my workers, indeed. But that is no longer so, it seems." A look of wistfulness passed over Elijah's face, before giving way to a grin more sincere than Rebecca remembered seeing in a long while. "This one, however, this apprentice is a bit special, as he is cut from a different cloth than his fellow boys at the furnaces." Shane appeared embarrassed at this, staring down at the soft grass between his brogans. "You know his father, Rebecca, whom you might remember if you ever spent any time with your thoughts on this earth. William Hughes, from Philadelphia Trust? You were introduced to him at our Christmas celebration. It was through the kindness and faith of Mr. Hughes that we built the new foundry building just last spring."

"Hughes," Rebecca repeated absently, the name playing on her tongue like a sorbet. She strained to picture the man who accompanied the name, the man who accompanied this Shane, but she had not even the faintest recollection of any such person. At this point, her thoughts were so scrambled, she could hardly recall a Christmas celebration. "Mister Hughes."

"Yes. Quite so," Elijah answered, apparently satisfied. "It was at that very party, in fact, that I learned of young Shane's interest in the iron industry. It seems he is most particularly enthralled with our new bridge company. With his education and ambitions, a managerial position seemed quite in order, so we arranged to have Shane here join us in the superintendent's building just a few weeks after the holidays. He moved all the way out here from Bryn Mawr, putting aside—at least for now, as I understand it—his studies at the university."

Rebecca listened to this as though it were another bedtime story her father was telling. It was all fantasy, a dream, and Rebecca still could find no foothold. Then, more impossibility, as her father reached out with those sure hands of his and grabbed hold of Shane's shoulders, the embrace of a proud relative, and Rebecca watched her father's gesture, as unexpected and miraculous as a disappearing act.

"Then do you know what this young man did, Rebecca?" Father asked, though he did not pause for an answer. "It was young Shane's wish, nay insistence, that he learn our business from the fires themselves. On the floors of the mill. As a furnace boy."

"This is nothing," Shane insisted, casting another glance of embarrassment at Rebecca.

"Far from it," Elijah responded. "It was one of the wisest requests of all my years, I say."

Shane added nothing to this, but kept his eyes focused squarely on the ground. Father continued to look on him with a wide smile, proud and pleased, and he waited for Rebecca to fill in the silence. Though she sensed the appropriate response would be obvious to anyone else, to any of these people trying so hard not to get caught staring at the scene beneath the magnolia, Rebecca could find no proper reply. Her words again failed her.

"I did not know," Rebecca finally said, again.

"Yes," Elijah answered, moving along, "well, yes. I shall let the two of you work that out, perhaps. Yes, perhaps so." Then, touching the brim of his hat, a fine bowler he bought last year when the seasons turned, Elijah said, "Mister Hughes, a pleasure to see you again, young man."

"The pleasure is indeed mine, sir."

Rebecca did not know whether to be angry, embarrassed, or pleased. So she simply stood there, watching her father take his leave and feeling the slightest touch of this young man's elbow brushing her sleeve. Rebecca could not tell if Shane was even aware of the touch, but there it was, a soft warmth like a candle's flame, and soon it was all she could think of.

"I have thought of you often."

The statement could have been her own words coming from her own dreams and Rebecca was at first concerned that this was so, but then she turned and saw her companion staring again at the grass, a touch of red showing through his gray cheeks. She noticed for the first time a smudge of something else on his face, apple butter perhaps, there at the corner of his mouth, and she realized at that very moment that she wanted to be nowhere else.

"Oh?" Rebecca replied, daring to respond at no more than a whisper.

"After that day," Shane explained.

"That day."

Rebecca repeated this with her best enigmatic tone, as if she in fact did not remember, as if the visions of the boy on the roof had not visited upon her every evening, so that the boy himself might not find too much confidence, too early.

"Yes, the first time we met," Shane said, slowly. "The roof?"

He paused and Rebecca felt his eyes upon her, deep and imploring, but she could not meet his gaze or else betray her own ruse.

"Would it be ridiculous," the boy asked, somewhat haltingly, "if I declared myself quite literally head over heels the first time I saw you?"

There was a moment then when Rebecca heard absolutely nothing, except the fading echo of the boy's question in the distance. Then, the emerging sound of her own laughter, a small chuckle she permitted herself, if only to let Shane know she understood his joke. She laughed only for a moment, so that the boy not suppose she was anything other than mildly amused. But surely, he could hear her heart, could he not? Thundering above the music, above the crowd? It rang within her like the smith's hammer on anvil and Rebecca placed her hand to her chest, smoothing the placket of her dress, feeling the pinch of the corset across her ribs, quieting the deafening drum.

"Is that an apology, Mister Hughes?" she managed to say.

Shane emitted an unseemly snort. "Apology? For what, may I ask, should I be apologizing?"

"You are not who you appear, sir. I did not know you knew my father. I do not ..." Rebecca said, stumbling for her words. "I do not appreciate being taken for a fool."

"A fool? You are no fool, Miss Wilton—"

"Rebecca."

"If there is a fool here this day, the role is mine to claim," Shane told her. Then, he smiled and added, "Rebecca."

The sound of her own name from those lips, so comfortable, stunned Rebecca, the way an errant clap of thunder might disturb a perfectly sunny August afternoon. She wished for him to say it again. She waited, choosing silence as her response. Let him think he is the fool, let him stake that claim, just as he said. Standing with him, sharing the shadow of the magnolia, Rebecca already knew this Shane was anything but a fool.

"I should have lingered longer with you on the day I fell," Shane muttered. Then, his tone shifted and he stood himself taller. "You do know that I work in the forge?"

"Yes, so I hear."

Shane continued as though he had not heard her. "I watch the blacksmiths all day long. You must, that is, it is imperative that one strikes the metal at exactly the right moment, when it is at exactly the right temperature, because if it cools too much it must be returned to the fires and reshaped." He checked Rebecca's reaction, which was impassive, though she understood. "That is what I should have done that day. Seized the moment."

"Carpe diem."

"Carpe?"

"The Latin," she told him.

Shane studied the young woman, this source of constant surprise, and then grinned. An impossibly beautiful grin. "Latin, indeed. Yes, that is what I should have done, and if I could not bear to speak to you that day, to find the right words, then I should have found you when the words came. There was no doubt where you lived, after all."

"It is a difficult house to miss," Rebecca admitted.

"Indeed."

Rebecca looked over at him, took him in once more.

"Regrets are useless," she said, knowing she had let this go on long enough, "in light of where the path arrives today."

As soon as they were spoken, these words so soft and quiet were borne away by the new music from the bandshell, out above the laughter of the crowd and the voices of the barkers, leaving not even a remnant in the air. But there was no doubt that the couple heard them. All pretense, all false elusiveness fell away, and Rebecca and Shane were together, just as they should have been.

"Quite so," Shane answered. "Quite so."

"You are an interesting young man," Rebecca said, though she regretted the innocuous statement almost immediately. "From what my father has said, that is. There is much to you, it seems."

Shane shuffled in his stance. "Your father is mistaken about some parts of his story, I should tell you. It is true that I am enamored of your iron business here—more so today than ever before—"

"Why?"

"Pardon?"

"Why are you enamored of the iron business?"

Shane regarded Rebecca as though no one had ever asked him this question, or as though the answer were perfectly obvious.

"Because it is the nation's ... the nation's very backbone. Quite literally. The railroads, the bridges, the buildings. Our work is the foundation on which everything is being built."

"Ah, so you are an idealist." Rebecca snickered. Then, hearing no response and fearing she had hurt the boy's feelings, she touched Shane's elbow and whispered, "It's all right. I am, too."

The young man's face washed with a new tentativeness. When he spoke again, his voice sounded fainter, difficult to hear over the band.

"I do enjoy the work. I say this not simply because you are a Wilton. I say this because it is true. I relish the work. It feels right to be building a part of this country with my own hands. You do understand, this is what we do here? We are building the nation, from Phoenixville to a hundred towns just like it."

"There are no towns like Phoenixville."

"No," Shane agreed, his voice revealing his discouragement, "I suppose that is true. Indeed."

Rebecca shook her head at her own damned nerves. She sensed Shane slipping away from her as easily as he had arrived, a boat floating farther from shore with each successive comment. She longed for this to be direct and uncomplicated, where nothing she said was wrong, or misunderstood.

She yearned for the rightness of this very morning, when she had taken her place on her rock at the cliff and gazed out toward the horizon. It was a beautiful morning, spectacular even, and watching it emerge Rebecca had wished to stay in that spot forever. In fact, she could not imagine ever leaving such a place. It was not the rooftops that captivated her so, nor the church steeples or the new clock being erected on the bank tower. It was the sky, a cloudless sky not so different from the way it looked now. All brand new. At first blush its color might have been mistaken for the hue of a periwinkle flower, soft and humble, or the tint on a crust of snow under a January moon. But neither of these did the color justice, for truly this was a shade heretofore unseen, a new color all its own. Looking out on this nascent blue, it occurred to Rebecca that morning, as it did again now, that this entire town stood with birth at its core. The birth of new colors and iron and houses. Birth from the flames of the furnaces. Birth from the water of the rivers and the mill's cooling pits. And the birth of new love from the wishes of a young woman at the edge of a tall cliff.

Now beneath this same sky, grown darker, Rebecca saw the times to come with this young man. She saw the ice-cream parlors and church socials and long walks along the magnificent cliff beyond her new back lawn. She saw it all, all impossibility. A dream, a wish, yet here it was, glowing red with heat.

At perfect temperature.

She took the boy's hand and held it in hers, their clasp hidden at her side within the folds of her skirt. Her heart raced ahead of her, to places unvisited. The boy's skin, so rough and callused, was surprisingly tender and she ran her thumb over his, back and forth, back and forth, like the beat of wings. And soon these wings bore them aloft, their feet lifting from that leaf-covered ground, the crowd slipping beneath them, the treetops falling away. As they rose, the music, once a joyous cacophony, faded like breath into the wind, until it was no more than a distant hum, a train slipping from the county, a river rolling by.

Still they climbed.

They were two angels, rising ever higher over it all, their hands joined, their wings as broad as magnolia branches, their strength beyond a hundred ocean waves. Here among the clouds, far from gravity's pull, Rebecca never felt more invincible.

"I do not know that I can stay in this town much longer."

It was a thought she had had a thousand times. But not recently. Not since she first saw her boy on the roof. So, when she realized these were his words now and not her own, the understanding arrived like an arrow, swift and sure, plunging beneath her wing, stabbing at her side. And she fell.

She fell.

"No?" she managed to ask, as the ground hurtled toward her.

"The war will be here soon," the boy told her, drawing his posture straighter, "and I shall be the first at its fires."

Broken now against the dirt, her wings wrapped around her, her boy as tall as an iron column above her, Rebecca found no thoughts of any coherence. Tears welled up from nowhere and she tucked her face within the feathers of her wing so that Shane would not see them. She knew of this war. Father spoke of it often, in the parlor with his men and their tobacco and drink and booming voices. War would be here soon. They said this, just as Shane did now. A rebellion from the South.

Rebecca could not imagine what that meant for her or her Shane. And Rebecca Wilton could imagine a great many things.

EIGHT

I could imagine a hundred different ways for the story to go, none of them good, and I ran through each of them, over and over, as I watched the minute hand tick ever so slowly around the classroom clock the next morning.

I was dying to talk to Boo, but he hadn't been at Tomney's before school and I hadn't seen him in the halls. I looked for him everywhere, asked everyone we knew. I listened for the familiar coughing, the high-pitched laugh, the breathless greeting. Nothing. By the time school ended, I was sick, thinking that Deacon and his Furnace Boys had found Boo before I had.

"Little man."

I pretended like I hadn't heard the voice as I unlocked my bike and backed it out of the tangle at the stand. When the voice repeated itself, louder this time, I had no choice but to turn.

Romeo and Payroll stood on the sidewalk over by the football field, their thick arms folded over thick chests, like prison guards watching the afternoon commotion in the yard.

"Yo, little man," Romeo called one more time. He even offered a slight wave. "Over here."

I swallowed hard, trying to clear my heart from my throat, and pushed my bike across the street. The Mongoose seemed to resist.

"Where is it?" Payroll asked, as he eyed my backpack. "You don't got the stuff on you, do you?"

103

"What are you talking about?"

Payroll frowned. "Fool, don't make me say it again."

"You can't be taking that shit into school," Romeo said.

I shook my head. "I don't got nothing on me."

Neither Furnace Boy looked as though he believed this, but they didn't push it. They knew they would get what they wanted in due time. Confidence well earned.

"The other one then," Payroll said. "Your fuglier half—he got it, is that it? I don't know, boy. That don't seem wise to me. You probably better off not letting him hold it, you know? Everybody knows you're the … the …"

"Responsible one," Romeo said, his eyes not leaving the group of girls crossing the street, their tight sweaters, the ribbons in their feathered hair.

"You're the responsible one, see," Payroll continued. "S'why Deacon was countin' on you to do this thing. Even though I told him otherwise. Can't send a boy to do a man's job, that's what I say. The boy only gonna screw it up. But Deacon believes in you, for some reason. Don't ask me none, I don't know."

"I haven't seen Boo today," I said.

Romeo still didn't look at me. "You two *did* get what we're looking for last night, right?"

I managed a lazy shrug. "I didn't go out last night. My mom, she wanted … I was home. If Boo went out, he went out on his own."

My words hung in the air. Saint Peter's three denials. Full of immediate regret, I tried to take them back.

"I mean, he was supposed to … I think he was—"

"That's fine," Romeo said, holding up his hand. "We'll talk to Boo. You tell him we're looking for him, you hear? Deacon was spectin' him to show at the Furnace last night, but none of you were out there."

"I was home," I said again.

"But Deacon was waiting on you all. That's not good, you know? Deacon was *waiting*."

"Deacon will get what he wants," I said. Then, I climbed back onto my bike. "Look, I gotta book, I'm gonna be late."

Payroll opened his hands at his sides. "Sure, sure. Just lemme ask you one thing, though. Your boy, Boo. He ain't come out of school yet. He's always with you, but he ain't here now. So, that's what I'm asking you."

"I'll tell him you're looking for him."

"Nah, nah," Romeo said, this time looking right into my eyes, "you got it backwards there. You boys should be looking for us. That's what you tell your Boo now—you boys come look for us tonight at the Furnace and you bring what we talked about. That's it, that's all. Deacon ain't gonna be patient forever."

"OK," I managed to say, as I let my bike carry me away.

I took the shortcut to Boo's house. I raced through the neighborhood around the school, cruised down the hill by the diner, and took the sharp right at the Revolutionary War monument. A couple of Slags were playing wall-ball against the beer distributor and one of them shouted something I couldn't hear. I kept riding. When I finally reached Boo's street, I half-expected more Furnace Boys to be waiting for me there, but the street looked safe. Lifting my bike up the wooden steps of the twin, I jumped when I spied the figure sitting on the porch next door, but my alarm was short-lived.

"How you doing, Batman?" I said.

The preschool boy, dressed in Batman pajamas and a homemade black cowl, kept watch over Hall Street. Peering through the slits of the mask, the kid's brown eyes expressed no greeting or recognition. He just fixed me with a look of supreme fearlessness. As fearless as one could look wearing flame-retardant pajamas before sunset.

"Citizen," came the high-pitched reply, except the boy's prominent lisp made the word sound like "thit-a-thin." I always made a point to greet Boo's little neighbor, just so I could hear the kid talk.

"That your Halloween costume?"

The kid shook his head. "Luke Thkywalker."

"Nice. May the Force be with you."

"Uh-huh."

"Joker behind bars today?" I asked.

"Yep."

"Good work. Who's next—Riddler, Darth Vader?"

"All of 'em," the kid answered. "All the bad guys."

I knocked on Boo's door, but no one answered.

Boo lived with his grandfather, Henry, a legendary heater who'd lost his left eye early in his career. After a successful stint as shop steward when the union was at its strongest, Henry retired as soon as he could, when the first scent of bankruptcy was in the air at the mill. He anticipated a grand retirement of seeing the country from a used Winnebago and living out his years anywhere but here. But when his wife succumbed to a particularly aggressive lung cancer, the plans were shot to hell and Henry instead retired into an alcoholic grief.

I had adored Boo's grandmother, because she'd taught me how to throw a curve ball when I first started Little League. Evelyn was a short, stout woman of questionable taste in clothes, who loved sports of any kind, especially her beloved minor-league Phillies up in Reading. Her loudest cheers were reserved for Boo and me, however, even during Wiffle ball games at the empty lot next to the hardware store, which she watched from the same ratty lawn chair every day. She and Boo were two of a kind and her illness only made it more so, their dueling coughing fits as violent as a firing range. Although she had been gone for a few years, I still felt her absence every time I was at Boo's house.

How Henry, despite his obvious affliction, became Boo's guardian was a matter of some debate. One fact was not in dispute: beginning when Boo was not much older than the Batman out on the steps, Boo's parents would skip town every September for jobs on oyster boats down on the Chesapeake, leaving Henry in charge of his grandson until Christmas. This annual abandonment of an only child fueled an endless stream of gossip up and down Hall Street. Some whispered the boy's illness was simply too much for the young couple to handle. Others claimed Boo's father wanted to return to his own Chesapeake roots. Still others believed the closing of the steel mill had chipped away some of the couple's sanity. For his part, Boo rarely mentioned his parents, except once implying that he couldn't go with them because all his doctors were in Phoenixville. Besides, he needed to finish school before he could go off on some oyster boat.

Truth was, Henry could have been a far worse guardian. He made sure Boo had enough food in the cupboard and clothes for school. He asked about homework from time to time and kept on Boo about working at Tomney's because "honest work never hurt no man." And he gave the teenager what Boo wanted most of all: the freedom to come and go as he pleased.

I let the screen door fall back in place and turned to the little Caped Crusader.

"You been out here a long time?"

The kid shrugged.

"I'm looking for Boo," I said. "Have you seen him?"

Batman turned his head and looked at me, but he said nothing.

"I can't find him."

"Like he's hiding?" the kid asked.

"Right."

"Are you playing a game?" He sounded hopeful.

"No, not a game," I said. "I just have to find him."

"I know the best hiding place," the kid said. "You would never find me."

"Oh yeah, where's that?"

The little Batman just sat there, smiling. "Psych—I'm not gonna tell you! Then you would know."

True enough.

I stared out at the abandoned lot, trying to remember the store that used to stand there. I found myself thinking about ghosts and memories …

And then I knew where Boo was.

NINE

The front entrance to Wishing Manor had disappeared years before into a tangle of overgrown brush and trees, where the cypresses grew together, branches intertwined. Two stone pillars, weathered green and overcome by moss and vines, framed the estate's entrance. Working harder than I expected, I stripped the rain-soaked growth from one column and uncovered a small black sign and the words "WILTON MANOR" beneath a carving of furnace flames. A thick, rusted chain stretched between the posts like a warning, though it now hung limp across a forgotten driveway.

Steeling myself with several deep breaths, I stepped over the chain. As I pushed my bike along the cobblestone path riddled with weeds, the great house ahead loomed large, cloaked in a misty afternoon fog. I told myself all those stories of Wishing Manor made no difference at all.

Nothing about the house was welcoming. With its high widow's walk, imposing porch, and dark windows, Wishing Manor was straight out of Hitchcock or Poe, a structure so massive it was best viewed at a distance, just to get a sense of the place. The cupola, a dilapidated structure with four large dormers and buckled iron cresting at its peak, only added to the threatening character. The house looked exhausted, as though defeated by its tragic history, with peeling paint and missing shingles and windows dark with grime, all Phoenixville gray, the thick blend of soot and years.

The porch groaned with my arrival and I thought for a second my foot would plunge right through the rotted wood. I didn't want to be there. The house gave me the creeps. I tried the doorknob, but it didn't turn. Finally, my own fears still whispering in my ear, I took the massive brass knocker and let it fall twice against the door. Its echo rolled through the house like a bowling ball at Phoenix Lanes, only to be swallowed into the silence of empty hallways.

Nothing stirred, no one responded.

I knocked again, this time with a little more force, then stepped down from the porch and waited in the driveway. Nothing. I waited some more. Finally, just when I was starting to think I was wrong, something moved across the window at the top of the tower. The smallest commotion of activity. I couldn't be sure what it was—a curtain, a shadow, a trick of the dying sun—until the window opened and Boo leaned from the cupola. He scanned the grounds of Wishing Manor and beyond, back and forth, until his eyes finally settled on me down below.

"I want to talk to you," I said.

"What about?"

"You know. Quit screwing around, Boo. Come down here and let me in."

He seemed to consider this for a minute, like he maybe wasn't going to do it. Finally, he disappeared back into the house and drew the noisy old window closed behind him.

Quite some time passed before the front doors finally opened. I remember Boo somehow looked even smaller than usual, swallowed up by his brother's corduroy coat and the darkness behind him.

"You didn't come to school," I said.

Boo only shrugged.

"You been hiding out here all day?"

Another shrug.

"What the hell, Boo?"

"I couldn't go to school, I couldn't go to work," he finally said, "not with them Furnace Boys looking for me. If they saw me 'round town, I was a dead man—"

"What are you—"

"Tomney's. Home. Nowhere. I mean, if I went home, they would just find me there. That's where they'd look, right? That's where you went, isn't it?"

"Of course."

"You went to my house?"

"Boo—"

"What did Pops say?"

"He didn't answer the door."

Boo nodded. "Probably passed out already on his afternoon drunk. Christ, what time is it?"

"Four. I don't know. Four-thirty."

"I knew you'd find me," Boo said. "Never doubted that. I figured you'd finish up school and then ride on out here and— how about that—here you are."

"And nobody else knows you're here?"

"They'll figure it out soon enough. Like you did."

I peered over Boo's shoulder, into a large foyer draped only by heavy shadows.

"What's it like in there?"

Boo laughed at me. "You're still chicken."

"I'm just wondering—"

"Come on inside, take a look."

"Nah. We should get you back."

"I ain't going back."

"Yeah, right. Just gonna live out here all on your own? Sure, that makes total sense, Boo. Dumb ass."

"Don't say that. You call me that too much. Don't call me that no more, hear?"

"Then stop being such a dumb ass."

"Shut up, Sketch, I'm serious."

Something in his voice told me he was.

"I'm serious, too," I said.

Boo looked out over the lawn and I followed his gaze. An aggressive swell of blackbirds, ravens, swooped down from the eaves of the mansion roof and across the great lawn. They searched for invisible prey, competing for it along the tree line. The birds darted in and out of the branches, down into the bed of leaves, then back up again as one, a black cloud against the gray sky. Finally, in unison, the flock disappeared around a corner of the house, their screeches fading as easily as they had arrived.

"I went to the Furnace," Boo said. "Yesterday, after school—"

"Yeah?"

"When you were with Tara."

"I wasn't with Tara," I said. "My mom was home, she told me I had to come home after school, help her with some stuff."

He studied me. "Whatever. I told them I couldn't do it. Like you said. I told them I couldn't get the guns."

"OK."

"But—"

"But what?"

"I told them about the other thing. I told them I would get the necklace."

"And they didn't want it, right?"

Boo shook his head. "Not at first, no. But I sold them on it, Sketch. You should have seen, I sold them. By the time I was done talking it up, they wanted that necklace all right. They got it, see. In your face, man! That Black Diamond—it's worth something right there. I know it."

"Deacon wanted the necklace?"

"Deacon wasn't there."

"What?"

"Deacon wasn't with them. It was too early, so I told Romeo about it. I told him my plan—"

"Romeo, shit. Romeo doesn't know his ass from his elbow, Boo. He can't make decisions for Deacon."

"I did what you said. I wasn't going to get no guns, wasn't gonna give them no guns. That's what I told them."

"That's not what I said. Well, not like that. I wanted you to stop stealing anything for those guys anymore."

"Romeo said they wanted the necklace."

"OK."

"So I told them I'd get it for them, have it for them by midnight back at the Furnace. I'd hit the library after dark, just like I said, get in there after closing and all. But then, but..."

"Boo?"

Boo shook his head. Then, he looked away, his hand rising to cover his face.

"Boo?"

When Boo turned back, his big charade was crumbling.

"This is all your fault," he said, his voice quivering.

"What are you talking about?"

"The necklace, the plan, all of this—it's your fault."

"My fault? You're nuts, you know that?"

"You told me not to take no more guns—"

"Right."

"But the necklace—"

"I told you not to touch the necklace neither!"

"Screw you, Sketch."

"Dumb ass."

And with that, Boo lunged for me, knocking me off balance, sending us both to the ground. It wasn't much of a fight, him flailing away with his bony arms, me covering up, reluctant to throw a punch. Lots of shoving and wrestling, the way boys do, until with one particularly hard push, harder than I'd intended, I sent Boo flying back against the porch. Slamming into the railing, sliding back down to the ground. Then, he was huddled there, shaking, sniveling, wrapping that old coat around his body. I wanted to go to him, tell him it would be all right, that everything was OK. That's what I wanted. So I stood, started towards him.

Then, I stopped. Frozen.

"Boo?"

The gun looked like a cannon in his hand.

"This wouldn't have happened if you—" Boo said, shaking with adrenaline or fear or God knows what.

I could hardly manage any words.

"Boo, what the hell?"

A crow returned from over the roof and landed on the ground between us. The bird just stood there, flicking its head, pulling at the grass. I glanced at it, watching the way it moved, the way the dull afternoon light revealed the sapphire streaks hidden within its black feathers. At last, as though tired of the attention, the crow spread its wings and took flight once more.

When I looked back at Boo, he was staring at the gun in his hands. Like it was all detached, not his hands, not his gun.

"I'm sorry," he said, as he slowly stuck the gun back into his coat pocket. "I wasn't—I'm just sorry."

"What the hell?" I couldn't think enough to come up with anything else.

I took a tentative step towards him, my eyes still on the bulging pocket at his side.

"Sorry, sorry. I'm just sorry is all," Boo said. Tears hung thick on the rims of his sunken eyes.

I didn't know what was happening, like I'd been thrust onto a stage without knowing my lines or even what play we were performing.

"Where did you get another gun?" I asked. "You said you weren't going to steal no more—"

"There was always another. The one I gave Deacon and this. I stole them both at the same time, but I kept one."

"Kept one, for what?"

"They were for us, man, you and me. Butch and Sundance."

I was shaking my head now. "Not guns, not us. Hell, no."

"I know. S'why I gave the one to Deacon."

"A necklace, Boo. You were gonna steal the necklace."

"I tried!"

"And?"

Boo said something I couldn't hear. I leaned forward.

"Boo?"

"We are so dead."

I crouched in front of him, the grass damp against the knees of my jeans.

"I told them I would get the necklace. I told them."

"All right."

"So dead."

"Boo," I asked, my voice hushed, "what happened last night?"

Boo wiped his hand over his eyes and drew a shaky breath into his rickety chest, the sound like a bellows with a hole in it. Then, he began to speak.

So I get into the library right before closing time, just like I told you, and grab myself some books, some thick Vietnam books with plenty of pictures, 'cause I got half the night to spend in there, right? There's nobody else in there—just me and that old guy who's always there. He's got me beat on the coughing, I'll tell you that, hacking up some big old phlegm ball every twenty seconds. I thought I was gonna go crazy sitting there, trying to read, while that guy coughed up a lung. Lucky for me, a couple of girls from the Catholic school showed up. Looked like they were waitin' on someone to come pick them up. They ain't that hot, but they're wearing those short plaid uniforms, and it gives me something to look at just the same. One babe keeps cracking her gum, which sets me crazy, worse than the coughing, but you would've been proud of me, Sketch. I don't say nothing because I don't want to call attention to myself, you know. That's gotta be part of the plan, right? I just keep nerding my way through that big pile of books and I don't spend a whole lot more time checking out anybody else, 'cause I got a job to do.

It's all right there, just like I told you. The exhibit, all in glass cases. They got books and papers, some kind of military uniform, a bunch of pieces of iron, you know, tools and things. And they got the necklace. It's a big thing, with this black gem right in the middle of it. I wander over to take a look, real casual. That's when it hits me. Nobody, not one goddamn person, is paying any attention to that exhibit. This valuable necklace is right out in the open and nobody cares. Think about that, what's it tell you? Exactly. Maybe you were right, maybe this jewelry ain't worth shit! What a smile that would be for all them Furnace Boys. Remember the time that idiot stole that worthless hunk of glass from the library? Of course Sketch was too damn smart for any of that, but not little Boo.

That's what I'm thinking, anyway.

Now all the time I'm stewing on this, the girl behind the counter, the librarian, she's starting to notice me. Nothing big, but little glances my way. I know it ain't no good that I've drawn her attention. I want to be invisible, a goddamn ghost. I finally got a babe looking at me, and this one, she's not half bad–better than those Catholic girls–and here I am trying to go unnoticed.

So now I got some new wrinkles in the plan. There's still plenty of people around and the chick behind the counter knows I'm here. That can't be good, right? I figure the only thing I can do is go on with the plan. At seven o'clock, one hour before closing time, I pack up my things—make a real big show of it so the librarian notices me—and throw on my backpack and head for the door. As I'm walking by the counter I get a little inspired and I say to her, 'Good night, thanks for letting me use your fine library. Time to go now. Big dinner plans tonight,' all friendly like, so she notices for sure that I'm leaving.

Once I'm out of her sight, I don't go out the lobby doors. I take the staircase down to the lower level, where the kids' books are. There ain't anybody down there, it being dinner time and all. Just another librarian, that grandmother one who's been there since we were kids, you know the one I mean, and it looks like she's just straightening up before closing time. Before she can see me, I sort of crawl past the book stacks and head into the bathroom.

Now I know what you're thinking. A bathroom is a pretty obvious place to hide and there's no way I can stay in there that whole last hour before the place closes. What if some kid needs to use it? Besides, the janitor or somebody probably comes in there to clean up at closing, so that just ain't going to work out.

Here's where the genius of the plan kicks in. You ever notice what's right next door to that bathroom? Of course you haven't. That's 'cause you don't keep your eyes open for things like that the way I do. It's a plain door, no writing, just a door, but right there at the bottom of the door is all you need to see. Slots. You know, ventilation. That's how you know it's some kind of mechanical room. They keep it locked, of course, but that's all right. Locks don't scare me.

What's that from? 'Locks don't scare me.' Come on, you know, it was in some movie. *Close Encounters*? Nah. Aw, man, you know it. Damn, that's gonna bug me all night.

Yeah, OK, OK, so anyways, what do you think I do once I'm in the bathroom? Very funny. No, I get up on the john, right on the back of the thing, and push out the ceiling tile. It's a nice big opening, big enough for me anyway, and I know this is going to work. I can just reach the ceiling tiles over the other room with my fingertips and I manage to pull one loose without too much trouble. I'm sweating though, and the backpack I got with me is heavier than I thought, but I finally get the thing up through the opening and over the wall into the next room. I can't see nothing from where I'm standing and the other room is all dark anyway, so I decide to just take a chance and drop the backpack down over the wall and right away, bam, it hits something and stops. The noise isn't too loud, but I wait for a minute anyway, to see if the librarian might have heard. But nothing.

Finally, I unlock the bathroom door, get back up on the john, and pull myself over the wall. Now, I don't mind telling you, it was a bear to pull myself up there. But I do it. I do it. I'm up into the darkness, then wriggling down into the next room like some kind of damn rattlesnake. Hell, maybe the CIA could use someone like me, all skinny like, able to go places no other man can get to. I could be a spy, James Bond and shit. None of those other Furnace Boys could do this. I'm not even sure you can get in there, Sketch. See, I was the best man for the job.

It takes a little fiddling to get the ceiling tiles back in place and then I need to rest myself. My breathing ain't doing so good and I'm shitting bricks that I'm gonna start a fit, but my luck holds out. For now, at least. I landed on some kind of shelf, only I can't tell for sure because everything is so damn dark. I keep waiting for my eyes to adjust but they never do. Real slow like, I find the edge of the shelf and twist my legs over the side. It can't be too far to the ground, but I don't want to land on anything and break my ankle, so I just hang down as far as I can until my toes touch the ground. When I stand up, I stay still and try to steady my breath. When I take my first step, that's when something scrapes me across the face. It's the cord to a light, one of those bare-bulb jobs. Even though I can't see a damn thing, I'm not sure a light is such a great idea right now, so I think about it for a minute, and I finally decide to pull the cord, just to see where I am. And where I am is perfect. Better than I imagined. It's not a mechanical room, but some kind of storage closet. There's two big shelving units full of crap like toilet-paper rolls and paper towels and office supplies. I look long enough to get my bearings, then switch off the light.

Now I'm thinking I still should find a place to hide in here, just in case the janitor wants to come in for some supplies. So I decide to spend the next hour on the bottom shelf, behind a couple of dusty boxes and some bottles of cleaning fluids. There's just enough space to wedge myself back in there, but it's a tight fit. You know me, I'm not claustrophobic or nothing, but after a time, with my arms pinned against my sides and my chest kind of tight, it starts to feel like a coffin under there. But I know I got less than an hour to go and then I'll have the place to myself.

And that's when I fall asleep. I know, I know, I couldn't believe it neither, but swear to God, that's what happened. Good night, John-Boy, damn! And listen, I'm only telling you this, Sketch, and nobody else needs to know. But it's the goddamn truth! I wake up and I have no idea what time it is because I ain't got a watch, but the light that was coming in under the door is dark now, so I figure it must be after eight and the library is all closed up and everything's all right. I get up from the shelf and flick on the light one more time so I can grab my backpack and then I open the door, real silent, and check the room.

It's quiet, and dark as hell. Did I mention how cold it is in there? They must turn off the heat at night, because I can just about see my own breath, which sort of helps me focus, making sure my breathing is slow and steady. I step into the hallway and creep back upstairs to the main room.

This is it now. The necklace is a few feet away and it's the moment of truth. Now I know those Furnace Boys probably think I ain't got the balls to do this, and I know you're probably thinking the same thing, and I don't mind tellin' you, that's what keeps me going. Seriously. Whenever I think of chickening out or just giving up, I think about you and Deacon and I tell myself it's time to show you what Boo can do.

Then everything goes crazy.

I'm standing ten feet away from the jewelry case, ten feet away from all that money for Deacon, ten feet away from becoming a Furnace Boy … and everything comes apart, just like that. First, it's the footsteps. So soft I think maybe my mind is playing tricks. Then I think maybe it's a cat or a rat or something. But no, there's something there. At least, I think so. Don't look at me like that—I know what you're thinking, but it was there. So I duck behind the counter, down between some book carts, and I wait. My eyes have adjusted pretty good now and the room is kind of lit up from the streetlamp outside and at first I don't see nothing. I stand up straighter and I try to steady my breath—I can feel a coughing spell coming on and I know I just need to get out of here as fast as I can.

That's when I see someone across the room.

God, even to say it now, out in the open like this, it scares the hell out of me … and it would you, too. Right there, all the way across the main room, something moves. It's a shadow really, nothing more than that. I know you said the place was haunted, but I thought that was all bogus. But now, I don't know. There was something there. Now I'm so busy trying not to piss myself or start coughing that I can barely think straight. I mean, what should I do, you know? Do I go after this guy, try to find out what the hell is going on? Do I grab the necklace and sprint for the front door? Or do I just get the hell out of there altogether and take my chances with Deacon?

Well, like my Pops always says, sometimes the decisions get made for you. See, I glance back at the stairs and think about making a break for it, just for a second, and when I look back to the room, the shadow is gone. Just like that. Now I'm not so sure I ain't going bonkers and I'm thinking maybe I was seeing things all along. Maybe I'm still waking up. Maybe this new medicine they got me on is messing with my head. Who knows? All I know is that the coast is clear and I'm heading for the exhibit case. This is my chance. But when I reach it, with my backpack open wide just waiting for the jewelry, it takes me a minute to realize what I'm looking at.

It's empty! The goddamn case is empty. There's a hole punched in the case and there's pieces of glass inside and the necklace, that beautiful Black Diamond, it's gone! Now I'm thinking I might just sit down right there and start pounding my head on the floor. What the hell is going on?

I don't have a whole lot of time to think about that right then, though, because before I know it, the world goes nuts. I mean, you never heard such a racket. A window breaks in the back of the room and the alarm bells go off, ringing like all get out. Then, another window shatters, this one right near me, and there's glass flying and I almost get hit in the head with a brick or a big rock or something. That's what happened. I'm sitting there on the floor and some kind of brick comes flying through the window from outside and the damn thing misses me by maybe a foot. Jesus, if that thing ... well, I sure as hell wouldn't be here talking to you no more. You'd be visiting me in the morgue. There's glass all around, all over the tables and the floor, and the fire alarm is just going batshit crazy.

Now I know you'll give me some crap for panicking right then, but I'd like to see what you would do with all that going down. So, yeah, I freaked out a little, but so what? I pull myself together enough to know I gotta get out of there. Right away, I gotta go. Fire engines and cops will be showing up any minute and there's no way I'm getting caught inside, especially when I didn't do nothin'. So in a heartbeat, I'm flying down the steps to the lobby and pushing on the front doors. Only thing is, the doors are locked together with some kind of chain. No, I didn't think of that. I'm banging on them, and kicking at the lock, and my breathing is gone and I'm tight and rasping and I feel like Deacon himself is sitting on my chest, but I got to keep going or I'm busted. I'm not thinking about who got to the necklace before me or who threw the rock. All I'm thinking about is living.

So I sprint back up to the main room and I look for the window that got broke and I climb up on that table there and I knock away some of the glass with my backpack and I jump through that window. Bam! I'm on the ground. It's a worse drop than I thought and my ankle is screwed and my elbow gets banged up, but I'm out. I'm hurt and I'm out of breath and I got no Black Diamond to give to Deacon, but I'm out. And when those first cop cars come rolling 'round the corner of Second Avenue, I'm halfway across town, running down the alleys like my life depended on it.

Running, Sketch, and I didn't stop until I got all the way out here to Wishing Manor.

ELEVEN

I was eight years old the first time I saw the ocean, on a family vacation with Rusty and our mother and some man named Bud who paid begrudgingly for an endless supply of caramel corn and pinball along the boardwalk.

The water was beautiful, with its roar and its foam and its Maxfield Parrish blue. It was the weight of the sea, the sheer enormity of it, that did me in. Rusty kept telling me that bodysurfing was the only way to ride and I did whatever Rusty said. But my big brother was twice my size and a wipeout—an all-out toss and turn, head-over-heels wipeout—was nothing but a rush to a teenager like Rusty. To a child like me, a lollipop with spaghetti limbs and not an ounce of muscle, a wipeout was an inescapable death spiral. I could swim, all the summers at the Y did that for me, but nothing prepared me for the way the waves got me in their hands, squeezing the life from me, toying with me, wrenching me down. My face breaking the surface. Stealing morsels of breath before going under again. Finding the shoreline, my mother there on the beach, just yards away, far enough to be useless. I still remember all of that.

This was worse.

Romeo had me against a fence, a tall fence in an alley near Boo's house, with its buckled pavement and broken glass and trash cans reeking of last Friday's fish dinners. I fought, the best I could, but it was too much. The weight of it all was just too much. The blows landed hard and fast, with fury and

125

determination. From time to time, I found the surface and, out of the corner of a blurred and swollen eye, I spotted Boo. He was a small figure on dry land, face down, Bigfoot Thompson knocking his motorcycle boot into Boo's ribs like he was crushing a Styrofoam cup. There were only two of them, Furnace Boys in black leather and boots, and they were taking turns with us like successive ocean waves. I made to call out to Boo, but my mouth was gagged with blood, thick in my throat. I called anyway with a gurgled voice, if that was indeed my voice I heard at all, and then Boo disappeared and I was upside down, head over heels, going beneath the surf once more.

Rising to the light of a lamppost, I heard words, snippets of nothing, that I later pieced together in a mosaic diary of the beating. "Necklace … cops … dead." The words belonged to Romeo, surprisingly breathless, as the Furnace Boy played the part of a fourth-quarter athlete still talking trash even as he lost steam. Then, as if reprieve was only a trick of the light, all went dark and quiet again, all except the pounding of the surf and the deafening sound of my own silent panic.

I didn't lose consciousness—it wasn't like in the movies—but instead I guess I simply let go. Let go of the will to fight, to protect myself, to raise my arms in defense. The will to keep my eyes open. The pavement was cold and hard and offered no comfort. But I stayed there, ashore, resting until the ocean quieted and the cries of the gulls faded and the darkness settled over us all.

Later. The hands that turned me over were massive and strong, but gentle. The palm against my cheek was rough as worn leather, but it held me there, my face to the streetlamp, until I could keep my eyes open for longer than a few seconds.

The man said nothing but instead offered something of a grunt, an echo in a distant canyon, and I couldn't be sure this wasn't a dream. Until I heard the sound again. I managed to prop myself to my elbows, with some assistance, and focused on the Samaritan at my side. Gargoyle. The man's face was as round as the moon, his shoulders heavy with a lifetime of brutal days, and he offered me a look of pity that said he had been down on the pavement himself not that long ago. I could say nothing at first. I just looked up into the man's face, recently shaved but poorly so, small pinpoints of burgundy scabs over his flabby neck.

"Boo."

I swiveled my head, slowly, as the pain gripped my body, and scanned the alley as though my friend would be right there beside me.

"Boo?" I repeated.

A beat.

"My friend. Where is Boo?"

With the patience of a parent looking under a bed for a monster he knew he wouldn't find, Gargoyle checked the alley, once, twice, before he turned back to me, a broken kid shattered on the concrete.

This was impossible. It was a dream. The only logical conclusion, this was all I could think, until the reality sank in that Boo was gone. Drowned in the depths. No, no. I had heard Boo, even when I was down on the pavement, I'd heard him. I'd heard ... the gulls. The cries of the gulls in the darkness. The piercing cries of my friend, clamped against a wire fence. Now, only memories, apparitions and nothing more.

I struggled to stand, even as Gargoyle tightened his grip on my arm.

"I'm fine," I lied. Everything hurt. My ribs were tight, as though a noose was fixed beneath my armpits and pulled taut by Hercules. The right side of my face—Romeo was apparently a southpaw—throbbed. My hands were on fire, bloody and burning with broken skin across the knuckles. I took stock of my pains. As best I could tell, the slit over my eye was clotted now, the blood there thick and tacky, like drying paint. My arms, my thighs, my ankle twisted on an errant and desperate kick, all seem manageable, albeit wracked with unfamiliar pain. I could make it through this. There would be no police, no ambulance, no need for assistance. I would do this alone.

Without expression, Gargoyle watched me stand, a small flag unfurling from the ground, and released his grip.

"Thanks," I said, trying to stay focused on the man's face, which kept slipping away into the night now and again. Gargoyle just kept staring at me. I extended my hand and winced when Gargoyle gripped it with pressure barely strong enough to crumple paper.

As I picked up my bike from the ground and walked away, other images arrived to me in the vapor, just long enough to be remembered.

We had made it halfway up Hall Street, Boo walking, me pushing my bike along the curb. Talking about nothing. The ability to burp the alphabet, the merits of pepperoni pizza, the wonders of bras that magically hook in the front. We were surprisingly relaxed for dead men.

"I'm hungry," Boo said.

"Vale-Rio?"

"Don't feel like diner food."

"Sal's?"

"Pizza neither."

"What then?"

Boo shrugged. "They got that new Pac-Man up at the lanes."

"Games don't exactly fill you up."

It had been easier than I'd expected to convince Boo to leave Wishing Manor. Even he could see that his plan to hide out in that old house for much longer was thick with problems. Not least of which was that he had no heat, no light, and no food. Never mind the fact that the Furnace Boys would find him sooner rather than later.

"We should go back to your house," I said. "You got food there. Plus, you can get rid of … you know."

Boo patted his coat pocket. "It's fine right here."

"Hell, no. You gotta dump that thing, fast. You can't get caught with that on you."

"I know, I know. I will. Let's just get some food first. Jesus, I'm starved."

"Fine," I said. "How about—"

"Hold up."

Boo saw them first, or heard them, footsteps in the gutter glass behind us. I glanced back over my shoulder. Romeo was a heavy shadow, moving with no urgency, but steady and sure as a tanker gliding down a current. Bigfoot Thompson was all agitation, a dog desperate to play, nearly bouncing right out of his boots alongside his slow-moving partner.

"Don't run," I whispered. "Just walk straight. Don't run." We were too far from anyplace safe. My house on the other side of Starr might as well have been on the moon.

We reached the intersection at the post office and headed south, toward the hospital and the pharmacy and freedom. People would still be out tonight, coming home from work, wandering back from dinner. We could hide among them, safe and sound in plain sight. But then what? We couldn't eat pizza all night. We couldn't duck endlessly in and out of stores. Besides, even if we did the impossible and got away, tomorrow was right there waiting. My Mongoose bucked beneath me like a rodeo bull, but as much as I thought about escape, I wasn't going anywhere. Boo had nobody else but me. I rode in tight circles, keeping pace with Boo as he began to walk a little faster.

"We're OK," I said. "They don't know nothing. Far as they know, you got the necklace. You got something to give Deacon."

"I don't got nothin'," Boo said. He was almost crying.

The Furnace Boys were gaining ground. I could hear the click-clack of their boots on the pavement.

"It's gonna be all right," I said, though I didn't believe it.

Boo sniffed, then coughed once into his hands. "How?"

"We'll tell them the truth. We'll tell them what happened. Somebody else got there first—a Slag, no doubt."

"Yeah?"

"Gotta be. Tell them and that solves everything, gets us right out of it. We'll just tell them—"

Boo shook his head. "No way."

"Boo, it's our only chance."

"I'll give them this, I'll give them the other one."

I grabbed his wrist as Boo stuck his hand into his pocket. "No way! No more guns."

He looked back at me, tearing up again.

"I'm serious, Boo. No more."

Finally, he nodded, sniffed hard. "Maybe I can still find it. Maybe I can get that necklace back from the Slags, you know, and ... and then I can give it to Deacon and he'll understand and everything will be all right." Boo stabbed a finger at a wet eye. "We can still be heroes, Sketch. We still can."

The alley appeared with a whisper and, without a word or a plan between us, we turned into it. By the time we reached the fourth backyard, we knew we'd made the wrong decision. In no time, the Furnace Boys were upon us. Ravenous, furious. Soon all four of us were against the fence.

"Where is it, little man?" Bigfoot hissed, his gnarled face right up in Boo's.

His eyes wide as a startled baby's, Boo croaked, "Where is what?"

I pushed off the fence, but Romeo held me there like a straw scarecrow on a post and simply shook his head in reproach. The Furnace Boy smirked, all hopped up and cocky, the muscles in his thick neck coiled tight, begging for an excuse to release.

"Let it be, Sketch," Romeo warned, his breath reeking of booze, his eyes wild from something else. "This ain't got nothing to do with you. Let it be."

"Bite me," I answered, even as Romeo pinned back my shoulders harder against the chain link.

The first strike was as sharp and sudden as a whip crack, Bigfoot's open palm catching Boo's jaw and sending him against the fence like a discarded wooden toy. Arms splayed, Boo slid to the ground, where he sat forever, stunned, before working up enough energy to reach for his pocket.

"Stop!" I screamed, hoping he would, hoping the neighbors heard me.

Romeo shoved me back, with more force this time. "I told you, man, you stay quiet and we keep you out of it. The little chickenshit is the one to pay here, not you."

I drew a breath and watched Boo, sputtering and wheezing through tears, pull himself up the fence. His back was to his attacker, his face pressed into the wire, his fingers hanging through the mesh. He was broken on the first hit, but he was on his feet again. There was something to be said for that.

"Don't, Boo," I said. Then, pleased that Romeo let this warning go without a reaction, I repeated it. "Don't."

Boo turned his head to look at me, his expression that of a suicide before the leap. Then, Boo pulled his empty hand from his pocket and with all the grace of a toddler on ice skates took a wild, spinning swing toward Bigfoot's granite head. The punch was easily avoided and, in one deft move, Bigfoot swatted it away, even as he thrust his own left into Boo's stomach with enough violence for me to exhale in empathy. In a split second Boo was on the ground again, coughing and crying now, choking on fear.

"You effed up, boy," Bigfoot said, sticking to his odd characteristic unwillingness to use any obscenity, no matter how appropriate. "You effed up real good."

"Tell us where the necklace is, Boo," Romeo said. "Tell us what you did with it and maybe we can work all this out. You think you're gonna keep it for yourself, is that it? Sell it on your own? Nah, that ain't how it works. The way it works is you go do the job and you bring the thing to the Furnace when you're supposed to. But you didn't show last night. We come to your school today and you're not there, neither. So, we come to get you now, we come to get what you owe." Romeo's voice softened, like he was Boo's best friend in the world. "C'mon, little man. Maybe you can set this right."

As Boo shook his head but said nothing, I scrambled for a coherent thought, even as I sent silent pleas toward the back windows of the houses lining the alley, begging someone, anyone, to throw open a storm door and see just what the hell was making all the racket. But no one bothered to check.

"He doesn't have it," I said.

"Riiiiight," Romeo said.

"No, Romeo, listen to me," I begged, "he had a plan. He went for that necklace, he did, but somebody else got to it first. Slags, probably, I don't know."

"Nah, naaah," Romeo said, even as he looked as though he was thinking it through. Then, he shook his head. "That's some bullshit story right there and I ain't in the mood for bullshit stories. Uh-uh, that story just ain't flying. You think we're nothing but fools, you two." Then, to Boo, "That what you think, you little shit? You think we're fools?"

Boo sniffed and raised his head toward Romeo. "It's true. I got nothing to give you." Then, in an unfortunate and misguided stab at bravery, he added, "It's also true that I think you're a dumb ass."

Boom, Bigfoot Johnson's boot, thick-soled and leather with long laces dangling like vipers, struck at Boo's side. Boom, again, the thudding sounds tempered only by the united howls of me and Boo. A third and final time, maybe as much out of anger as for Boo's use of a curse word, Bigfoot landed a particularly aggressive blow to Boo's shoulder.

It was the match at the flint for me, igniting my own fury, swift and desperate, and I ducked out of Romeo's grip and thrust myself forward with everything I had. I collided with the Furnace Boy and then, unexpectedly, miraculously, we were both on the ground, a tangle of arms and legs, a chaos of fists, as we rolled together away from the fence. Bigfoot Thompson was frozen, momentarily paralyzed by this turn of events. But his indecision didn't last, as Bigfoot soon realized Boo wasn't going anywhere and that he could easily insert himself into the new fray.

I was pulled to my feet again, two hands under my armpits, squeezing at my sides and lugging me upward. I felt quite distinctly as though I were rising on my own volition and I looked down on Romeo and the pavement and all of it and knew in that instant that my ascension would soon change direction. Romeo was still on his knees and shaking his head like a disapproving father and I, in a light-headed moment of wishful thinking, thought the Furnace Boy just might stay down there. Then, as the muscles along Romeo's shoulders tensed, the inevitable became dreadfully clear. I spent my last moment looking over at Boo, still shattered there not ten feet away. Boo was awake but unmoving, the only signs of life the quivering breaths he took as he surrendered to his own cries. His hands stayed away from his pocket, away from the gun. I wanted to tell him to stop crying, to shut up, to not let them win even in victory, but I found my own words drowned in the thickness of my bloody mouth.

The first solid punch caught me in the sternum, breaking it into a thousand pieces I was quite sure, and I fell backward into the embrace of the devil behind me. Bigfoot propped me up again, preparing me as Romeo stood, with a grimace of pain that gave me some small measure of satisfaction. This satisfaction was short-lived, however, as the second shot hit me at the temple, a devastatingly accurate blow that sent me easily, gratefully, back to the ground. I collapsed onto the cold concrete with a clatter of limbs and sank into it with resignation and relief.

As the Furnace Boys took their exit, there was a stirring around me, waves breaking on the surface, but I stayed down, enveloped in the warmth and quiet. My eyelids were heavy, all of it was so heavy. I wanted to raise my head, to tell Boo we would be all right, but the undertow was too strong, seizing at my arms, my neck, my legs stretched out behind me. Soon, its grip was around me and I was slipping under, without argument, letting it pull me down, into the depths and the silence and the darkness.

I remembered all of this, as I reached the corner of the alley and turned back to Gargoyle, my Samaritan, and offered a smile I hoped looked something like confidence.

TWELVE

Boo was going to die.

I can't tell you when I realized this. I just knew it from our earliest days together. Not in the sense that sooner or later everybody was going to die, but with the very real understanding that came with Boo's illness and hospital stays at a young age and too much fear and too many unknowns. For his part, Boo lived his life like he too knew he only had limited time. Despite his coughs, his weaknesses, despite it all, he never stopped taking his chances. I guess I always thought it was left to me to do the worrying for Boo, to save him from himself. As though I could do anything anyway, as though I had some kind of superpower.

Superpowers were at the center of our longest standing argument. We could go for days debating which was greater: invisibility or flight. In Boo's mind, there was no contest. Invisibility was his missing ingredient. The ability to slip in and out of convenience stores or to watch girls undress in locker rooms, the gift to move about without detection, that was Boo's choice by a long shot. But I always argued for flight. To soar above the clouds, move with speed from place to place, to escape. If I could fly, then everything would be different. That's what I always said, anyway. Not that it mattered who was right. Superpowers didn't come to kids like me and Boo, not in a place like Phoenixville.

"My God," Tara said when she opened her back door. Her hand snapped to her mouth and she stifled a sound into her palm. I'm sure I looked a mess, a horror even. As a new rain fell around me, I propped myself against the storm door and looked back at Tara through the fog of swollen eyes.

"Don't say anything," Tara said, guiding me by the arm to the small kitchen's dinette set. She grabbed a bag of frozen peas from the freezer and placed it against my face, watching with concentration, the way a nurse watched for allergic reactions to a shot. When I recoiled from the shock of the cold, Tara pushed the bag back against my skin and held it there, her hand over mine.

"You have to keep it there," she told me. "Best you can."

"It makes it hurt worse." To my embarrassment, I found I was close to tears. I looked down at the faded mustard tiles of the linoleum floor.

Tara caressed my hand, still pushing the bag against my cheek. "It'll only be worse if you don't."

The cold stung so much that I could think of little else right then, until my skin grew numb and the pain ebbed and my focus cleared a little. I moved the bag to the other side of my face, against the eye socket which hurt the worst.

"Where are your parents?"

"Church meeting," Tara answered.

My neck was too sore to nod, so I just closed my eyes in response. Tara's parents lived at that church. Praise the Lord.

After a time, when I finally lowered the bag of thawing peas to the table and Tara placed her hand, soft and warm, once again over mine, she asked the question I came there to answer.

"What the hell happened, Sketch? What's going on?"

And just like that, under the swelling drumbeat of the rain on the kitchen windows, the story—or most of it—poured out in a torrent of jumbled fragments. The words and emotions tripped over each other, despite the promise I had made to myself on my way over to keep things simple and direct. I had skulked behind Tara's house, sifting through the truth, catching glimpses of Tara as she walked by her bedroom window. I'd waited there in the dark and the rain, rehearsing the story, until the kitchen light went on and I saw Tara through the café curtains and I finally seized my chance.

"We need to call the police," Tara said when I finished my story.

"We can't call the cops. That would change everything. You understand that, right? It all changes," I told her. "Besides, my mom doesn't need another cop showing up with more bad news on her doorstep again."

Tara sighed, but didn't take the bait so easily. "I'm just saying, it's the kind of thing the police—"

"We're not calling the cops." I slumped back into the chair. My body hurt in places I didn't remember ever feeling.

"I don't understand why Boo thought Deacon would want a necklace," Tara said, almost to herself.

"He thought it was valuable."

"But what's Deacon supposed to do with it? How would he get rid of it? Who would give him enough money to buy guns or whatever you think he—"

"I told you. It's not like Boo thought it through."

"No shit. You know, maybe the thing is actually worth something, if a Slag got in there to take it—"

"It's not worth anything."

"How do you know?"

"'Cause it was too easy to take. Sitting out there in the open like that ..."

Understanding slowly emerged on Tara's face, like sunrise on the horizon.

"Oh my God, Sketch."

"I couldn't let him go through with it. I had to stop him, don't you see?" I said, my voice rising. "It's what you told me to do—"

"Me?"

"You said I had to make a decision. This was my decision. This is what I decided to do—"

"What did you do, exactly?"

My hand was already in my pocket.

"What did you—" Tara asked again.

The necklace was no less striking there in my outstretched palm than it had been at the library. Despite the darkness and the rain, a light seemed trapped inside the onyx. A captured wish, burning bright within the black, shining there in the palm of my hand ...

"I thought if I took it, if I got to it first, then Boo would be protected, you know? I would keep him safe," I said. "If Boo couldn't take the necklace, then he'd give up the whole idea of stealing for Deacon. We'd be out of it. Stealing anything at all. But I guess I'm no better at plans than Boo is. I see that now, I get it." I placed my head into my hands, gingerly holding on. "The Furnace Boys, they didn't believe us, they're not gonna believe anything we have to say. They beat the hell out of us, Tara. I mean, they could have killed—"

I stopped. I'd said enough. And I'd said everything I was capable of saying right then.

"He'll be all right," Tara said, after a long time of just listening to me crying and the rain drumming against the kitchen window.

"Boo's bad," I said. "Worse than me. He can't take a whole lot of this shit, you know what I mean? He ain't made for it."

Boo was no fighter. For all the fights I had gotten myself into through the years, I could count on one hand the times Boo had joined me. There was this fight years before—not much of one, really—when Boo got so angry at a kid over some perceived insult during a pickup baseball game that he chased the boy all the way to the creek with a Louisville Slugger. Of course, when Boo finally caught the kid, he didn't have a clue what to do with him and finally just slapped the guy, open-handed like some girl, while the rest of us neighborhood kids roared with laughter. I couldn't decide which was funnier, the fact that the kid got caught by someone as slow as Boo or the sight of Boo weak-wrist slapping at the boy.

"No one is made for this," Tara said, shaking her head. "God, why are guys such idiots?"

The clock on the wall, a black cat swinging a pendulum tail, counted the minutes with ambivalence. The plastic white eyes in its plastic head shifted back and forth with each second, scanning the room in constant vigilance for plastic mice. It was almost nine o'clock.

Tara leaned forward over the Formica table.

"Did you actually see them take him?" she asked, not as accusation. "Did you see where they went?"

"I know where they went."

"But how do you know? Did you see—"

"No. I didn't see anything."

"What do you mean, how could—" Tara asked slowly, as the reality dawned on her. "You were unconscious?"

"I guess."

"Oh my God, Sketch, we have to get you to a doctor. We're going to the E.R."

I shook my head, emphatic, stiff and sore. "No doctors. They're the same as cops."

"And your mother, what about her? She could help—she's a nurse, for chrissake."

"I'll deal with this myself."

"She'll find out soon enough, Sketch."

"I'll deal with this myself!" I repeated, rubbing at my temple and wincing from the pain still burning there.

Tara ran her fingernails through her hair, which I just noticed had a fresh streak of green in it. Admiring her calm, I watched as Tara tucked the streaked lock behind her ear and returned her hand to mine.

"I'm going to the Furnace," I said. "I have to go get him."

The statement just hung in the air as we held hands and the rain hit the window and the cat on the wall swung its tail from side to side. Even in my battered state, I understood the implications of what was to come. Maybe not all of them, but enough. A war of sorts had begun, without me ever hearing a single warning shot. When I think about it now, I can see there were signs, but at the time I was regrettably, woefully oblivious.

"I'm going with you," Tara said.

"No way."

"Why else are you here? You need help, you need me—"

"I was hurt," I insisted, "I needed to see you. That's all."

It was true, I had gone there because I wanted to talk to Tara, but I also knew I didn't have anywhere else to turn.

But Tara couldn't solve this.

"But you—"

I needed my brother back. Rusty would know what to do.

"Alone," I said. "I'm doing this alone."

I thought of my bike again, the wind at my back, my drawings tucked safely into my backpack, my legs pumping hard against the pedals. Flying. I could slip into the wind and let it carry me away from Phoenixville, this town full of nothing but ghosts and ashes. I could fly! Invisible? Hell, that was nothing. Give me flight any day and I would be gone. Gone for good.

"Sketch," Tara said, her voice far below me.

As I returned to earth, I managed something like a smile. "Sometimes, you have to make things happen yourself," I said. "Sometimes, you got no choice."

Tara took my hand again. "That's why I'm going with you."

THIRTEEN

In the distance, a train howled a curse as it passed through the outskirts of town on its way to someplace else. Everything was dark, the shadows and the rain playing tricks with each other. The cold wind was a malicious exclamation point, as it rattled the loose metal roofs of the millyard and tossed about the debris discarded over the ground.

Tara led the way, under the padlock and through the mud and weeds. I followed slowly behind, my injuries revealing themselves with every step. I limped, more pronounced when I thought Tara wasn't looking. My right side hurt like hell, a sharp stabbing pain where Romeo's blows had landed in quick succession, and I figured I'd probably be pissing blood for a few days. I was having trouble taking deep breaths and wondered if maybe a rib was broken, but I didn't share any of these concerns with Tara.

"Nobody's here," Tara said as we approached the empty shed.

I had expected as much. "Raining too hard."

Harley's absence was a particular disappointment, considering how useful some muscle would be right about now.

I pulled Tara into the shed. With its lookouts vanquished, the Furnace could be considered vulnerable, just another worthless building among the ruins.

"You sure you're up to this?"

Tara looked up at the foundry walls, dark and foreboding. "How do we know he's even in there?"

"There's no other place Boo could be."

"There are a hundred other places! The canal, the park … maybe he got away, got himself to the hospital—"

"He's in there, Tara. No place else."

Tara started to speak, but then stopped and her argument drifted into surrender. The moon, a voyeur slipping through the black clouds above us, illuminated the green streak in her hair. And in that moment, like the day she had first wandered into my class, I was certain Tara was the most beautiful girl I had ever seen.

"Do you feel all right?" she asked. "Enough to do this?"

I looked at her, this brave and beautiful girl, and was ashamed by my own fears. I closed my eyes and tried to picture myself as the hero, brave and bold. But in no time, this vision dissolved, replaced by another—a broken figure, lying on the ground, crumpled beneath the weight of a boot. I heard the cries of the gulls once more, in concert with the wind and rain, and the distant train making its own escape into the night. I opened my eyes.

"Let's go," I said.

Beneath the night's cover, we crept the last lengths through the mud to the old building. There, without even a brief hesitation, I pulled open the heavy metal door, hinges cried out with neglect, and we stepped into the darkness.

Darkness.

The faintest hiss, like a rush of blood to the head or the whispering quiet of an open tomb, absent until one truly listened for it. My aches and bruises forgotten now, I was aware only of the pounding of my own heart, the nausea in my gut, the dizziness behind my eyes. I wondered if Tara was feeling this, any of it at all, but I didn't ask. I took her hand and guided her up the stairs.

Leaning forward with his elbows resting on his fat thighs, his thick wrists hanging limply over his knees, Deacon was seated as usual in that damn fake-leather throne. The king cocked his head toward the staircase when he detected some movement there, then offered in greeting a slippery grin full of white teeth from the dark.

"Surprise," Deacon said, a hush.

"Damn, boy," Romeo sneered, glaring at us from his perch on an upended wooden crate beside the window, "we seen you coming a mile away. You two scurrying like a couple of river rats down there. All secret and shit."

Romeo let out a belly laugh, which echoed around the room, supplemented by the sudden laughter of other Furnace Boys who stepped forward like spirits from the shadows. Twelve Hops was there. Little Hal, too. Identical smug smiles on their lips, a shared nectar.

"Where is he?"

Tara's voice was strong, absent any obvious nerves. If the Furnace Boys were surprised to see her here, much less opening her mouth, they didn't show it. They looked only to Deacon, who sat back in his chair, folded his clasped hands over the mound of his Buddha belly, and sighed.

"Now, I'm not gonna play all dumb for you two and ask you who you mean or anything like that," he said, "and I'm not gonna suggest I don't know where your boy is. I'm just going to tell you one thing. This don't concern you. None of this concerns you. And that means you all need to just turn around and leave."

"Bullshit."

My voice this time, to my own satisfaction. The sight of Romeo there, nursing no apparent injury from our brawl, served only to piss me off even more and strengthen my newfound resolve. I wanted to smack that shit-eating grin off that face, but there was something I wanted even more.

"Give us Boo back," I said, "and we'll go."

Deacon smiled again, though its luster faded this time, and the big man shifted forward in his throne. "Give him back? After what he's done, Sketch? Give him back?"

"Yeah," I said, my tone no longer convincing.

"I don't think so. We ain't done with him just yet, see."

"Deacon, please," I said, my voice breaking too soon, suddenly pleading, "you know he can't take much of … anything."

"Sketch," Deacon said, his gaze flicking over Tara, "Boo done this to himself. Just talks himself right into things, don't he? But that's not my fault, no matter what you two have to say. The thing of it is, he said he could do a job, that's what he promised my boys, and he didn't do the job. Broken contract. So I deal with it the way any businessman deals with it. Simple as that." Deacon brushed his palms together and opened them clean, Pilate at the washbowl.

"He didn't do anything," I implored. "The necklace—"

"The necklace, the necklace. All that boy talks about. I never wanted no damn necklace in the first place."

"But you could sell it," I said, Boo's plan sounding more stupid with every airing. "You could sell it and use the money for all the guns you want."

Deacon touched his double chin, like he was thinking about it all, even though I knew he wasn't. "So where is this damn necklace?"

I opened my empty hands, even as I felt the weight of the Black Diamond in my pocket. "Somebody got to the necklace before Boo did. Like he said. He doesn't have it."

Romeo laughed. "Bullshit."

Deacon said nothing. He just gave me a dismissive glance, then returned his attention to Tara, this time working a path from her ankles to her eyes, as slowly as an asp slithering through a garden.

"That's the goddamn truth, Deacon," I said, "and you know it. Don't you think Boo would give you the thing if he had it, especially after you had your meatheads jump us this afternoon?"

"Careful little boy," Romeo hissed.

"I don't know nothing about any of that," Deacon insisted. "Alls I know is he said he would have something for me last night and he ain't coughed up no necklace and no guns—and he's coughed up a whole lot of other shit—so we got to keep talkin'."

I didn't know, couldn't tell, if Deacon really believed Boo had the necklace and was holding onto it for some reason. I suspected this was all some twisted act of bravado, macho garbage—everyone knew Boo wouldn't be stupid enough to hold onto the necklace now, if he did have it at all. He would give it back. If he was capable of such a thing, if he was capable of anything at all at this point. It was unclear just what any of us were capable of now.

My hand slipped into my pocket, my fingers wrapping themselves around the Black Diamond.

"What about them?" I said, waving my free hand at Romeo without looking at him. "Maybe one of your boys got to it first. Maybe they're lookin' to make a quick buck, sell the thing to the Slags or something. D'you ever think of that?"

Romeo slid down from the crate. "Shut your face now—"

For his part, Deacon seemed to consider this, but not for long. His eyes never left Tara, but he did offer me a smirk. "Nah, your boy got it, Sketch, or he knows what happened to it. So, he's gonna have to stay with us a little while longer ..."

Tara folded her arms over her chest as Deacon's gaze lingered there a little too long. "You can't do this. You have to let him go."

"Or what, girl?" Deacon said this last word with a precise enunciation, making sure his acrimony was clear.

"Or, or the cops are going to roll up here any minute now and bring Boo out for us."

Deacon laughed like he hadn't laughed before, loud as the blast furnace itself, his grin wide and open, full of flame. The laughter didn't last long, however, because suddenly Tara was moving toward Deacon and Deacon was bracing for her and Romeo was heading toward them and I was moving like I was going to get between them somehow and it felt as though all hell was rising up from the black. But then, just as the world was about to end, a sound came from somewhere else.

A cry, muffled and faint, but there.

Boo.

I peered into the shadows behind Deacon as something moved in the darkness. Then, the cry again, still quiet, and the louder sound of footsteps. I tried to find my breath, to steel my legs beneath me.

Bigfoot had Boo by the scruff of his neck, Boo's sweatshirt balled up in his fist. Boo's eyes were swollen, already a couple dozen shades of purple. There were cuts on his left cheek and the right sleeve of his brother's coat was torn loose. A red bandana was tied over his mouth and appeared tight enough to be slicing into him. But I barely noticed any of this. I was too busy staring at the gun.

The gun, clenched in Bigfoot's left hand.

The gun, pressed to Boo's temple.

The gun.

And, in that moment, as the gun glistened blue in the moonlight, I felt the seismic shift working its way beneath the old structures of Phoenixville.

"Put it away."

Deacon's voice, soft but stern.

Bigfoot laughed, uncertain. "Aw, I'm just messing—"

"Put it away." Same words, same inflection.

"He had it on him."

"What now?"

"Thing was in his coat pocket."

Deacon raised his eyebrows and looked at me. "You boys holding out on us, huh. He got us another gun after all."

"I don't know nothing about that," I said. God forgive me, that's what I said.

Deacon studied me for a long while. Like he was looking for the lie, listening to my heartbeat. His face gave away nothing. He was trying to figure it all out and trying to hide the fact that he didn't quite understand. Finally, he turned back to Bigfoot. "Put it away."

This time, the gun disappeared behind Bigfoot's back and got tucked into the waist of his jeans. His expression was one of a reprimanded child who'd just lost his favorite toy.

"Now, take that off."

Deacon again, pointing at the bandana. This time, Bigfoot didn't protest.

He untied the gag from Boo's mouth and gave the boy a small shove. Sprawling forward, Boo tripped over a loose board or his own shadow and fell with a sickening thud onto the floor. There he laid on his side, a crumpled heap, his arms tucked beneath him, his head tilted at an unnatural angle. Immediately, Boo erupted into a round of violent heaves, coughs and tears in pained harmony, and his body rose and fell with each emission. At the mercy of his reflexes and his injuries, he was no longer under his own control.

A Nightingale, Tara took a step forward, but I reached out and grabbed her arm.

"Wait," I said. Then, I looked at Deacon. "Can we help him?"

"Damn it," Tara said. She went for Boo, but I held her fast.

Deacon studied the scene for an interminable amount of time. A dog barked someplace far away. A steady yelping, at precise intervals, its own perfect rhythm. The rain grew harder on the roof. Finally, with apparent reluctance, Deacon disengaged from his appraisal of Tara and nodded, almost imperceptibly.

Tara reached Boo first and tried to help him from the floor, but she could only get him as far as the old oil drum lying beside him. Boo draped himself over it, like a washrag set out to dry. His coughing increased, violent and raw.

Between the coughing and the injuries from the fight, his pain must have been unbearable.

"We're here, Boo," I told him as I struggled to kneel beside him, my own pain not quite forgotten. "We're here now."

With as much force as I could muster, I pounded Boo's back, breaking apart the phlegm and the illness, the way I had too many times, for too many years. Boo was lying facedown over the rusty oil drum, propped on his elbows, as I slapped at him just below the shoulder blades. Over and over the blows rang out with dull echoes that died premature deaths in the emptiness of the Furnace.

"Son of a bitch," Boo said, smothering his raw coughs with his sleeve, which he also used to wipe the streaming snot and tears from his face. "Son of a bitch."

I knew it was killing him to shed those tears, in front of the Furnace Boys, in front of a girl. Tara, for her part, seemed attuned to Boo's shame. She stroked his hair, her fingers tangling in the red locks matted with what could only have been blood. She didn't draw back her hand.

"Easy," she whispered, as soothing as a lake lapping at its shore, "easy, Boo."

Boo was a shattered mess, bruised and bleeding and heaving. I looked over at Tara with encouragement. Keep at this, I tried silently to tell her, even though it felt as though we were doing nothing. I pushed up Boo's coat and shirt, exposing the raw skin to the cold, and ran my hand slowly just beside the spine. Then, finding heat, I lashed out again and brought my hand down against Boo's bare back, hammer to anvil.

"We have to get you out of here," Tara said. Then, to Deacon, "We have to get him to the hospital."

Turning his head, his body twisted into an odd angle over the drum, Boo looked back at Tara and said, "No, no hospitals."

"Boo—"

"Just get me home."

"I'm calling the police," Tara said, defiant.

Some of the Furnace Boys laughed.

"Then what you gonna do?" Deacon asked. "You gonna come visit your friend in juvie? 'Cause that's where they'd be putting little Boo. Yeah, they'll patch him up and get him healing right and all that, but then they're hauling his ass into court and asking Boo about the library and the missing necklace and he's gonna have to tell them he was there. You think they'll believe some bogus story about somebody else stealing the jewels? With all his stereo pops, that punk's got more priors than the rest of us ever did at his age. Nah, he'd take the fall, no matter what. Is that what you want?" Then, he stopped and sneered at Tara. "Don't think so."

Tara frowned. "You're not making sense."

Boo's whimpering interrupted the argument. I leaned closer.

"Boo, it's all right—"

"I'm sorry," Boo was saying.

"Shh," I told him, "you're gonna be fine. We'll get you home."

"I'm sorry..."

"Boo," Tara said, "you didn't do anything wrong. It's these assholes..."

"Bitch should shut her mouth." Romeo stepped down again from his spot, but Deacon stopped him with a raised palm.

Boo shook his head, too vigorously, like a little kid throwing a tantrum. "No, no. I screwed up. I should've stayed in the house, Sketch. I should've stayed inside. I screwed up."

"It's all right, Boo," I insisted.

"I'm sorry."

"You did great," I said, easing Boo from the drum. "We'll get you home now. Come on, let's see if you can walk." Then, to Deacon, "We're going to take him home."

I knew this was a request, though it was said with all the confidence I could summon. At first, there was no reaction. Then, finally, Deacon made the smallest of gestures. A slight wave, a dismissal, an emperor casting out soiled whores. And exactly in this moment I realized just how much hurt and hell I would bring down on Deacon one day.

Tara helped me to my feet and, despite my own injuries, I put on a good face. Then, together we grabbed Boo tenderly beneath the arms and lifted him from the barrel. He weighed nothing and we managed to haul him up with little effort.

As we stood, I dared a glance at Bigfoot, who remained only a few feet away. The weight of the revolver tucked into his waistband seemed to draw his posture straighter.

For everything I knew about Deacon, I knew nothing about this sudden need for guns. Sure, a Furnace Boy lived on the wrong side of the law, but never more than a few inches over the line. The crimes they committed were non-violent irritations, more than anything else. They were still children, despite their years, committing the crimes of children. Yes, there were rumors of some of the Boys dealing drugs, weed and speed, nothing more threatening than that. I had never been sure those stories were even true. But guns?

Deacon sat motionless in his chair. He still possessed the air of the leader, but his expression had shifted since we arrived. The smile was no longer wide, the eyes no longer confident. As though a lie had been uncovered.

"What the hell are you doing, Deacon?" I heard myself ask. "What do you need a gun for?"

Time passed slowly. Between there and somewhere else, the Furnace Boys hovered like souls in limbo. No one moved, no one even drew an audible breath. Tara and Boo stopped where they stood, looking at me and saying nothing. I saw none of them anyway. I concentrated only on Deacon, this overgrown boy playing king. For a moment, it looked as though Deacon would respond, but just as the tepid smile faded altogether and he opened his mouth, Boo let loose another angry flurry of coughs. Then, my splintered friend hesitantly shook his head.

"Not one gun," Boo whispered, his gaze never rising to Deacon. "He's got a dozen guns back there. A hundred! They all got them. This ain't about one or two guns."

I looked back into the black. "More?"

Tara's voice broke beside me. "Oh, God ..."

One look at Deacon, whose face in the shadows was nonetheless easy enough to read, told me the truth.

"Deacon?"

Deacon didn't even blink.

"There are more guns?"

"He made a promise, Sketch. Your boy promised me something and broke that promise. That's all this is about."

Tara started moving us backward to the stairs, to escape. "Come on, Sketch—"

Stalemate.

"Is this what you thought would happen?" I asked.

Narrowing his eyes, Deacon placed a finger to his chin, to create the illusion that he was giving careful contemplation to a response, even if he most likely didn't fully understand the question.

"I thought Boo might surprise us all," Deacon finally said, smiling with pleasure at his own answer.

"No, that's not what I mean," I said. "What I'm asking is, is this what you thought would happen when everything in Phoenixville went to shit, when how it used to be went and changed?" I swallowed and looked into Deacon's eyes, as deeply as I possibly could, no matter how difficult it was. "When my brother died, he left you alone, didn't he, just like he left me? I never thought about that, but it's true, isn't it? Alone in this place, alone in this town. And now we all have to find our own way. Everything was planned for us before. We were supposed to be Furnace Boys and go to work in the mill and live here our whole lives. Then our destiny got yanked right out from under us and all the sudden we're trying to figure it out for ourselves. So I'm asking you again, is this what you thought would happen?"

From his throne, Deacon peered down on me with something that looked like pity. Pity for my lack of understanding, my apparent naiveté, or pity for the future we were now hurtling toward.

"Time to wake up, boy. We ain't playing Wiffle Ball no more. You're still living in that little dream world of yours, head in the clouds, where everything is all perfect. Look around you—the world is changing and you're missing the whole damn thing."

Boo and Tara made their way down the stairs and I followed behind. I said nothing more, but I knew Deacon was wrong.

I did know the world was changing.

I knew this was only the beginning.

Best of all, I knew Boo would not die tonight.

THE LORD WILL WATCH OVER HIM

There were guns in the hands of the furnace boys.

Rebecca Wilton could focus upon only this as she watched the parade of soldiers make its way down Main Street.

The boys—her neighbors, friends, employees—her boys, every last one of them, were holding guns. Guns not for hunting, but for war.

With their whiskered chins held a bit too high and proud expressions masking any fears, the Phoenixville Artillerists of the First Pennsylvania Volunteers marched toward the railroad depot, where the train was waiting to take them into Philadelphia. Standing atop her carriage seat like Guinevere reviewing her knights, Rebecca was overcome with emotion, even as she struggled to recover from the initial shock of seeing her boys dressed in their new blue military uniforms. It was all too much—the guns, the uniforms, the music, and the stars and stripes—and within moments, Rebecca felt the hot tears well up. Reaching out a trembling hand, she steadied herself upon the arm of her new chaperone, the heavy-set Negro woman named Constance, who Father took on only weeks before to serve as the family cook and housekeeper and to fill the void of the overbearing governess Rebecca finally convinced him to dismiss. The woman placed her warm hand over Rebecca's and smiled.

"He will come back to you," the woman said, the certainty in her voice lending the weight of truth to her prediction. "Worry ain't nothing but a waste of that imagination of yours, darlin' girl. Your boy will be back."

How Rebecca wanted to feel this same faith! She had attempted to convince herself of such beliefs for all these past days and nights, but somehow the declaration sounded more persuasive coming from this kind soul at her side. Rebecca returned the smile and looked back to the parade.

There were eighty men or more, none much older than twenty years, and so similar in their uniforms that at first Rebecca could not find Shane in their midst. In this moment, she hoped, if only for a fraction of a thought, that Shane had changed his mind and made his way for the hills in the cover of night. But then, there he was, in the very thick of the formation, and to Rebecca's eye the only soldier who looked utterly comfortable in his uniform. Even at a distance, she recognized the familiar confidence across Shane's face, the eagerness for his journey ahead. He was the very picture of a warrior. With her handkerchief held high, Rebecca waved to her champion and called his name as he passed, but the other cheers were too loud, the music too boisterous, the crowd too thick for Shane to find her. In fact, he never looked to the crowd, marching instead with his eyes fixed straight ahead, focused on the flag in the hands of the young boy at the front of the parade.

Although this added more heaviness to her heart, Rebecca was not surprised that Shane did not look for her. They had agreed, after all, that she would not come here today, that the pain of seeing each other one last time would be too much for either of them. They had shared the evening before and that would have to suffice. This was the agreement, but in the end, Rebecca could not stay away. As the daughter of Elijah Wilton, she knew very well she could not sit at home. She needed to be here, not only for Shane, but also for all the boys from the Iron Works and the church and the rest of Phoenixville. She needed to be here, as one with the rest of the crowd, which now lined Main Street three people thick on both sides. Rebecca looked down at the withered men watching the parade, with their eyes lowered out of respect and guilt, and at the women waving their own small handkerchiefs and torn pieces of cloth. As children shouted from the branches of the park dogwoods and well-dressed citizens cheered from windows along the parade route, Rebecca added her voice to their chorus, singing the songs and joining the cheers, as her soldier marched by, seemingly oblivious to her presence.

As the company paraded toward the turn at Bridge Street, Rebecca found herself smiling with the sincere hope that this army's success would not depend on its ability to step in time, because their disjointed cadence betrayed the soldiers for the country boys they were. They looked a ragtag division indeed. This should have been no surprise, as just yesterday these young men were farmers and grocers and clerks. Furnace boys as well, of course. Indeed, the furnace boys comprised the bulk of the company, as they were perhaps most willing to exchange the fires of one hell for another.

This was the rationale Shane offered Rebecca when they sat on their rock and spoke once more of his plan to join the Union Army, a plan appearing more inevitable with each passing day. Although the war had only just begun, towns across all of Pennsylvania were calling for arms, pulling their men and boys from the fields and factories for the service of the nation. Shane saw no higher calling. War, he insisted, was the only way to preserve the Union and towns such as Phoenixville. A Union victory would ensure the free navigation of the rivers, which any furnace worker knew was necessary for the success of a mill. It was said the war could even abolish slavery, though Rebecca found few who would claim such a cause as the primary objective. None of this mattered, in any case, as Rebecca cared not a whit for these rationalizations. As her Shane spoke, the brass buttons gleaming from his fine blue uniform, his confidence further bolstered by the emblems at his shoulders, Rebecca wished only for one thing: for this boy from her roof to remain with her there on that rock forever.

In the nine months since Shane surprised Rebecca at the Harvest Festival, theirs had been a most enthusiastic if hurried courtship, made more urgent by the impending threat of war. Though the long hours of his shifts made it difficult for Shane to visit Rebecca as much as either of them desired, he made the journey out to the parlor of Wilton Manor as often as he could. They sat together on the chaise, their knees touching occasionally, or daring to hold hands for a moment whenever Constance left the room. Though Elijah was spending more time at the mill, overseeing the production of weapons and materials for the Republic, Father still managed to linger at Wilton Manor whenever Shane came to call. He took a particular and obvious shine to the boy and often asked him to join the family for dinner, where he regaled the young couple with stories of his own courtship of Rebecca's mother. Several times, Elijah and Rebecca each prodded Shane to accept that supervisor position at the Iron Works, so that his hours might be more amenable to a developing courtship. The ulterior motive of delaying Shane's enlistment was obvious to all, and Shane would only smile politely and shake his head.

The couple became a familiar sight at every social gathering and the source of constant whisperings. The only child of Elijah Wilton taking up with a furnace boy was irresistible gossip, a blessed distraction from all this talk of war and bloodshed. No matter where they appeared—walks through town, the church socials, the Saturday night dances—Rebecca did her best to satisfy the audience, holding Shane's hand in public and combing back his hair whenever the renegade locks fell over his face. Once, in front of a small crowd of youths waiting on the steps outside the dancehall, as Constance went off to find the carriage driver,

Rebecca seized the moment to plant a long goodbye kiss on Shane's lips. Shane pulled her tightly against him as she did so, pressing his chest against hers, his hands sliding along the side of her bodice, and Rebecca felt for certain she would faint away. Later, after Shane returned to his room at the blacksmith's house and the Wilton carriage crossed the long bridge over French Creek, Rebecca still tasted the salt of that kiss.

At the end of supper one night, as she placed a dish of her marvelous lemon custard in front of Rebecca, Constance pronounced, "You love this boy." It was a statement of fact, indisputable, and Rebecca felt her cheeks grow warm under the woman's gaze. Rebecca wanted to dismiss the words, as though a denial might soften their blow, but she found she could not, and simply returned her attention to her dinner.

"Yes," Rebecca admitted after a few moments, her voice a low rasp. "As though my chest will explode with it."

"Then, trust," Constance told her, "trust that the Lord will watch over him."

For a time, Rebecca found some solace in the conviction of her housekeeper, but as the certainty of war and the inevitability of Shane's departure grew nearer, the girl's strength was eroded by intruding sadness, drawn over her by invisible hands like a dark shroud. Matters were made worse by Shane's own distractions as he seemed to take such pleasure in each preparation for battle. He basked in the arrival of his new Federal uniform and was stunned speechless when Elijah presented him one night with a specially made single-shot rifle. To Rebecca's mind, Shane never showed any trepidation at his coming journey, and his strength and calm, traits Rebecca once considered so attractive, now served only to bring her more darkness. Why, it was as though he were actually looking forward to leaving Phoenixville behind. Thus, Rebecca awoke more confused each morning, this love and anger and confusion at battle within her heart.

Her surprise therefore could be well explained when, one late afternoon as they shared iced tea on the wide front porch overlooking the manor's entranceway, Shane asked her, "What will we do, Rebecca, when I return?"

Not understanding at first, Rebecca answered too quickly. "I imagine we shall put on quite a celebration, a party here at the house."

"No, what I mean is," Shane told her, "where will we stand, you and I, when I come home? Will you, that is, will you wait for me?"

It was the closest they had ever come to discussing their future, perhaps because the future was so obvious to anyone who saw the two of them together. The future was certainly clear to Rebecca.

"I will wait," Rebecca told him, taking his hand, "for no less than forever."

Shane allowed himself a proud smile. He seemed anxious to say more, but no words arrived. Instead, the young man reached into his jacket pocket and extracted a package, wrapped in a white silk handkerchief.

"'Tis all I could ever wish," Shane said, "that you would wait for me."

He placed the gift onto Rebecca's lap, then watched as she peeled back the handkerchief.

"Oh, Shane," she whispered. "It's breathtaking."

The necklace was unlike any Rebecca had ever seen. The jewel, a large black gemstone, was cut as a hexagon, framed in silver, and hung from a thick filigree chain. Despite its black hue, the gem seemed as bright as a flame, even against the shining sterling. Rebecca did not dare put it on. Instead, she hesitated, holding the jewel higher, so that she could admire it as the afternoon shadows fell over the manor grounds.

"An onyx," Shane told her. "Queen Victoria herself is wearing such jewelry now. If it is good enough for a queen, then ..."

"Look how it shines," Rebecca said. "Like a black diamond."

Gently, Shane took the gift from her hand and Rebecca allowed him to place the necklace around her, so that it draped just so. The onyx was striking against the pale of her skin. Rebecca watched Shane's reaction. She could see the wish in his eyes and she knew then all of this was real. In that moment, the girl fell against her soldier, burying her face into his chest. She let him hold her there, until her breathing returned. When she finally spoke, her voice was strained.

"Why must you leave?" she asked.

"Rebecca," Shane answered, "it is not that I wish to leave. What I wish is only that my leave might be brief, so that I will soon return to you, to this town, where we might build a home and a life. Together. That is worth the fighting."

Smiling up at Shane, Rebecca touched her necklace, so that the afternoon sun took its final breath just beneath her slender fingertips.

Shane left his work at the mill three days before the train arrived and spent his remaining time on the grounds of Wilton Manor. To the pleasure and surprise of the couple, Elijah even permitted the boy to take a small room on the first floor beside the kitchen, though Father made it clear that any abuse of his hospitality would not be tolerated. Because he himself was spending much of his time at the Iron Works, Elijah depended on the watchful eye of the new housekeeper and three dogs who slept on the kitchen floor outside the boy's room. Still, Shane and Rebecca managed to spend most waking hours together, due in large part to the discreet distance Constance kept.

On the afternoon of their final day, Shane led Rebecca on a long walk that took them along the cliff and out toward the old Indian trail at the property's western border. They walked slowly, holding hands, heads down, hardly speaking. A persistent mist enveloped them as they walked, though neither seemed to notice. The sounds of the mill across the creek rang like distant church bells, unheard. The emerging mud of the path only served to slow the couple's pace, until they came to a stop at the farthest corner of the property, beside the small grove of weeping willows Father had planted last summer when the house was under construction. They looked at each other, their thoughts easy to translate. When Shane kissed Rebecca now, the hot days of the previous summer and the sight of the boy on the roof seemed as distant as the streets of Paris. She kissed him in return, allowing his hands to slip over her, feeling every second of these final moments and praying, praying the afternoon would last forever.

"Are you frightened?" she whispered, squeezing her arms around the furnace boy as tightly as she could.

Shane broke her grip gently and pushed her away, so that he might look at her. His usual reply, confident and dismissive, was ready at his lips. But then, his expression shifted and he pulled Rebecca close to him once more. They stood there, sinking into the mud at their boots.

"A little," he confessed.

"Then, let us run away," Rebecca quickly replied, seeing the opening for which she had prayed. "Flee this war, all of this, as fast as the wind will take us. No, say nothing yet. Listen to me. This is what we must do, we must. We can be gone with tonight's sundown. Father will lend us horses, I know he will, and we can take the old roadway along the Schuylkill, back through the forests. The same path the Negroes take on their way to Canada."

Shane sighed. "And is that where we might go, to Canada? Like runaway slaves?"

"To the mountains then, to the west," Rebecca answered, her voice rising. "Anywhere. It does not matter. You understand that, surely? It does not matter, Shane, as long as I am with you."

Chuckling softly, Shane cupped Rebecca's chin and lifted her face so that she might see his eyes, so green, so rich.

"You have thought about this," he said, not unkindly.

"Every waking moment," she answered.

Standing there, Rebecca was quite certain they were the only two beings on this earth. How she wanted to be with him, not just now in this moment, but in all times, in all ways. So lost in this fantasy, she did not hear his words at first, though she was quite certain of his response long before he ever spoke.

"We cannot flee our destiny, Rebecca," Shane told her, his voice as light and soothing as the mist.

Rebecca knew he was right, of course, no matter how difficult this truth was to hear, to accept. She could not argue. There was only one response which made any sense to her now. As the tears exploded forth, Rebecca tore away from Shane and ran. There was no grace to her movements. She sprinted wildly, like an Appaloosa tasting first freedom. As Shane raced behind her, Rebecca stole glances over her shoulder, her steps veering closer and closer to the cliff's edge, her footfalls more than once tearing loose a thatch of soil and sending it plummeting to the creek far below. She heard Shane's voice behind her, his pleas, but she was the wind, the rain, and she rushed away from him with everything she had.

Not until Rebecca was within a few steps of their rock did Shane reach her. His hand grabbed her wrist, pulling her to a stop and turning her to face him. They were both in tears now, rain mixing with it all, and their breaths came in deep, heavy waves. Neither spoke. The soft patter of raindrops fell on the leaves all around them as they kissed once more. Between them, the necklace shimmered with a fire barely contained.

After a time, Rebecca pulled herself away from Shane again, but this time, she did not seek escape. Taking hold of his hand, she led him the final few steps to their rock, cantilevered out over the creek, and she pulled him down onto her. As she gave herself to him there upon the rock, the coolness of the wet stone against her back, the warm strength of the young soldier upon her, Rebecca surrendered all thoughts of war and anger and confusion.

Afterward, they sat against the granite, tossing pebbles over the cliff and looking out on the iron mill and the rest of the town spreading around it. There on her high hill, wrapped in the arms of her soldier, Rebecca felt invincible.

"With all my being, I promise one thing to you, Rebecca," Shane said to her, softly at her ear. She dared not lean back to look at him, she just let him hold her there, close to him, feeling their heartbeats united. She did not need to look into his eyes to know his words were true.

"Yes?" she said, even more softly.

"I will return to you," he whispered. "I will return to you and we will have this day again, just as we have it now. All will be exactly the same for us."

Rebecca swallowed and tried to breathe. Her eyes filled.

"I wish for nothing else," she said, crying once more. "Nothing."

The young couple remained there as quiet as snowfall, clinging to each other at the cliff, until the raindrops slowed against the branches and Constance's distant voice carried through the trees, calling Rebecca home.

Now, as Shane and his parade finally disappeared around the bend, Rebecca sank to her seat in the carriage beside this small woman with the enormous smile and was taken aback to discover Constance's own eyes full of tears. This was enough to break the dam and Rebecca covered her face with her hands and sank to the bosom of her chaperone, as the driver untied one of Father's strongest horses from the hitching post and began the long return journey up the hill to the sanctuary of Wilton Manor.

FOURTEEN

"Mister Walker, let me see you for a minute, please."

As the rest of my classmates filed out of homeroom, some shooting me looks of curiosity or even sympathy, I slouched my way to Crowe's desk.

"Can we do this later?" I muttered, eyes on the floor.

"No."

"I'll be late for first period."

"I'll write you a note." Crowe gestured toward a front-row desk. "Sit down, please." I slumped into a seat. "Now, I still haven't heard from your mother."

I stared back at her and shrugged.

"I think it might be a good idea if I give her a call. It's important that she's in on what we've been talking about," the teacher suggested, as she chose a pencil from the cup on her desk and twirled it between perfectly manicured fingers.

As usual, Crowe looked spectacular. Her hair, long and sun-washed, was pulled back in a tight ponytail, revealing four silver studs along the rim of her left ear. Best of all, she was wearing my favorite shirt, a billowing peasant blouse with a wide neckline that fell open whenever she bent over. Along with every other guy in my homeroom, I spent most of the days she wore this top concocting ways to get her to pick up things from the floor. As she walked through the maze of desks inspecting our work, there was always a conspiracy of pencils dropping hopefully at her feet. Rarely to any avail.

"You can call her," I said, trying to sound indifferent, "but she ain't never home. She's pulling a lot of double shifts over at the hospital."

Crowe frowned and sat back, her arms folded over her pregnant belly, which looked noticeably larger in this position. I couldn't help thinking she looked a little like Deacon in his recliner. "Why do you do that?"

I studied my hands, clasped too tightly in my lap, and started picking at my fingernails. "Do what?"

"Say 'ain't'? You're better than that, you know. It isn't you."

It isn't you. What was that supposed to mean? Like she knew better than I did just who I was. Like she knew anything.

Then again, just who the hell was I, anyway?

Nothing but an impostor, that was my answer. A damn impostor. Nothing different from anybody else in this town, a place full of pretenders and phonies at every turn. That was how I saw it back then. Phoenixville was the land of the lost, people caught between who they used to be and what they were becoming. The unemployed lingered around the remnants of jobs like dogs sniffing at the curb on trash day. The politicians insisted the town would return to its glory any day now. And the churches actually believed they had a prayer of saving a soul. The land of the freaking lost.

Sometimes it seemed like the only person in Phoenixville not putting on some kind of act was Deacon.

Goddamn Deacon.

I stared back at Crowe. It isn't you. There were guns in the hands of the Furnace Boys and this woman wanted to argue about grammar. She was lucky I even got my ass to school that morning. I'd been this close to ditching, on account of everything. After I finally got Boo and Tara home, it was well after midnight and I just made it back to my own house before my mother's car pulled up at the curb out front. I did my best out-cold act when she came in to touch my shoulder and whisper her love before shuffling off to her own bed. After replaying the night's events on an endless loop, I finally did drift off, for a little while maybe, but I awoke before the dawn and, with a hastily scrawled note on the kitchen table to explain my early exit, headed out into the morning. I thought about going back up to Wishing Manor and killing the day—it would buy more time before I had to explain my bruises to anyone. More time for the swelling around my left eye to go down. But I didn't really feel like riding all the way up there and I didn't have any other place to go. So I showed up at school. Hoping to slouch through another day with my head down, without too much drama.

It isn't you.

"You mean it ain't me," I said. Then, I offered a friendly little smile to ease the sarcasm.

To my relief, Crowe laughed and leaned back into her cracked vinyl chair, sliding the pencil behind her ear in that way she had. Through her classroom window, the light caught the woman just right and I was struck again by the beauty of her face, the high cheekbones, the elegant nose, the easy smile. If the opportunity ever presented itself—and I was just about sure it never would—I would have to reconsider my refusal to draw portraits and human studies. I'd make an exception for Crowe.

"You came to me," Crowe finally said, with a stare so pointed that I had to look away. "Isn't this what you wanted?"

"I guess."

"You guess? The Blake School is without question one of the finest schools on the East Coast. You must have recognized some of the alumni names in the packet I gave you? Poets, presidents, musicians. And artists. The Wyeths themselves have sent their children to school there. I thought for certain your mother would support your interest. And yet she doesn't call ..."

"I know," I said, because it was all I could say.

"I'm confused. Didn't you say you wanted a different school, an art school? We had this conversation already—"

"I said I wanted to get out of this school."

"To work on your art."

"But not at another school."

She stared at me for a good long while. "What, are you thinking of dropping out? Being a starving artist already?"

I shrugged.

"It's just that this—" Crowe stopped, abruptly, and looked out the window toward the staff parking lot. "Oh, God."

"What?"

"I almost said this is for your own good," she replied, snickering at her own presumption. "That isn't right. Well, it is right, but that isn't something for me to decide."

I nodded, still not understanding, and wished the conversation would just come to an end so I could get out of there. I needed to check on Boo, to talk with Tara. It wasn't that I dreaded time with Crowe and on just about any other day I wouldn't have minded the chance to be alone with her like this. But not today.

"Here's the thing," Crowe said. "Maybe I shouldn't have done this—some would say I've overstepped my bounds—but I've done it nonetheless. I went ahead and set up an interview for you at The Blake School. I sent your transcript over to an old friend in Admissions there, along with some of your work from art class and, well, they would like to meet with you."

My cheeks burning, I leaned forward at my desk and sputtered, "What? Meet with ... but, but what if I don't want to meet with them?"

For the longest time, Crowe said absolutely nothing. She just sat there, staring at me, her arms still folded over her unborn child.

"What is it you want to do?" she finally asked. "Once high school is over. What will you do?"

I shrugged again.

"Is it too far away to think about?"

"Maybe."

"Maybe not."

I stayed quiet, maybe out of defiance or annoyance. Maybe because I was lost, because I didn't know what to say.

"Do you plan to go to college?" Crowe asked.

I scoffed. "We can't afford no col—. We can't afford college."

Crowe ran her tongue along the front of her teeth and didn't respond.

"And besides," I said, "what would I need college for? It's just more school. More putting off the, you know, the inevitable."

Behind the teacher, a large Picasso print, the hands holding flowers, was framed in cheap black metal that didn't do the picture justice. I would have used a nice light oak, something natural. Then again, I never would have bought the print at all. Too obvious, too popular.

"It is more school, yes," Crowe agreed, "but I would argue the inevitable is what happens if you don't go to college. Look, I won't bullshit you."

I was startled by the word coming out of her mouth, like a thousand flashbulbs just went off.

"You have a chance here," Crowe continued, unaffected, "a very good chance to make it out of Phoenixville and there aren't too many people—students or adults—who can say that. Most of your classmates, this is it for them. You know that. Even the bright ones, the ones with good grades, good tests, the odds are not in their favor. How many kids do you know who have even talked about going to college?"

"Not many," I mumbled, thinking only of Tara and her mother's school in Boston she had mentioned once or twice. Boo had never said one word about college. It wasn't like Boo's grades would get him in anywhere, anyway, and if his illness kept up it just might hold him back in high school until he was thirty years old. Harley could end up playing football somewhere, but even if he did, he'd be right back in Phoenixville the day after graduation, probably working in his dad's garage.

"You're not going to college, because no one around you is even talking about it. It's not because you can't afford it, Sketch. It's because of your surroundings."

She was right, probably, but I still stayed quiet and instead just waited for the hard sell.

It came quickly.

"So," Crowe said, "my suggestion is that you change your surroundings. Go to Blake. Do something for yourself—take this step in the right direction. You'll be boarding with students from all over the world—all of whom will go on to college."

"Boarding?" I repeated. "You mean, like, I'll live there? That ain't gonna happen."

"It's a boarding school, yes. And it has an art program unparalleled, I guarantee you that. You'll be able to work on your craft and learn from great teachers and get yourself ready for college."

"I'm not going to some boarding school," I said, thinking not only of being apart from Tara, but also being surrounded by little rich snots with emblems on their blazers.

Crowe sighed. Then, she reached for a folder at the corner of her metal desk, a thick folder packed with brochures and information about The Blake School, and handed it to me. I took it without even opening it and shoved it into my backpack.

"Blake wants students like you, Sketch."

"Students like me ..."

"Yes," she said, "and they're willing to pay for that diversity. A scholarship, a full scholarship, is certainly a good possibility here. Do you understand that? You and your mother wouldn't have to pay a cent for a top-notch private-school education. And if you can't get a scholarship based on your financial need, well, you can be assured they would be very interested in your talent."

"My talent."

"Your art."

"It's nothing," I insisted, shaking my head. "Cubes and perspectives and bowls of fruit. A monkey could do that stuff."

Slowly, Crowe rose from her chair, her belly coming first, then the rest of her, and she walked around the desk. She smelled like a warm bath, vanilla and flowers. She leaned on the corner of the desk, her body only inches from me. At this point, I was convinced my head was going to explode. I fidgeted with the zipper on my backpack.

"Why are you doing this?" I finally asked.

"Because you have a gift," she said, opening her hands as though the answer were self-evident. "And I believe in gifts."

"Nothing I believe in ever comes true."

"This is true, this is real," Crowe said, the calm of her voice never wavering, "I have no doubt. I believe in this."

"Then," I told her, "prepare to be disappointed."

She didn't flinch. "Tell me you will at least go see the school. I'll drive you. Your mom and you. We'll drive up there and take a look. You could transfer in for the second semester of this year and be well on your way to a Blake diploma. After that, provided your grades are all right, you'll have your pick of some outstanding college art programs."

I just shook my head again, a mixture of exhaustion and sadness. Then I stood and pulled my backpack over one shoulder.

"Is this what you do?" I finally asked, a harsh edge to my voice.

"What?"

"Get off on trying to save people?"

"I don't ..."

"Not everyone wants to be saved," I said, "and not everybody is cut out to be a hero."

With that, satisfied, I reached for the door. That would end it. We wouldn't talk of The Blake School and scholarships and college again. My defenses held.

"Mister Walker?" Crowe asked, just as my hand turned the doorknob. "You want to tell me how you got those bruises?"

I paused, my hand still on the knob, my head bowed.

"No," I answered.

FIFTEEN

The afternoon air still smelled of showers as I stepped out of school and the gray of the clouds suited my mood. Things only got worse when I spotted Deacon on the bench near the bus stop. He took up nearly the entire bench, one of his legs crossed at an awkward angle over the other, his long arm stretched along the back of the bench like it was made for him. He watched the kids streaming from the doors of the high school with a smug expression of ownership and feigned disinterest.

I did my best to avoid Deacon's gaze and nearly made it to the bike rack before I heard the shrill whistle from across the street. I looked—despite myself, I looked—and Deacon beckoned me with the slightest flick of his head.

"What's happening, Sketch?" Deacon purred when I reached him.

"Nothing much." I looked down at my sneakers.

"How you feeling?"

Harley always said that football players, after they got hit by an especially violent tackle, made a show of getting to their feet quickly, to let their opponent know they were unfazed.

"Never felt better."

Deacon looked me up and down, lingering at my black eye.

"I've seen you look better."

"Yeah?" I replied. "Well, I didn't get a hell of a lot of sleep the past couple days, so maybe that's it."

I could barely stand to look at him. When I did, I didn't even really see Deacon at all. I saw Boo. Boo, with his eyes swollen shut, the rim of his mouth caked with dried blood, the tears coming in endless and emphatic streams. I heard the cries and the brittle coughing and the pounding of my own open palms against his bare back. I relived all this pain, as I knew I would for some time to come, and standing there now next to the guy responsible made me more furious than ever. God, I hated the bastard.

Apparently oblivious to all this, or maybe just indifferent, Deacon cleared his throat and spat into the grass. "Me, I sleep like a baby. Always do, man. There's no substitute for a good night's rest, you know what I mean?"

Over Deacon's shoulder, I spied Big Hal and Little Hal on someone's front lawn across the street. They were wrestling, Big Hal laughing and sitting with his knees pinned on his brother's biceps, Little Hal wailing and wriggling like a snared trout. A tree in the yard had a yellow ribbon tied around it for the hostages over in Iran. A carpet of leaves covered the ground beneath the tree and Big Hal was shoving a generous handful into his brother's mouth. This must have set off Little Hal, because with one sudden move, he swept his boot up and around his brother's throat and sent Big Hal sprawling. With that, the wrestlers reversed positions and Little Hal was seated atop his brother, if only for one brief stunning moment, until Big Hal tossed him aside like a used towel and got to his feet. Then, dusting himself off and still laughing, Big Hal suddenly snapped his head up and spied me staring at him. He stopped laughing. I returned my attention to Deacon.

"Whatever," I said, shifting my pack. "So, like, take it easy."

I turned to leave, but Deacon grabbed for me, his hand wrapping so tightly around my forearm that his fingertips overlapped.

"Hold up, where you going?" Deacon said, sliding over against the bench's arm rest and clearing a narrow space for me. "Sit down here a minute. Sit down." He lowered his voice. "C'mon now, if I was gonna hurt you for real, you'd be dead already."

Even though Deacon said this with a nice wide grin, I wasn't sure if he meant it as a joke and I sure as hell didn't take it as one. Despite the overwhelming desire to run, I took a seat beside the fat man, so close our legs touched.

"Good," Deacon said, "that's good. I was just thinkin' I might run into you out here and now here you are. Ain't it funny how that works out sometimes?"

"It's where the bikes are," I said, pointing at the rack.

"Easy, boy," Deacon said, dragging out the words like he was exhaling smoke.

"So, what do you want?"

"Want?"

"Come on, man, I don't have time—"

"Come on, man, I don't have time—" Deacon repeated in a near-perfect mimic of my thin whine, too high-pitched to sound anything near tough. Then he placed his hand firmly on my knee and slapped it twice. All the while, his eyes stayed focused on the school, studying the steady parade of departing students. "You got time, boy. Much as I give you. You got time."

"All right."

"So, lemme ask you, this necklace Boo was bragging about," Deacon said, "what do you know about it?"

"I don't know nothin' about it."

"The Black Diamond. That's what he kept calling it. Some kind of—heirloom or something."

"I guess," I said, still avoiding Deacon's eyes as my mind slipped and slid. "It's not like Boo always knows what he's talking about. He's full of shit half the time, you know that."

"True enough. But still, you think it's worth something? Old jewels like that."

"Me? I don't have a clue."

I could feel Deacon's eyes studying me, but I couldn't look at him. I suddenly couldn't do much of anything.

"Well, somebody must think it's worth something," Deacon eventually said, "seeing how somebody went to all that trouble to steal the thing."

I tried to swallow, but my throat was knotted up like a kinked garden hose.

"I don't like losing," Deacon said. "It's just that this seems like maybe some kind of missed opportunity, you know. Like maybe, just maybe, Boo knew what he was talking about. Maybe this necklace is worth more than anything else he could have picked up for us."

I shrugged, because I wasn't sure I could respond any other way.

"You boys think the Slags got it, huh? That's what Boo kept saying—"

Another shrug, then I managed a few words. "Probably, yeah. If somebody got to it first, makes sense that it's them. Sure."

"Sure, yeah," Deacon said. His voice was eerily calm, even kind. It scared the crap out of me. "So, listen, you'd tell me if

Boo had it, right? You know that'd be the best for everybody. To come clean and all. You'd tell me."

I nodded.

"Of course you would. Nobody ever called you stupid."

Suddenly, Deacon stopped talking to watch Crowe leave the school, slipping out early with the student dismissal. The teacher waddled down the steps to the faculty parking lot, then dropped, not without some difficulty, behind the wheel of her increasingly too small Honda Civic, the one with a "NO NUKES" bumper sticker.

"That is one sweet ass right there," Deacon said. "Even all knocked over, she is f-i-n-e."

Although I didn't want to prolong this, I couldn't just let that go.

"Knocked up," I said.

"What?"

"You knock them up, not over."

"Shit," Deacon answered, still watching the teacher and waving his hand imperiously at my correction, "you know what you're doing, you don't do neither, little man."

"Whatever."

"So, who the hell is that, anyway?"

"Some teacher," I said, although I considered the answer pretty obvious.

"Da-yam, teachers didn't look like that when I went here."

"Which was what," I asked, "all of five years ago?"

Deacon snorted. "Something like that. 'Course, I wasn't on the four-year plan."

Not until Crowe's car slipped down City Line Avenue did Deacon turn his attention back to me.

"So, the thing is, Sketch, I visited the library myself this morning. Just to see what's what," Deacon said. "I got to talking to some cute librarian. College girl, Ursinus, I think. Anyway, I got her spilling about the necklace and she said they're all broken up about it. I couldn't ask too much, you know, so she didn't get too suspicious or nothing."

I just nodded my head, hoping this was an adequate response. My stomach was thick with anxiety, foaming up inside me. I stayed fixated on the laces of my sneakers and tried my best to keep my voice under some control.

"Anyway, she said they figured the robbery was just some stupid prank. A truth or dare."

"Truth or dare," I said, if only to test out my voice.

"Right."

Deacon reached down and scratched with vigor at his fleshy calf, where the elastic of his tube sock had left a deep imprint. To get at the itch, he pushed up his pants leg to reveal a fine full-color rendering of a majestic bird, a phoenix in blue-green ink, rising from the ashes with its wide wings outstretched.

"That new?" I asked, pointing at the tattoo, and praying the shift in subject wasn't too obvious.

"A couple of weeks ago," Deacon answered, seemingly pleased the tattoo had been noticed. "Cool as shit, don't you think? A good old phoenix, coming back from the dead and all that."

"Hell of a metaphor," I mumbled.

"What'd you say?" Deacon snapped.

"I said," I answered, in a louder voice, "it's quite a metaphor."

"No, asshole," Deacon replied, his eyes narrowing, "I heard you the first time. What I'm asking is what the hell you talking about?"

I pointed again toward the tattoo and stammered, "It's a metaphor, you know, a symbol. The dead bird that comes back to life. Like they're always promising about this town, right? Phoenixville will rise again, and all that bullshit. I just thought that's why you picked it. A metaphor."

"Yeah, a metaphor," Deacon said, looking as if sometime long ago he once had heard the word. "It's a damn metaphor. You wanna know the truth, I never thought I'd get one of these things. Always thought they looked stupid. Maybe not so much now, but what about when you get older, you know? Nothing sadder than a washed-out tat on some saggy-ass skin. Old people just ain't made to wear no tattoos."

"So, aren't you gonna regret it when you're old?"

Deacon sighed and looked away.

"We ain't gonna get old, boy."

Across the street, Tara exited the school with a small mafia of Jordache and hairspray girls, all of them laughing loudly at some shared joke and clutching identical denim binders tight to their chests. The other girls didn't exactly seem like the kind Tara would hang with, but I liked seeing her with someone other than us delinquents. I watched her intently, trying to imagine what they were talking about, and willing Tara with everything I had to not look my way. Soon, she turned the corner, without ever seeing me.

"So, I don't got nothing to do with no necklace, Deacon. We've been through all this already," I said. "Why don't we talk about what you're really into ..."

I can just about count on one hand the number of people I have truly feared in my life. There was Ferguson, an older kid who used to live up the road when I was in first grade. We neighborhood boys were convinced that Ferguson ruled the streets with an old hockey stick and too much Pabst Blue Ribbon in his system, but I always believed the fear was instilled through reputation more than anything else. Still, like any kid with half a brain back then, I stayed clear of Ferguson just the same.

There was Five, one of my mother's boyfriends back when Rusty and I used to give the guys numbers instead of names, just to keep them all straight. He was a drunken Teddy Roosevelt bear of a man, lumbering and clumsy, who moved like he was quite capable of knocking over anything in his path and didn't give a shit. Five also was prone to rage, never directed at us or our mother, but at the great indignities of life itself. Grocery prices, athlete salaries, the suits who screwed up the steel plant, he would bitch about anything, but it was an explosive bitching, far beyond a level that fit the subject at hand, and I lived in fear of whatever might set Five off on his next fiery rant.

Back then, there were teachers who scared me as well. A batshit-crazy girlfriend of Rusty's. The old crossing guard with the lazy eye. The butcher who seemed to enjoy cleaning all the blood from his knife whenever he was sure I was looking.

And there was Deacon.

"What I'm really into?" Deacon repeated, flashing his familiar grin. "I ain't into nothing, little man. Nothing t'all."

"Right."

"Right. Simple as that," Deacon confirmed, and again lapsed into silence. Actually, silence is not exactly the correct description as Deacon made about as much noise breathing as a struggling window-unit air conditioner. It wasn't the breathing of the afflicted like Boo, but the laboring of a person for whom a flight of stairs posed the day's most daunting challenge. I listened to this, the rhythmic breaths of this fat young man beside me, and I waited.

"You might not believe this," Deacon said, "but I actually give a shit about you."

"You're right," I told him, "I don't believe you."

"Your brother and me, Sketch, we were tight. He watched out for me, took me under his ... you know ... his wing and whatnot. He made sure I was doing all right whenever anybody else was giving me shit."

"I don't think anybody gave you too much shit, Deacon."

"You'd be surprised," Deacon answered, his eyes straight ahead as if focused on some distant yet vivid memory. "But Rusty, it wasn't just me he took care of, neither. Even back then, when you knew the mill was a goner and the town was dying, you felt all right with him around. Rusty took care of things. He knew the right way to get things done, to make things happen. He always did."

"I don't want to talk about my brother."

Deacon stopped for a moment. When he continued, his tone was actually contrite, barely above a whisper. "All I'm saying is, what you said last night—about how your brother left us alone, you and me—that's what got me, man. You were right. We're all just trying to figure this out, you know, find our way."

"Find our way? You almost killed Boo."

"Nah," Deacon said, smiling, "they didn't come close. But I'll tell you what—everything that boy got, he had coming to him."

"He didn't do anything, Deacon. He told you the truth."

Deacon returned his arm to the back of the bench, wrapping it around me. I immediately leaned forward to pluck a tall shaft of ragweed from between my shoes and, in one fluid motion, stripped the buds from the stalk and tossed it all back to the grass.

"Maybe," Deacon said. "Maybe he didn't. All I know is, your little Boo lost me a good shot at one easy payday."

"Bullshit. You don't even know if that necklace is worth anything. You said so your—"

"Librarian was all knotted up about it. That's what I said. Like they lost something valuable. Worth a lot of cash."

"And what do you need the money for, Deacon?"

And there it was, the million-dollar question, all framed up and ready to be hung on a wall.

"What does anyone need money for, boy?" Deacon laughed.

In this laugh, however, I sensed just a little less confidence. I rephrased my question.

"All right, so what do you need the *guns* for?"

If Deacon was surprised, he didn't show it. The only indication that the question had thrown him in the least was the fact that he stayed absolutely stock still. Above us, the sun cowered behind a cloud. The air took on a noticeable chill.

"Supply and demand," Deacon finally answered, spreading his hands wide. "I'm a businessman, an entrepreneur. I'm just providing what the people are asking for. Look, this town is changing. Even a punk like you can see that, right? And people, they ain't doing a thing about it. They just stick their heads in the sand and pretend we're all still living in yesterday. It's like the world's gone backwards, you know? People, they think the future is the past, like what lies ahead is everything they had before. They go 'round talking about the mill and the old stores on Bridge Street and all that shit. They can't let go of the past, but the thing is, the past let go of them a long time ago. It's all gone and it ain't coming back." Deacon folded his hands, letting them collapse together into his lap, a pose of mourning. "And then, there's people like my moms, right, who want to keep moving forward, want to do the right thing, but they ain't got no idea what that is. So they spend their days like she does, camped out in front of soap operas and talk shows and cashing their unemployment checks. You think that's any kind of life? Shit, that ain't no life at all, man. No life at all."

I wasn't buying it. Maybe Deacon took comfort in that rationalization, that he was just some kind of salesman giving the people what they wanted, but I just thought he was full of shit. And I was all too aware that my original question remained unanswered.

"My mom told me a Slag came into the emergency room with a gunshot wound in his leg just last month. Probably a drug deal or something," I said. "We don't need no guns in Phoenixville."

Deacon acted as though he didn't even hear me. "You remember the fair, Sketch, over in Kimberton? When we were kids, I couldn't wait for that thing to start. Every year, a whole week of rides and food and loud music and lights, man, all those lights. Christmas in July, that's what it was. The whole town would turn out for that thing and I'd spend every hour and every nickel I had just being there. Even when I ran out of money and couldn't scam my way onto the rides no more, I couldn't leave the place. Hell, I'd even watch the cow judging and all that animal crap just to soak everything in. You remember that, don't you? 'Course you do. That's what I'm talking about now. People can talk all they want about the steel mill, but that fair was the thing that brought people together. Brought them out of their houses and ... aw, shit ... I don't know. We were together, that's all. You remember, right? You remember. And all those places ... we don't have places like that no more. They don't come back."

"Deacon ..."

"Somebody's gotta to do something, is all. We can't just let them take the whole town away from us."

"Who?"

"Everybody, man," Deacon said, his voice rising, his breathing growing more pronounced. "The fool politicians, the schools, the churches, the Slags—everybody."

I couldn't argue with him. Not really. Phoenixville wasn't the same. Dying or changed or whatever, it definitely wasn't Phoenixville any more. My God, I actually agreed with Deacon. I kept this to myself.

"Shit, boy, open your damn eyes," Deacon said. "It's happening now. Rent is cheap, houses are cheap, come on in 'cause everybody else is gone. Ain't nobody else wants to live here no more. You can't sit here and tell me that ain't true— the only new people moving in here is that trash blowing in from 'cross the river. You just sit back and let that happen and pretty soon you don't got no town no more."

"But there are others coming," I said, thinking of Tara and her parents. "New people, I mean."

"You ain't hearing me, boy. I'm not talking about some little trickle this way or that. I'm talking about the whole dam bursting. It's time somebody stood up and did something about it."

"With guns?"

Deacon snorted. "Guns ain't nothing but the tool. There's people out there who are tired of waiting for others to give them a way out, you know? People want to take matters into their own hands. They want to provide their own living."

"How? By robbing places? Each other?"

Another shrug, all innocence. "Like I said, everybody's got a right to earn a living. Look, I'm just meeting a need. That's all I'm doing, man. I'm running my business."

I frowned, tried to process it all, tried to think of the next thing to say.

"Preservation," Deacon said. "You asked me a question and there's your answer. The guns are for preservation."

I was spent. I reached down for my bookbag, then stood and slung it over my shoulder. The bag was heavy and my body was sore and I was beyond exhaustion now. I just wanted to get away.

"You're gonna ruin this town, Deacon."

I wasn't sure why I bothered saying this. I don't know why I didn't just walk away. Walk away without a word, before the conversation began all over again. But Deacon simply looked up, his lids heavy over surprisingly watery eyes, and sighed.

"Already ruined, boy. Already ruined."

Big Hal and Little Hal, who apparently had stolen a pumpkin from a neighbor's porch, were tossing it back and forth in the middle of City Line Avenue. There was a loud, fleshy splat when Big Hal deliberately missed a catch. Without another word to Deacon, I turned and walked away.

I didn't get too far before I heard Deacon's thundering steps coming up behind me. I sped up, stepping out into the street and heading for my Mongoose, before my bookbag was wrenched backwards and I was brought to an abrupt halt at the curb.

"Boy, I got one more thing to say to you."

Deacon leaned in so close I could see the small beads of sweat along the bridge of his nose and smell the bitter coffee on his breath. His brow squeezed low over his squinting brown eyes, Deacon glared at me. Any friendly pretense had vanished.

"You get in the way of this and I'll kill you," Deacon said, without a smile. "And, believe me, that ain't no fucking metaphor."

SIXTEEN

The path to Wishing Rock was pock-marked with deep puddles splattering with fat raindrops. Tara and I left our bikes beside a tall pine tree and tried to avoid the muddy pools as we walked the rest of the way along the edge of the cliff to the rock.

"Are you scared?" Tara asked.

"I don't like heights all that much."

"No, about Deacon. Are you scared about Deacon?"

I drew a breath, let it out. "Nah."

"He threatened you, Sketch ..."

"I guess."

The rain had picked up again from the time we'd left Tara's house. She was dressed for the weather, with a yellow raincoat, polka-dotted rubber boots, and a big cowboy hat that she'd studded with buttons and pins, decorated to look like some kind of rodeo punk rocker. Tara liked to say that her "new-girl honeymoon period" at school lasted exactly ten minutes before the preps in her French class started making fun of her fashion sense, her streaked hair and her bohemian clothes.

I loved everything about how she looked.

"I still don't understand why you don't just tell Deacon the truth," Tara said, as we settled onto the slick surface of Wishing Rock. "You could end everything, just by giving him the necklace, before ..." She pointed at my black eye. "Before all this."

194

Wrapping my arms around myself, my ribs still sore, I stared out over Phoenixville. "I don't know."

"It would have solved—"

"It wouldn't have solved shit!"

"You can't be sure."

"I am done with Deacon, OK? I can't just keep handing him whatever he wants: no more car stereos, no necklaces, and no goddamn guns. I'm not giving him a thing, no more. Not one thing." I shoved my hands deep into the pockets of my painters pants, found the Black Diamond still there, wrapped the necklace around my finger. "He doesn't deserve it. OK?"

Tara shrugged. "Then you'll just have to put it back."

"I can't do that neither."

"Why not?"

"Because then everybody would know. The cops, the Furnace Boys, they would know I took it."

"I'm sure you could figure out a way—"

"Boo. Boo would know. And if he knew I had it all this time … when we, when he—" I touched the onyx one more time, then took my hands out of my pockets. "Look, things are really screwed up. Boo and me, it's different now. I mean, he never would have done that job on his own like that. Without me. But now that you and me are … I don't know, he thinks because I'm with you now, or … shit. Everything's just different, everything's changing." I took another look at Tara, but I had a hard time meeting her eyes. "Because of you."

"You can't put this on me," Tara said. "You stole the necklace, Sketch. No one else."

"I only mean—"

She took my hand, rubbed her thumb over the scabs at my knuckles. "I know what you mean."

We sat there for a while, as Tara wiped the mist from her face and I wondered when the goddamn rain would ever end.

"I don't know what to do about the guns," I finally said.

Kicking her boots against the granite, Tara weighed her response.

"Why do *you* have to do anything?"

"Because, it's wrong," I answered. "Somebody's got to do something ..."

Tara removed her hat and ran a hand through her hair, the green streak slipping between her fingers. Then she reached out and gently touched the swollen spot around my eye. "Maybe fighting isn't really your thing."

"We did pretty good. Stood our ground and all that. Boo, he's tough as hell, considering."

"And did it help anything?"

I thought for a minute. "I guess not."

"Then the fight wasn't worth a damn."

I put my arm around her. She leaned into me. We didn't look at each other.

"It's not just Deacon, you know. It's not even just the Furnace Boys," I said. "He wants to sell them, put them in everybody's hands. Can you picture that, the Slags with guns? It'll be a goddamn war."

"But not your war."

Slipping down from the rock, Tara left me to grapple with the conversation's tail as it writhed away just out of reach.

"Fall has the prettiest flowers," Tara said, as she bent slowly and pulled a tall wildflower from the edge of the cliff. "Have you ever noticed? Never made sense to me, that the season when most things die is exactly the time when other things just start going." She stood again, spots of mud clinging to the knees of her jeans, and held the flower out to me, before the breeze took it from her hand and stole it away over the cliff. "So there's that."

"Right," I said. "There's that."

Suddenly, Tara started walking away from me.

"Where are you going?"

"I want to see the house," she said. "We should go inside, get out of the rain."

I shook my head. "We can't go in there."

"Why not? Boo went—"

"Yeah, but only the one time. We never go in. I don't know, I just never felt—it's somebody's house."

Tara peered back through the trees at the decaying structure of Wishing Manor, its broken windows, the vine-covered walls, the weathered trim.

"Not anymore," she said.

Then she was away, through the brush, into the pines, and headed for the great lawn behind us.

But Tara never went inside the house.

I caught up to her at a small garden of some kind, something I'd never noticed on any of my other visits. Ringed with white speckled rocks the size of grapefruits, the grass there was rich and thick, grown longer than the rest of the lawn. Flowers, colorful and fragrant from the rain, were scattered across the plot. And over it all, from a small pedestal at its center, stood a stone angel with her head bowed slightly, her hands opened at her waist, and wings reaching toward the sky. One wing, her left, was broken in half, its fragment nowhere to be seen. I took Tara's hand when I reached her and we stood there together in silence, gazing at the broken angel, its face only a suggestion of features, after so much time and weather.

This wasn't a garden.

"Who do you think—?" I heard Tara ask.

I didn't know the answer.

"Someone who lived here, I guess," I finally said, "a long time ago, probably."

Tara made no acknowledgment that she agreed. Instead, she said, "Why do they call it Wishing Manor?"

"Who knows?"

"But aren't you curious?"

"No, not really."

Wishing Manor rose over us like a protector, sheltering us from the wind in that quiet corner of the yard. I walked over to a wide window near the back door and wiped my palm over the glass. When we pressed our foreheads to it and peered into the darkness, we could just make out the floorboards from the second story, rotted and collapsed through the ceiling into the kitchen. Every surface was black, covered in a thick layer of dust and dirt. Tara took a few steps back and I followed her gaze along a tall dogwood tree to one of the second-floor windows, the panes dull and covered by the impressive architecture of an enormous cobweb.

"There's a story in there," Tara said.

"I don't really care about the past," I answered with a shrug. "Sorry."

But I wasn't sure if Tara heard me. She seemed miles away.

"It's nice here," she finally said. "Even in the rain."

It wasn't yet five o'clock, but darkness was coming early, and we would have to go home soon. My mother wasn't working that night and I would need to face her, show her the bruises, endure all the questions.

"You and Boo," Tara said, "you think you'll be all right?"

"I haven't seen him," I answered. "I doubt he'll be coming to school for a while and he doesn't pick up the phone when I call. Maybe I'll get him to come to the parade tomorrow. We'll see. I can't remember a day we didn't talk. Me and Boo talk every day."

The angel, regal in thick drapes of robes, tinges of green in the stone folds, watched us there. Her shoulders were slumped with the weight of more than wings. Her hands cupped the rain, cradling it for a moment before letting it flow over her fingertips and down to the thick grass below.

"What are we doing?"

"I just wanted to come out here," I said. "To get away—"

"No, not this. I mean, what are we doing, you and me?"

"I thought it's what you wanted."

"Am I your girlfriend?"

"I think so."

"You think so?"

"Well, I don't, I — I know this is new and all. Only it don't feel like that. It feels like we've known each other forever. At least, that's how I feel, anyway."

Tara let slip a smile, apparently content with this answer. "Yeah."

We kissed, in the rain and beneath the watchful eyes of Wishing Manor and the broken angel. After a time, we made our way back to the rock, hand in hand.

"I'm sorry," I said. "About the necklace. I probably shouldn't have taken it. But that was the only move I had left, you know? I tried to talk Boo out of it. I did. But Boo isn't exactly the type—"

"—to listen—"

"—to listen, once he's decided he's gonna do something."

The rain was easing and we returned to our place on Wishing Rock, beneath a sky now that perfect Phoenixville gray.

"Anyway," I said, as I pulled the Black Diamond from my pocket and handed it to Tara, "I think you should have this."

She raised both hands in alarm.

"What? You're crazy. I'm not taking that."

"But we already said, I'm not giving it to Deacon and I'm not putting it back in the library—"

"So?"

"So. Far as anyone else is concerned, this thing is vapor, vanished," I told her. "Come on, it's not like it's really worth anything. We would have heard by now if it was, don't you think? The town would be going nuts looking for it. No, it's like they're saying, probably just a stupid teenage prank over a piece of worthless, sentimental jewelry."

"Maybe. I don't know."

"And I think it's better if this necklace just disappears for a while," I said. "Let them all forget about it. Let it be lost to the ages. Look, you don't even have to keep it forever, if you don't want. Just keep it until all this dies down, until everything goes away. And then, if you really want to give it back to the library or whoever, you can figure out how to do that. If that's what you want."

"But what am I supposed to do with it? I can't wear it in public or anything ..."

"Of course not, no," I said. "But you would have it and I would know you have it. And that would make me very happy, to know that."

"Sketch, I—"

"Please."

Tara finally took the necklace in both hands and looked at it, really looked at it for the first time, before placing it around her neck. The necklace didn't exactly go with what she was wearing—the rain slicker and the cowboy hat—but it looked perfect on her just the same. Like it was meant for her.

"Beautiful," I said.

And Tara actually blushed a little, as she closed her collar over the Black Diamond.

Somewhere in the west, a car horn blared, a reminder that neighbors were in fact just over the tall hedges that separated Wishing Manor from the rest of the world. For a few minutes, I had forgotten all about them.

"Did you draw today?" Tara asked.

"What? No, I didn't draw. Not in a while—"

"Did you want to? The sun's gone, but there's still some color there."

Truth was, I would have loved some time to get back to my drawings. Maybe it would make more sense to just hide out for a while, away from Deacon and his Furnace Boys and Boo and everyone else, and simply bury myself in my artwork. The steeples of the Three Sisters had been giving me trouble for weeks and it would be good to catch them in the dying light.

"I got too much going on," I said.

Tara nodded, as if that was the end of it.

"Did I ever tell you about my uncle?" she asked, after a time. "My father's brother. He's my favorite relative, my hero really, even though I don't get to see him all that much anymore. He's crazy looking, with legs like a whooping crane and he's got this Adam's apple, big as a golf ball. Actually, that's what my father calls him. Apple." Tara said this like she'd only just remembered it, permitting herself a slight smile at the memory. "Anyway, he's a writer, a poet, and he carries this beat-up notebook everywhere he goes, this ratty thing shoved down deep in his pocket. And every chance he gets, every time I look at him, he's scribbling something in there. Maybe quotes he hears or little observations or just a list of groceries he has to pick up on the way home, who knows? But I'll tell you what, that notebook is the best friend my uncle's got. It's like he can't live without it. He spends so much time with it, you would think his hand would fall off from all that writing. One Thanksgiving, after we were all fat and happy sitting around the living room, I finally decided to go ahead and ask him just why it is he spends all his time scribbling in that notebook. And you know what he told me?"

"He's got no choice," I answered.

Tara broke into a wide grin, the rare kind of smile a person seemed grateful for, the kind that illuminated her whole face.

"Yes. Exactly."

"That's not me." I shrugged, an unconvincing gesture. "I don't have to draw."

Tara raised her eyebrows. "You sure about that? I don't think even my uncle would come all the way out here to some rock to work on his writing."

As though under Tara's direct command, the fog eased just then and a horizon of rooftops and flagpoles and filigreed spires revealed itself, the structures glistening like minerals in a riverbed. And with one last breath of muted ambers and reds, the day gave way to evening.

"It's raining."

"It's stopping."

"There's too much going on, " I repeated.

"Do you have your stuff with you?"

"Back at my bike," I said. I'd left my knapsack hanging over the handlebars of my Mongoose back at the tree.

Tara opened her hands at her waist, mimicking the gesture of the stone angel. Her only response.

I know I probably should have told her then that drawing was just about the last thing on my mind. All I was thinking about was running away, leaving Phoenixville, leaving them all. I should have told her about my big plans: The Blake School and art and all of it. That was the moment, right there.

"I never expected to find you," I said, "not here in Phoenixville."

Tara's smile took away all the rest of it.

"Maybe you weren't looking hard enough," she answered, as she turned and headed back toward our bikes.

I didn't say anything about leaving Phoenixville. Not a single word.

BRAVERY TAKES A THOUSAND FORMS

Rebecca Wilton could not sleep.

On nights such as this, when the moon was full and the music of the forges laid a raucous symphony over the city, when the rest of the world seemed so awake, Rebecca Wilton could never sleep. This was not for lack of trying, as sleep was her only remaining refuge and she welcomed it as often as she could find it. But on this night, she seemed much too desperate for its arms and sleep stayed warily at a distance. Still she tried, reading by the lamp until the fuel burned low and her hands grew too heavy to hold the book, but even when she closed her eyes and placed a feather pillow over her head, she could not sleep. Today had not helped matters.

Elijah Wilton was in his element when he escorted the visitor around his mill as though Mister Lincoln himself had graced Phoenixville with his presence. The day for Rebecca was a command performance. She was decoration and nothing more, there to be admired, but certainly not heard. For his part, the visitor appeared less an army general than a lawyer or a banker, attired in a well-tailored suit of imported wool, his military uniform apparently left behind in Washington. As they walked through the mill, the general was polite enough, enduring Father's endless boasting of the Wilton workmanship and the many years of success with which the town had been blessed. Indeed, the general's attention frequently appeared focused elsewhere—that is, until the tour left the mill and came to a halt on a vacant field at the end of the Iron Works property.

The cannon, a remarkable gun fashioned less than a month before by the new weapons division at the furnaces, sat alone in the field atop an enormous caisson. Its apparent target—the skeleton of a dead oak—stood in a small field across the creek.

"So, this is it?" the visitor asked, running the admiring hand of a marksman along the cannon's long barrel.

"Yes, General Geary," Elijah told him. "I dare say it is the finest weapon you will see. Your bursting problem with other models has been solved. The secret is in the way we have rolled the wrought iron rods—"

Geary interrupted without even acknowledging that he had heard Elijah. "Does it shoot straight?"

"What's that?" Elijah answered, momentarily thrown. "Why, yes, of course. This is why we brought you all the way up here, General. The Wilton Cannon shoots straighter, its load flies farther, than any gun currently in the Union's arsenal."

"Show me."

"Would you like to hear how—"

"Mister Wilton," Geary said, "if this gun fires as straight as you have said, I don't give one good goddamn how you have made it." Then, with a glance at Rebecca, he added, "Pardon me, Miss."

As Rebecca offered an appropriately demure smile and bowed her head, Elijah called to his men, who were standing by, "You heard the general, boys. A demonstration now, if you please."

The first shot rang out like nothing Rebecca had ever heard. Though she stood far back at the edge of the field, with her hands cupped over both ears, she was quite certain she had gone deaf. Because her eyes were closed, she missed the cleaving of the old tree as the ball passed through it. The second shot was just as accurate, tearing off a branch as easily as a turkey leg at a banquet. By the time the third shot pierced what remained of the trunk, Phoenix Iron had received an order for one thousand cannons to be used in the service of the Union Army.

As General Geary heartily shook hands with each of the workers present and her father beamed with pride, Rebecca remained obediently quiet. But it was on the way to the dinner, a spectacular afternoon feast at the Hotel Phoenix on Bridge Street, that Rebecca could keep her thoughts to herself no longer.

"It is wrong, you know," the girl said.

"What is that, angel?" Elijah answered, hardly looking up from the pages of the Independent Phoenix.

The carriage had only just slipped past the twin stone columns marking the entrance road into Wilton Manor. They were ugly markers, Rebecca thought, these columns—far too big and brash and adorned with the name she was coming to detest. She considered the iron signs depicting furnace fire on each tower a further undignified conceit.

"Profiting from the war," Rebecca told him. "It is wrong."

As he removed the half glasses from the bridge of his nose and folded the newspaper neatly in his lap, Elijah stoically considered his daughter seated across from him as the carriage turned toward town. His jaw, so strong, so sharp, was clenched, his cheeks a deepening red, and Rebecca steeled herself for the admonishment to come.

Instead, her father spoke with a soft voice difficult to hear.

"We cannot all be soldiers, Rebecca."

Rebecca followed her father's gaze through the carriage opening to the lush balustrade of trees along the roadside. The sycamores and the oaks swayed, their leaves turned upside down, the harbinger of another rainstorm.

"I do not know what that means."

With a heavy sigh, Elijah explained. "We cannot all do what your Shane is doing. That is what I mean."

"This has nothing to do with Shane."

"Of course it does. You miss him, as do I, and there is nothing wrong with that. But the way you are going about it, this mourning, this sadness, it is not healthy. Look at you, you are wasting away."

It was true. Before she could catch herself, Rebecca looked down at her mother's dress, which once fit her perfectly and today hung too loose from her shoulders. Her appetite was gone, her meals spent writing more letters to Shane or re-reading his long epistles from the front, which came in thick monthly packs bound by twine.

Nothing helped. The darkness that visited more often these days was soon upon her again. It was not a sudden sickness, but rather one which crept over her like the sunset, slow and steady, easing her into its shadows until she forgot the very feeling of daylight. It might be expected that this darkness began when the train left the station nearly two years before, taking with it her soldier and his company of men. Rebecca herself might admit as much. But, in truth, Rebecca showed remarkable fortitude in those days and weeks following Shane's departure. Indeed, she became the very picture of a war mistress, spending her days gathering supplies or consoling other women far worse off than she. The girl even took to the mill when the workforce grew so depleted that the soft hands of a woman were better than no hands at all. But her back was weak for the work and she found herself an obstruction to the blacksmiths and fillers more often than not. Soon, when she learned that Shane had re-enlisted—this time for a two-year term supporting the 51st Pennsylvania Infantry Regiment—Rebecca surrendered and took more permanently to Wilton Manor. Though she busied herself there with her books and the gardens and her father's household affairs, she could keep the darkness at bay no longer. It consumed her at will.

"This cannon will do nothing to end the war," she argued, diverting the conversation away from her health. "It is a toy for these generals, so they might prolong the fight until ... until the last soldier falls. You must see that, Father."

As tears welled, Rebecca wiped a furious palm at her eyes. Her father looked on her with pity.

"I see nothing like that, angel," Elijah said. "This is merely a case of supply meeting a demand. It is you who will see. This cannon will become the Union's greatest weapon. The Rebels will fold at its first volley. Much good will come of this, a swifter end to this war. I promise you."

Rebecca's eyes burned. She was enraged: this man, this wealthy man, sitting here in his cushioned carriage on his way to another succulent meal, while her Shane, her soldier, slept with mosquitoes and snakes in some godforsaken field. What did Elijah know of war? Of courage?

"If it is not profiteering," Rebecca said, her voice trembling, her fists opening and closing, "then it is cowardice."

"Rebecca!" Elijah started, his face flushed with fury.

But then he stopped and Rebecca heard only the creaking of the carriage springs as they bounced along the ruts of the back road.

"You are young," Elijah said, finally.

"Nonsense."

To this Father offered her no response and Rebecca nearly drowned in the subsequent silence. Finally, she spoke again. "I do not even know where you stand on this war."

Elijah sighed once more. "Where I stand is no longer of any consequence."

"Father—"

"Child," Elijah snapped, "that is enough! We are nearly in town and I should rather finish my newspaper than continue this manner of conversation with you."

So it stood. Father and daughter did not speak for the rest of the evening, each maneuvering through the party at a careful distance from the other. When the carriage took Rebecca home, Elijah remained behind, so that he might entertain the general into the early evening.

Unable to sleep and aching for conversation, Rebecca opened the door to her bedroom and peered down the hallway toward her father's room. The house was dark, but for a sliver of yellow light beneath the distant door. She had heard her father return an hour before, but Elijah had not stopped to see her. She had no sense of the time now, but she knew her father would welcome her apology no matter the hour. Inhaling a breath for confidence, she crept down the hallway, the wide floorboards complaining with every step. Her actions were all impulse—she possessed no plan, no earthly idea what she would say when she reached the end of the hall. She had every reason to expect Father would tell her to return to bed, but she would make the effort nonetheless. If she found him awake, reading one of his favorite books or more likely poring over his business ledgers, she would take him by the hand and lead him downstairs to the kitchen, where they might finally talk of it all.

The room of her father stood empty.

Rebecca placed her hand on her father's bedspread and could tell immediately that the bed had not yet been used this evening. A novel sat open, spine split on the arm of the upholstered chair in the corner of the room, but she couldn't be sure that Father had not left the book there days before. The lamp on the end table burned low.

Rebecca crossed the room, intent on the mystery, but knew the open book on the chair would offer no assistance. She was stalling, an irrefutable trepidation growing around her with the silence of the enormous house. When a loose shutter rattled against the wall outside, Rebecca's breath caught and she froze in the center of her father's room. She listened for more sounds, any other sounds, but there was nothing. It was all ridiculous, poppycock, she told herself. Father was downstairs, she knew, asleep at his desk in his study or gnawing on a late platter in the kitchen. Perhaps it would be best if she simply returned to bed and spoke with him in the morning. The conversation had waited this long, after all. This was what she told herself, even as she crossed the room.

It was no more than a shadow at first, a ghost in the corner of her eye. A wisp of her own hair perhaps, or a passing moth. She dismissed the vision even as she turned to it, toward the large window overlooking the great lawn behind the house. Pushing aside the thick draperies, Rebecca pressed her forehead to the window panes and stared out into the darkness of their property.

She saw nothing. Not at first. Then, there! The same shadow stepping from the trees, the faint glow of a lamp spilling forward at its feet.

Father?

Although the shadow bore resemblance to her father in its stride, the figure was too faint, the distance too great, and Rebecca felt no immediate certainty of its identity. In fact, her fears raced ahead, concocting new possibilities, conjuring ghosts and phantoms from her storybooks. Or perhaps someone all too real. Father had spoken of Night Thieves before, evil souls who used the cover of darkness to rob the wealthy while they slept. There was no question the added burden of the war had brought even more desperation to the town and Rebecca now knew there was no telling just what a person might do.

She was moving for the staircase before her fears could truly overwhelm her.

The first floor was even darker than upstairs, hidden as it was from the moonlight by the wide wrap-around porch outside. When she reached the foyer, the girl stopped at the bottom of the stairs and drew another breath, which quivered as she took it in. She inhaled again, her hand placed to her chest in a rather futile attempt to calm herself. With unconscious yearning, her fingers danced over her precious onyx necklace. Then, not the least bit fortified, Rebecca plunged ahead, hurrying for the backdoor, slipping in her bare feet when she reached the kitchen tiles, and bruising her thin hip against the table corner. Cursing herself for not bringing a lamp with her, she stepped tentatively outside. By the time she crossed the stone patio and down into the grass, the dew cold on her soles, the figure had disappeared.

Her father—Rebecca now told herself the figure was indeed her father—had been quite close to her rock when she spied him from above, but there was only darkness back there now, a shadow web of tree branches shimmering in the moon's faint silvery light. Was he in there still, perhaps on the rock itself, or at the cliff? A small wave of uneasiness suddenly stirred at her stomach, Rebecca stood stone still and strained to focus on the open field, but there was nothing there, no movement at all, save a flurry of bats swooping down from the manor's cupola for their own inspection of the proceedings. The air was far cooler than inside the house and Rebecca drew her night dress around her, with little result. With expanding guilt, she regretted her earlier accusations of cowardice and begged for her father's appearance now. She would rush to him, throw her arms around him, hold him close, just as she did as a child. She thought about calling out for him, but reconsidered on the small chance that this indeed was not the shadow of her father she was chasing, but a thief in the night.

It was then she looked toward the eastern corner of the property, where the stone cottage stood. Even at this distance there was no mistaking the lamplight spilling forth like a betrayal from the small bedroom Rebecca once called her own. She had not set foot within the cottage since Constance made it her home and, as far as she knew, neither had her father. If this was indeed Elijah she was following, Rebecca could not imagine what he was doing visiting the woman's cottage in the middle of the night.

And then, she did.

This past July marked five years since her mother's death at the hands of her consumption. By all accounts, and not just from their daughter's perspective, Elijah and Clara shared a loving marriage, uncommonly so perhaps given the hours Elijah worked and the few occasions the couple actually spent in each other's uninterrupted company. But when they were together, hosting one of their grand parties or walking the streets of Phoenixville arm in arm, the love of Elijah and his wife was as obvious and as true as summer. After her mother's death, Rebecca and all of Phoenixville knew that Elijah would never find another woman to take Clara's place.

Rebecca also came to understand, however, there were certain things a man still required, needs he must fulfill elsewhere.

Like a hare in the garden, Rebecca crept along the edge of the cottage, bending low beneath the window sills, her bare feet sinking into the damp mulch of the flower beds. She heard nothing at first, only her own sounds, thundering within her head and chest. But soon, when she reached the spot just below the bedroom window, she held her breath and discerned the muffled voices of a man and a woman, more tones than words, entirely indecipherable. To Rebecca's ear, the man's voice sounded like her father's, enough so to dismiss the threat of the Night Thieves. Almost. She knew she could simply lift her head over the sill and peer into the bedroom, but she dreaded what she would most likely see there. Run away, she told herself. Turn your head and return to the house, where you can take once again to your bed and allow your father his peace. She knew this was the prudent course, but she could not bring herself to do it. Something kept her at the window.

Rebecca raised her head.

Constance was seated on the bed, her back to the window, her nightgown slipped down over her right shoulder, exposing brown skin crackled and dusted with gray. Elijah stood before her to the side of the bed, his own dressing gown, a burgundy robe he found on the trip to Massachusetts last year, drawn across his bedclothes. He was talking to Constance, merely talking, passionately but not in argument as best as Rebecca could tell. Her father's eyes did not glance to the window, but instead stayed focused on the woman on the bed and occasionally darted toward the corner of the room that Rebecca could not see. The girl remained at the window, hearing bits of the conversation and trying mightily to discern the events there, when it all become clearer and more confusing in an instant.

When the other man in the room appeared from the corner and, with his head bowed like a confessor, approached Elijah at a slow shuffle, Rebecca got no more than a glimpse before throwing herself to the ground. She dropped like a shot, a retreat out of fear perhaps or more likely embarrassment, for the man was clothed in mere rags, naked by most accounts.

When she returned to the sill, the man was standing before Constance, his unblinking eyes fixed on the kind face Rebecca knew well. Mesmerized, the girl crouched at the low corner of the window, her face barely exposed as she dared to watch with only one eye, as if viewing the whole scene through a sailor's looking glass. The Negro man was as tall as Elijah, taller perhaps, but his broken posture made him appear far smaller. He was weathered and thin, impossibly so, dark leather stretched tight over bones, and his cheeks were sunken around a mouth of yellowed teeth. At his wrist was a cuff of iron, the remains of a metal shackle with one link of chain still intact. The arm which held this shackle was no more than kindling wood, though the tightness of the muscles indicated a past of work and strength, a strength which remained in his chest now held high. Indeed, there was something almost regal about his bearing and Rebecca considered that in any other life, at any other time, this man might have been a prince or a warrior.

Lost in these thoughts, Rebecca did not notice the shift of her father's gaze until it was too late. The world jolted forward as Elijah said something in haste to Constance, pointed at the man in rags, and then raced from the bedroom for the cottage door, as Rebecca sprang from the garden and darted back into the night.

"Rebecca!"

Elijah came running like a jungle predator, dangerously fleet, unwavering on its prey. Rebecca ran even harder, though she knew it was futile. Even if she could keep a faster pace, outrunning her father offered no more than a temporary solution. She needed evaporation, complete disappearance. Escape.

"Stop, girl!"

His voice was a roar, vicious and commanding, and there was only one appropriate response.

Rebecca stopped.

They were at the rock again, for Rebecca had run oblivious to her path and headed straight into the trees, the branches scraping at her exposed legs, the pine needles stabbing at her feet. When Elijah reached her, his breath gone, his chest heaving, he immediately seized his daughter's shoulders for fear she might run again. They stood there facing each other, panting, the mill's own bellows hissing from across the creek, until Rebecca collapsed away from her father, onto her rock, and awaited her own voice.

"Who ... who is he?" she asked.

Elijah pursed his lips, as if the answer were right there but he was reluctant to share it.

"A friend."

"A friend?"

Her father's response made no sense to her, but as Rebecca studied his white eyes in the darkness, she found no further explanation.

"Yes, Rebecca," Elijah answered, impatience showing at the edges, "the man is a friend."

"A friend of Constance, perhaps. Is that it?"

Her father shook his head, slowly, the answers still emerging. "No. He is a friend of ours, all of us."

Rebecca stared hard at her father, not much more than a silhouette in the darkness.

"What is he doing here? We don't have ... they ... what is he doing here?"

"He came to the fire," Elijah told her, patiently, "on the gate."

The fire on the gate? Then, Rebecca remembered the manor's entrance and the placards mounted on the twin stone pillars. The black iron signs depicting the flames of the Wilton furnace.

Seeing his daughter's confusion, Elijah continued, his voice hoarse and tired, "The sign marks us as a station, Rebecca. If he can find it, then a man is certain of safety, if only for a night."

Rebecca had heard only a little of the railroad running underground, the whispers of conductors and stations, but she had always thought such talk little more than the wishful thinking of a guilty people.

"That man, Father, he is a runaway?"

"Yes."

"And you are helping him?"

"Of course."

"But ..."

"Rebecca," Elijah said, "this is no small matter. No game. This man's very life is at stake here and our movements must be swift and silent. Above all, silent." In punctuation of his words, Elijah again squeezed Rebecca's shoulders and brought his face so close to hers that she could feel the warmth of his breath, which still reeked of his evening tobacco. "Do you understand this?"

At first, Rebecca did not know why her father was so concerned about her discretion. With Shane gone now, it was not as though she had anyone to whom she would ever confide such matters. But perhaps it was her bond with Shane that brought Father such worry. Rebecca considered the letters she wrote to her soldier, the careful descriptions of even the smallest matters back home in Phoenixville, and she knew her father's concerns.

She could not write of this.

"I understand," she answered.

Satisfied, Elijah relaxed his grip, though his hands remained at his daughter's shoulders, soft and strong.

"Now, these are dangerous events, my child. You must return to your bedroom and think not again of what you have seen here. Consider it no more than a dream, one of your nighttime fancies, yes?"

Rebecca did not answer directly, but instead asked, "What will we do with him?"

With another sigh of reluctance and impatience, Elijah paused and again considered his words.

In the lull, Rebecca prompted, "Will he go to the north borough, with the others? Constance has her family there, I believe. Up near the dam."

"No," her father said, "he will not go with the others. He will need to go much farther north than that, child. Canada perhaps, or the mountains. There are men after him—slave hounds—and they will be here soon."

Fears renewed, Rebecca looked behind her, down the path along the cliff. She found only deeper shadows and blackness.

"Not yet," Elijah reassured her, "but soon. So I must get back to the cottage and you must get back to the house."

"But tonight, where will he go?"

Another sigh, smaller. "We will hide him beneath the cottage—"

"Beneath?"

"There is a cellar, behind a trap door, built for this very purpose."

"Then," Rebecca said, slowly, "you have helped others?"

Elijah nodded. "For years."

Rebecca thought again of her father's tales of the thieves in the night.

"We must give him whatever he needs, Father," she blurted out. "We have so much, more than any person should ever need, and if we could give it all away, we should. We must give it to him, to all of them that come. Food, clothing, whatever it is they need."

Elijah smiled and helped Rebecca to her feet. "Yes, we shall do these things, dear angel. Of course, we shall do them. But none of that is what is most needed now, Daughter."

Rebecca looked up at Elijah, a faint orange glow on his skin, a reflection of the furnace fires or the emerging sun.

"What is needed then?"

"Hope."

Rebecca found herself collapsing again, this time toward her father, into his arms, against his chest. Her tears were quiet, subdued. Tears of relief and celebration more than anything else.

"So brave," she managed to whisper.

"Yes, bravery takes a thousand forms," Elijah agreed. "This man, he is braving all there is, my child. He has come to us from hell itself, come to us on his own feet through woods and storms and an ever-present threat of death. His journey is not over, but he is almost there, and we shall do all we can to help him reach his destination."

Rebecca knew Elijah had misunderstood her words. It was not the slave to whom she was referring when she whispered of bravery. Here, in the arms of her father, Rebecca felt the sadness of the past years ebb away like a tide, soon to return, but for now leaving only a trace of light foam. Bravery takes a thousand forms. The girl looked up again at her father and smiled. In this light, the glow of his open hearths upon him, Elijah Wilton looked to his daughter every measure a hero.

SEVENTEEN

Phoenixville's Homecoming celebration occurred that year on the kind of Saturday when the weather took center stage. A few clouds from the previous week remained, billowy and gray, but gorgeous shafts of sunlight streamed through them like maypole ribbons. As the parade began its journey down Bridge Street, the crowd kept looking to the skies, jaded from the week's rain and hopeful that any storm would hold off for the Duck Race and that night's Firebird Festival.

The streets were closed all around Bridge & Main and a swell of townspeople strolled ahead of the parade, visiting with friends, chasing after children, and stopping only when they found a perfect curbside seat beside thin saplings entwined with strands of white lights. The sidewalks and surrounding parks were filled with booths and displays, fresh-painted and eager. Outside the new bookstore, a group huddled around two steaming coffee urns. Next door, the bakery was handing out free doughnuts, and a juggler was tossing bowling pins, which kept clattering to the ground to the delight of a small crowd of laughing children. Overhead, banners stretched across Bridge Street, emblazoned with "Phoenixville: Welcome Home!" in purple and white.

Tara and I huddled arm in arm, waiting for the parade beneath Tomney's new awning. Boo stood by himself a few paces away, head down, hands shoved firmly into the pockets of that big old corduroy coat. A mesh baseball cap was pulled low, red hair, greasy and unruly, jutting out from beneath it.

Boo was still a mess, the worst injury a gash over his swollen right eye that probably needed stitches to heal right. When he coughed into his bandana, a cough exceptionally hollow and grating that morning, Boo looked particularly fragile, as though it was an effort to stand with us at all.

After I got home from Wishing Manor the night before, I thought about going straight to bed. It was still early and I wasn't all that tired, but I knew my mother would have some questions about my injuries when she got home from work and I figured bed was a good place to hide. I was starving though and stayed downstairs, vegging with a M*A*S*H rerun for the hundredth time and eating half of an Entenmann's cheesecake. By the time my mom came in from her shift, I was sprawled on the couch, working on my drawing of the library again. My mother barely gave me a look, but she smiled when she saw me drawing and said it was a nice surprise that I was home. She thought she might have meat for tacos and even said she would go to Foresta's if she didn't, because she knew they were my favorite.

She didn't notice my black eye at first, but when she came back out to the living room, she saw it. I didn't think it looked as bad as before—it was already changing colors and the swelling had gone down—but my mother still gasped and overreacted the way she always did. When I told her I'd just gotten into a little fistfight at school, she asked if the principal knew (I was already on "thin ice" with the principal from a few prior incidents). When I insisted no one knew and that the fight was just a quick act of self-defense against some Slags, my mother seemed to accept that. At least she stopped asking questions. We got out the Scrabble game for the first time in years and I forgot all about guns and boarding schools and the town's rumblings of a new war.

When I finally fell asleep, I dreamt again of Tara. This time, she was standing behind a second-floor window of Wishing Manor, her eyes on the horizon. From the ground, I studied her face, the drape of her hair, the shape of her body, the graceful way she held her hand to the glass. In my dream, I took hold of a pencil and I drew her, my hand moving with magical speed, as quickly as I could draw, as though I might keep her there in that window forever if I only moved fast enough. If only...

The cop was upon us before I even saw him. He must have come around the corner when our attention was on the invisible parade now heard somewhere in the distance. I felt my whole chest tighten as the cop approached, the blue uniform strangling me as it closed in, the man's eyes boring into me like an auger. I shot a warning look at Boo, but he'd already seen what was coming and he'd sunken deep into his coat, pulled so tight the zipper could probably touch in the back. The cop came closer. I managed a thin breath, then another. Closer. Finally, he stopped right in front of us and gave us all a good look up and down. The guy appeared impossibly strong, his chest and arms inflated from hours on the weight bench. His face was framed by lopsided sideburns and marked by a thick white scar splitting one eyebrow, similar to Boo's new wound. His nose pointed at an odd angle to the left. The cop wore no jacket despite the cold and walked like he couldn't have cared less about the weather.

"What's up," I grunted, when the man stood there a little too long without saying anything. Boo said nothing, no doubt convincing himself he was doing his best Han Solo in the face of local authority. In reality, Boo looked like he was about to wet his pants.

"You all over at the high school?" the cop finally asked.

"Yeah," Tara answered. "We go to PAHS."

"Good school?"

I just stared, knowing the guy was toying with us. Good school? Who gives a shit? He knew something, the guy knew something. I could feel it—the cuffs were coming out, me and Boo were about to be slammed into the bricks, frisked and humiliated, right there in front of Tara, in front of everyone. We'd finally pay for Boo's lame-ass plan. We'd pay for all of it. The end was near.

"School's OK," Tara replied.

The cop wasn't going anywhere. He leaned against Tomney's window glass like he had all the time in the world. He smelled of an ongoing competition between soap and drugstore aftershave. The aftershave was winning.

"My wife and I just moved down here and we've been wondering about the schools. Our boy is only in kindergarten right now, but you can never start too early thinking about high schools. Education is everything, right? We're looking at the Catholic school over in East Pikeland, of course, but it might do him some good to meet kids outside the parish. You boys aren't from Saint Basil's, are you? I see you around, but I don't think I've seen you there."

We both shook our heads, then Boo started off on a string of coughs. Tara slapped his back a few times. Boo shifted away from her. I stayed focused on the cop.

"What happened to you?" the cop asked, pointing at the bandage over Boo's eye.

The coughing got worse.

"Bike accident," I answered. "The ramp was too high."

The cop studied my face. "And how about you, Evel Knievel? You standing on his handlebars or something?"

Before I could answer, Gargoyle emerged from Tomney's store, a broom in his hand. He made a few slow stabs at the pavement before noticing us standing there. Recoiling, the big man stared at us as if we'd just appeared out of a fog. A sneer formed, like a dog making up its mind, but then Gargoyle saw the cop in the blue uniform. He appeared pleased by this, as his expression shifted, and he even offered the policeman an odd little smile. I thought for a minute he might blab all about me and Boo and our fight with the Furnace Boys, but I wasn't even sure he recognized me from the alley. Still, I kept watching him as he pushed the broom a few more times, until he shooed some leaves into the gutter, picked up a crumpled paper cup, and finally retreated inside the store.

"You guys ever box?" the cop asked.

"Huh?" I was momentarily distracted when Tara took my hand.

"Box. Have you ever been in a boxing ring? Or do you just do your fighting in the streets?"

Thrown again, I could only shake my head.

"No?" the cop asked. "Well, listen, you guys should come up to the civic center after school sometime. The Police Athletic League's putting together some activities for kids in the afternoons."

"To keep us off the streets," Tara said.

"Something like that."

"I don't know," I said, checking the invisible parade again. A bass drum boomed somewhere beyond the horizon.

"Well, think about it," the cop said, as he tipped his cap at a woman who shuffled by with her lawn chair looking for a place to sit. "A little boxing might do you some good."

He offered us a wide grin, which was not returned, and started to cross the street. Then, the cop stepped back onto the sidewalk. "Let me ask you one more thing. I just was wondering whether you know anything about what happened at the library the other night. You must have heard the sirens, the alarms, all that. You heard that, right? So, what I'm wondering is, do you know anything about it?"

I was shaking my head before the guy was even finished talking. I played dumb and gave my attention to Tara, squeezing her hand and leaning against her. But Boo, he didn't move. The guy was paralyzed. He was going to say something though, I could sense it, he was about to open that fat mouth of his, clear out his lungs, and then cough up some sort of confession. And there wasn't a damn thing I could do about it.

"The library?" Boo croaked, his eyes lighting on me for the briefest of moments. The cop took another step forward. Then, Boo shook his head too, as he bent down to re-tie his perfectly laced sneakers. "Nah, I ain't much of a reader. Us delinquents don't even know where the library is."

The cop took this in without showing much reaction. Then, he simply nodded, told us to enjoy the parade, and crossed the street.

Tara's hand slid to the small of my back and then to my hip. "You could tell him."

"No way."

"About Deacon, and the guns, Sketch."

I sighed and glanced over at Boo, who pretended he wasn't listening.

"He threatened your life," Tara insisted. "You have to go to the police sometime. You have to."

"Deacon was just talking," I replied, attempting to sound nonchalant. "He's not gonna do nothing." Boo made some kind of scoffing sound, but his eyes remained fixed on a crack in the sidewalk. "Besides, even if I did rat out Deacon, even if the cops lock him up or something like that, I'm still a dead man. Hell, we're all dead. We're the only ones who know what's going on in there. If the police grab up Deacon, we're the only ones who could've tipped them off. We could do it all anonymous or do it right here in public and either way we're the obvious rats. Even an idiot like Romeo would figure it out. And don't think they wouldn't come after us."

Tara removed her arm from me and looked away, as a cheer erupted from the crowd and the color guard from the Veterans of Foreign Wars finally turned the corner from Starr Street.

"Look, I agree with you," I said, "guns are some serious shit. They scare the hell out of me. Did you see the big-ass revolver strapped on that cop's belt? Man, I hate even being that close to the things."

Tara turned on me. "So, then—"

"The Furnace Boys, they'd kill us, Tara. Dead."

I thought I caught a small nod from Boo, but it passed too quickly. Except for an occasional wince at some lingering pain, Boo seemed to have slipped back into his catatonia, mesmerized by patterns in the pavement. I understood. I usually looked forward to the parade, but I was having trouble getting into it all. Nothing connected. My arm around Tara, the approaching music of the marching band, the scent of hot chocolate and popcorn, all of it seemed so distant, unreal, like a television show. I found myself drowning instead in distractions—guns ... art classes ... girlfriends ... steel mills ... old mansions—and the persistent feeling that I was being watched. Furnace Boys and Slags must have been everywhere, but when I scanned the crowd, no one was looking at me at all.

"I have to stop him," I said, checking the nearby spectators to make sure no one was listening, "but I don't know what to do."

Tara seemed to hear my confession for what it was and her expression softened, as a string band of Philadelphia Mummers passed by playing "Camptown Races."

"No one knows what to do," Tara said. "No one ever knows."

Boo showed no sign that he heard any of this. He kicked at a discarded cigarette filter with the toe of his sneaker. He cleared his throat and shuffled his feet. He gave off a whiff of antibiotic ointment. He still wouldn't look up and when he spoke I could barely hear him above the parade.

"We could join him."

That was what Boo said.

"Join him?" Tara asked.

Boo kicked again at the ground. "When you think about it, there's something—I don't know—heroic about what Deacon's doing. He's protecting our town. Preservation, that's what he told you, right? You gotta respect that. Look, Deacon gets it, he sees what's happening here and he's doing something about it. What else is he supposed to do? There ain't no jobs here anymore. Deacon's planning his future, taking charge of his own destiny. I don't care what you think. That's heroic. So, maybe, what I'm saying is, maybe he'd let us join him."

"Seriously, Boo," Tara said, shaking her head in disbelief, "sometimes I think you're certifiable."

At this, Boo finally looked up.

"You don't even know me," he said.

"Boo," I said, before Tara could respond, "you actually want to be a part of this? A Furnace Boy, still, after everything?"

"You got some other idea?"

I had spent much of the morning thinking of nothing but other ideas. Everything from tipping off the Slags that the guns were in the Furnace to stealing the guns myself and dumping them into the Schuylkill River. At one point, I even considered ratting out Deacon to his father. Somewhat surprisingly, Deacon still lived with his parents in a house over in Puddler's Corner. Although a basement apartment with its private entrance sounded like a dream to just about every teenager who heard about it, it had its rumored down sides. There were stories that Deacon's father, a large man in his own right, had beaten the crap out of Deacon a few times for mouthing off to him or coming in late at night, though I always considered these stories wishful thinking more than anything else. Ultimately, I realized talking to Deacon's father would be the same as talking to the cops, with the same likely result.

"All Deacon cares about is money," Boo said after a while.

"Yeah, so? What, you want to buy the things from him?" I replied, laughing sharply. "Here, I got seventy-five cents. Tara can kick in another buck or maybe two. And how about you, Boo, you got a penny for the cause? What do you think? Think Deacon'll take three bucks for his, his arsenal there? That should do it, yeah." I shook my head. "Jesus, Boo."

Boo retreated again into his stupor and I immediately regretted my sarcasm, but I didn't say anything else. A convertible arrived, this one a fin-tailed classic carrying some distant relative of E.J. Wilton. Her round face flush with the contented look of a trust-fund baby, the woman waved to the crowd with practiced enthusiasm.

"All right," Boo finally muttered, drained before the day was old, "maybe we shouldn't do anything."

"Maybe," I said.

As we lapsed into silence again, strains of Cohan wafted over the sidewalks crammed with what now appeared to be every resident of Phoenixville. People cheered the music and the floats from each church and social organization. The float from the Police Athletic League rolled by, two kids whaling on each other in a makeshift boxing ring, their hands in gloves the size of pillows. The cop from earlier presided over the ring in a referee shirt pulled over his uniform. When he spied us on the sidewalk, he offered a small salute. We pretended not to see him. Firemen dressed as clowns handed out balloons, the school mascot did cartwheels, and the high-school band marched by, dressed in new polyester purple uniforms probably purchased for the occasion. Beaming and flushed, the musicians took obvious pride in their playing and the townspeople beamed right along with them, oblivious to any missed notes.

I imagined The Blake School had a band that won a lot of awards.

The loudest cheers of the morning were reserved for a contingent of former Phoenix Iron & Steel employees who walked the parade behind a banner proclaiming the town's "150 Years of Service" to the country's steel industry. Boo's grandfather held one end of the sign, his posture erect. Several dozen workers in all, a weathered lot, with hands and faces scarred and blemished by years at the furnaces, held their heads high as they strolled through the town their predecessors built. Smiling and waving, the steel workers threw handfuls of candy toward the spectators, sending children scurrying along the curbs in pursuit.

"I'm out of here," Boo said, gazing down Bridge Street.

"What are you talking about?" I asked. "It ain't over."

Boo shrugged and walked off into the crowd, without looking back. I thought about going after him, but Tara's hand felt so good in mine and the crowd was cheering again and soon the fire engine sounded its siren like it was never going to end.

EIGHTEEN

"Do you like it?" Tara asked.

After the parade, we stopped at the coffeeshop so Tara could grab a free hot chocolate before heading to the creek for the Duck Race. Waiting for her, I was examining a display of student artwork in the window of the arts center next door. No more than a dozen works in all, the eclectic arrangement of frames hung beneath the words "Local Phoenixville Artists." There were several still-life pastels, a nude in charcoal, a splatter painting that looked more like a tragic mistake than the Pollock it imitated. There was a black-and-white photograph of the rolling mill demolished last year. And there was the small pencil rendering of a trio of church steeples.

"It's all right," I answered, hoping my ambivalence was enough to end the conversation before it began. "Not bad."

"Those are the Three Sisters, aren't they?" Tara asked, pointing at the small sketch. "That's what they call them, right? The churches over towards your house."

I nodded, eager to retreat, to escape, but unable to pull myself away. I remembered drawing that particular depiction of the spires two summers before, when the sky had been a perfect August blue and the sun filtered by an occasional smudge of clouds. I had spent most of that day at Wishing Manor, daydreaming over the creek, devouring the snacks I'd lifted from 7-11, and drawing a few sketches into my notebook. The steeples, three churches standing tall at the center of town, had come at the end of the day, easily and completely in one frenetic burst.

"They look like the ones in your book."

"A little," I said. "Maybe."

Tara leaned closer to examine the tag beneath the drawing. Each piece had a small card noting the artist's name, a phone number, and a price. As Tara read aloud, I turned away.

"Anonymous," I heard her say. "Very mysterious."

I remembered the drawing, but I couldn't for the life of me remember what I had done with it. And I definitely didn't know how it got in that gallery window.

"Why would someone ever want to be anonymous?" Tara asked.

I didn't want to talk about this. I just wanted to get going, down to the creek, to the Duck Race, anywhere.

"Hell if I know."

"Not me, baby," Tara said. "When I do something, people are going to know I'm the one doing it. Otherwise, what's the point?"

I stepped away from her. Not a lot, not more than a step, but enough for Tara to turn and look, with a question at her lips. My question arrived first.

"Do you really believe that?"

"What?" Tara replied. "Yeah, I guess. Oh, I don't know. Maybe. Sometimes I think the only way to prove you exist is to do something big, you know? Big enough to be remembered—leave a legacy and all. You got to let people know who you are, what you can do." She placed her hand over the glass, like her slender fingers were wrapping themselves around the church steeples. "Living anonymous, living in a vacuum, it's all just like singing in the shower. Kinda pointless if no one hears you, right?"

I didn't know what to say. I stared back at the drawing again and then I remembered. The church steeples were in the small notebook I'd given my mother last Christmas, when I needed a gift and was out of money. I knew I could swipe something from Woolworth's or over at the pharmacy, but stealing a Christmas gift didn't seem quite right. So, in a fit of desperation on Christmas Eve, I wrapped one of my smaller sketchbooks in the Sunday comics and gave it to my mother after church the next morning. She adored the gift, as I knew she would, and examined the sketchbook again and again throughout the day. When I told her (belatedly) that the gift came with the caveat that it could be shown to no one else, she didn't protest, even as there was a hint of disappointment in her slow agreement.

I had forgotten all about the drawing, the way a musician discards hundreds of melody fragments or an author forgets drafts of his own stories. If I remembered it at all, it would have been with the mistaken confidence that the artwork was tucked safely in one of the many sketchbooks I kept locked in the chest at the end of my bed, where no one would ever find it.

Yet there it was, hanging in the window for everyone to see.

"C'mon," I said, "the race is gonna start." The small smile on Tara's face had me concerned.

I started for the creek, but Tara didn't follow. Instead, she headed into the arts center. The woman behind the counter was on the phone and paid Tara no attention. The rest happened in slow motion. Tara soon appeared in the gallery window, surrounded by the frames, and pulled a ballpoint pen from her pocket. She took down the small piece of paper beside the Three Sisters drawing and scribbled something onto it. When she taped the paper back onto the glass, my own name stared back at me.

"This is nice," Tara said, as we headed for the creek, hand in hand. "I see why my parents wanted to live here."

"I was wondering about that."

"Why we moved here?"

"Right."

She took her time, like she was deciding to tell me something. "They wanted to get me away from the big city."

"Too many bad influences?"

"I guess. They didn't like my friends. Said I fell in with the wrong crowd, whatever that is."

"Did you?"

Tara shrugged. "We all have our little demons and rebellions, you know. Anyway, my dad got a job down here in King of Prussia and I guess they figured that was the right time to move. He's in computers, mainframes."

"I don't know what that is."

"Me neither, actually. But anyway, my mom grew up this way, little parks and corner stores and, yes, even parades, and I think she wanted that for us."

I made a sound, something like a laugh. "Plenty of other small towns to choose from. The Main Line is full of them."

"I don't know," Tara said, sweeping her arm towards Bridge Street. "This place, it's different. They put on a show like this and it still feels all Mayberry, don't you think?"

"I think Mayberry is long gone. Just like the steel mill and the jobs and—"

"God, everybody here is so hung up on the past."

"Phoenixville is nothing but past," I said.

Tara shook her head. "My mom thinks this town has potential. That's what she always says. Potential."

We were among the last to arrive at the Duck Race. Throngs of spectators crowded the shores of French Creek, watching Jacob Tomney and several of his Kiwanis brethren take their places atop High Bridge with the bags full of plastic ducks. Gargoyle was up there too, his hulking frame beside Tomney, his arms wrapped around a particularly enormous bag. The mayor, who also taught Biology and coached tennis at the high school, stood on a makeshift platform at the center of the bridge. At the mayor's signal, the ducks would be dropped over the bridge railing into the flowing waters of the creek in frantic and utterly uncontrolled pursuit of the finish line, a white rope stretched beneath Low Bridge.

"Do you think he's all right?" Tara asked, squinting up at the bridge, momentarily bright with sunlight.

"Who?"

"Boo."

"Oh, yeah, he'll be all right. He's just scared, is all. He's not good when he gets too scared."

Tara shook her head. "It seemed like he was more than scared. Does he always get quiet like that, when he's so upset?"

In truth, I was hard-pressed to remember seeing Boo retreat so far into himself. Boo had always been more the type to work out a problem by talking—usually endlessly—about the situation. There was no question the morning's performance had been out of character.

"He'll be all right," I said again, slightly less convincing this time.

Using a bullhorn full of static, the mayor made a speech no one could hear as the Kiwanians held up their bags of ducks and the children on the shore scurried too close to the water in anticipation of the race. The mayor said something about the amount of money raised and gave special recognition to Tomney, who apparently had sold the most raffle tickets for seven years in a row. Then, the mayor reminded everyone to attend the Firebird Festival that evening over at the high school.

"You don't think he'll do anything crazy, do you?" Tara asked.

"Like what?"

"I don't know," Tara replied. "It just seemed like Boo was thinking about doing something."

"You mean like revenge or something like that? I'm sure he's thinking about it," I told her, "but that don't mean he's going to do anything. It's not like he'd ever go up against the Furnace Boys all by himself. He's just sore, that's all." I smiled, attempting to diffuse Tara's concerns. "Literally."

Biting her lower lip, Tara stayed quiet for a while. She reached down for my hand as the mayor fired a starter's pistol into the air and Tomney and his boys opened the bags and an avalanche of plastic ducks hit the water in rapid succession. Kids cheered, adults laughed, and Tara and I held hands. And all the while, I could think of nothing except Boo's strange silence earlier and the obvious distraction on his face. The ducks, all bright yellow with faded red bills, rode the current at a surprising clip toward Low Bridge. To the delight of the children, some floated hopelessly off course, veering toward the shore as if by their own accord, but most calmly floated straight ahead.

Boo is hurt, I knew, humiliated even.

A cheer rose from several nearby on-lookers as a group of ducks caught a sudden swell in the creek and shot out in front.

But he's not capable of revenge. Not at this point.

Two young girls brushed against me on their way down to the creek for a closer look. The smallest one was squealing as though she had never been so happy.

Boo won't do anything stupid.

Three ducks were in the lead and the children were running alongside them, urging them on. Waist deep in the water down by Low Bridge, a man in waders and a hat full of fishing licenses gripped one end of the finish line, while a woman on shore held the other end.

Boo won't go after Deacon. Not without talking to me first. Not on his own.

More cheers, louder still, as a duck finally slipped beneath the rope. Tara led me through the crowd to get a better view and we found a space just as the fisherman in waders lifted one of the ducks into the air. Tara was smiling now, clapping along with everyone else, as several spectators reached for their raffle tickets and hungrily awaited the reading of the winning number. I spied the mayor pushing through the crowd, on his way to the finish line, so that he could officially declare the victor.

In that moment, the noise of the crowd suddenly dropped away and I again felt eyes upon me, like rays of morning sunlight slicing through bedroom curtains. I let go of Tara's hand and turned back toward the town. Nothing. I scanned the faces in the crowd, but everyone was focused on the Duck Race. I was turning, a full 360, around and around as I tried desperately to find ... to find ... there!

Deacon.

Deacon stood on the opposite side of the creek, away from the crowd, surrounded by his Furnace Boys down at the water's edge. The others were rowdy and jovial, jostling as they played catch with Little Hal's hat, Romeo and Bigfoot passing it back and forth between them. As all this activity swirled around him, however, Deacon stood motionless, a statue on the bank, his arms folded over his belly, his eyes fixed without expression on me. Only when he saw that I'd noticed him did Deacon come alive. A thin smile crept over his face. Then, slowly, Deacon raised his hand to chest level and pointed toward me. His thumb was extended toward the sky. A cocked gun. His thumb came down, the shot was fired, and Deacon blew wisps of smoke from his fingertip before lowering his hand once more to his side. My breath stolen, I couldn't help but look away.

"Don't worry about him," whispered Tara, who had seen the whole episode.

"I'm not," I answered, my lie as loud as a mill whistle over the crowd. "He should be worried about me, if anything, that son of a bitch. He should be worried about me."

Then, when I saw that Deacon was still watching us, I fired my own shot across the creek.

A middle finger, artfully extended.

NINETEEN

"Tell me what to do."

My words were whispered like a prayer, but for all their stillness they were the loudest sound in the room. The evening's soundtrack, side one of *Darkness on the Edge of Town*, dissolved into the background. The hum of the hot-water heater disappeared. A car passed along the street outside and then faded away like a dream. And Tara and I were left with those five words.

"Tell me what to do."

"This is good," Tara said. The music swelled again and Springsteen sang about racing in the streets.

The basement was cold, like a room long abandoned. The temperature was a topic because it provided Tara with her initial excuse for leaving on her flannel shirt. It was faded red-and-green tartan plaid, which looked good on her, though I desperately wanted it off her at that moment. My fingers fumbled at the buttons again and again, until Tara finally revealed herself, a vision in white lace and cotton and her oldest jeans, with rips at both knees and the snap undone. The flannel shirt dropped to the floor. Almost in disbelief, I just stared, frozen and awkward.

"This is good," Tara repeated, as she leaned forward to kiss me again.

Maybe it was the confidence of an empty house born of her parents attending the Firebird Festival, or the dusky setting of the paneled basement, but we were less inhibited than at any

242

other time together. Still, the nerves remained, underneath it all. We kissed, our tongues frantic, even as the rest of our bodies stayed remarkably still. I was terrified. At first, one arm remained propped around Tara along the back of the sofa, the other stayed frozen at my side, for fear of doing the wrong thing at exactly the wrong moment. I wanted everything to go perfectly, like in my dreams, like in the movies. I wanted to soak it all in and hold it there, like the deepest breath. I pushed Tara away, only so that I could steal another glimpse of her body. She was small and smooth and perfect. My hand slid forward, testing, awkward, and landed on her stomach. Tara started and I retracted the move immediately. She told me my fingers were cold, that was all, then she took my hand and returned it to her skin, warm and ripe and alive. She was softer than I had imagined. And I had imagined everything.

We came up for air only occasionally, Tara glancing toward the door at the top of the basement stairs, me nuzzling my face into her hair (now absent any dye and smelling of floral shampoo) as if I were afraid to lose contact. As if breathing her in made the two of us one somehow.

At one of these intermissions, my lips were at Tara's ear, just there, breathing.

"I love you," I slurred, because it seemed the right thing to say. Because it might make her happy. Because it might lead to other things. Because they always said it in the movies. Because I thought in that very moment that it just might be true. Because.

Tara moaned, as she took my kiss again, more furtive this time, leaving me to decipher her silence.

When we first heard the faint tapping, the sound didn't seem real, nothing more than water dripping from an invisible faucet. Still, I lifted my head, but Tara pulled me down to her again and the sound was quickly forgotten. It soon returned, insistent, and we raised our heads and squinted into the dimness of the room, as though this would help us hear more clearly. Silence again, except for the scratching of the needle at the record's end and the turntable's arm as it swung back to the beginning. Then, once more, tap-tap-tap.

The face at the small window across the room was distorted by the grime on the glass, giving the vision an altogether ghostly appearance. There were eyes, not much more, and skin moving in and out of focus like a swimmer underwater. On the sofa, everything moved in frenzy as limbs untwined, hands flew to zippers and buttons, the flannel shirt was retrieved, and brilliant flares subsided. Recovered, Tara reached for the lamp. As bright light washed the room, the face at the window disappeared.

Stuffing my shirttail into my jeans, I raced up the basement stairs and out the front door without so much as a breath. I was still sore but I felt none of it and I leapt down the porch steps like a Doberman. My hands were on the figure crouched at the window in a flash and I tugged at the shirt and the two of us were suddenly tumbling over each other onto the patch of grass.

"What the hell—"

His hands raised in front of his face as a shield, Boo cowered. "I'm sorry, man. I'm sorry."

I sat back onto the ground and exhaled.

"How long," I said, "how long have you been out here?"

"Not long. Swear to God, not long. I just was looking for you, that's all. I went by your house, but nobody answered and I knew you weren't up at the Firebird with everybody else, so I figured you was here. I been ringing the doorbell and knockin'..."

"Boo—"

"I didn't see nothin', man."

I could have killed him. Then, seeing Boo's genuine anxiety, I just laughed. "You perv."

The storm door swung open with a creak and Tara stepped onto the porch, looking down on the two of us tangled on her front lawn. Her clothes intact but her hair disheveled, she scanned the street and saw that the neighborhood was quiet and oblivious. Then, like an exhausted parent, she sighed.

"You guys coming inside, or what?"

Boo looked to me, then rose slowly to his feet, brushing dirt from his pants and rubbing at his elbow.

"Yeah, all right."

"Boo..."

"This'll only take a minute," Boo insisted, looking up at the rising moon. "I don't got a lot of time as it is."

After stopping in the kitchen for some sodas, we all trooped downstairs. Slurping his drink like he'd had nothing to eat all day, Boo took a seat on the worn carpet remnant covering the basement floor. Coughing only slightly, he wiped his bandana across his mouth.

"I got an idea," Boo said after a while.

I glanced at Tara, who was already frowning, and felt a familiar sinking in my stomach. I said nothing, hoping Boo would make this quick, hoping everything would be returned soon to where it all had been just a little while before.

"But," Boo said, "I'm gonna need some help. Not that I couldn't do it myself, I guess, but it'll probably take more than one person to pull it off is all. It could be perfect, goddamn perfect. That's what I'm thinking, anyways. So, I wanted to tell you and, seeing how everybody else is over at the bonfire and you guys said you weren't going, well, that's why I come here. I didn't want to interrupt or nothing, but I just thought you might want in on it."

As Boo gathered steam, I was struck by the obvious change in his demeanor. The distractions and catatonia at the morning parade were gone now, replaced by a rambling excitement, enthusiasm even. Though Boo was still having trouble making eye contact, his gaze flitting from one thing to another in rapid succession, there was more here than his usual agitated state. His arms wrapped tightly around his legs gathered to his chest, Boo quavered with it, a secret he could barely contain.

I drew a breath. "It depends what it is, Boo."

Boo finally looked up at me. "It never used to."

Flushing, I folded my arms and somehow resisted a response. But Tara sighed again with impatience and asked, "Look, Boo, why don't you just spit it out? What the hell are you talkin' about?"

Boo looked at her, like he was deciding whether he wanted her to hear. I knew he would spill.

"The Duck Race."

Boo said nothing else, as if that were explanation enough. He picked at a loose strand of shag carpet and twisted it between his fingers.

"The Duck Race? C'mon, Boo—can you not speak in riddles for once in your life?" I said, snapping a bit more than I'd intended. "You said this was only gonna take a second."

"I know, I know. I'll let you get back to ..." Boo said, waving his hand at the sofa. "I just thought you might want to hear—"

"For God's sake, we do. What do you want us to say?"

My voice rising, I was going to keep going, but Tara quieted me with a touch on my arm.

"What about the Duck Race?" she asked.

Boo kept looking at me. "You remember how Tomney was saying this was the biggest year ever? How there were all them prizes?"

Tara stiffened. Not enough that anyone else would have noticed, but I could tell. I was pleased that I was beginning to sense these things about her.

Boo just kept twisting that carpet strand.

"What, Boo?" I asked. "You pissed off you didn't win one of the big TV sets or something?"

Boo shook his head. "The money."

"You wanted to win the money? Who wouldn't?"

"All cash."

"Yeah, it's a lot of cash. Right."

"I wanna steal the money, Sketch."

No one moved, no one spoke. The noises of the house arose again, as if from a deep sleep, and the turntable restarted one more time.

"The old man," Boo explained, "Tomney's got all that money in his store, see. He's been selling raffle tickets forever, right, and that group he belongs to, they've been doing the same. For weeks now. Hell, you saw how many goddamn ducks they dumped in the creek today—"

"Yeah."

"Well, those ducks are money, cash money, and it's all there, in his store. Don't you see? Tomney, he's been taking all the cash and collecting it into his back office. Never once taking it to the bank, because he wants to just make one trip and he needs to collect it all first. Every day he goes in his office and fills his stash a little higher. And it just keeps growing. You saw him this morning—the guy was still selling tickets during the parade. Swear to God, if I hear him say one more time how many he's sold, I just ... I ... swear to God."

Trying to focus, I leaned forward from the sofa.

"All right."

Boo seemed to take this attention as enthusiasm and smiled up at me. "So, it's all set. I did it this morning during the breakfast rush before the parade, before Tomney closed up the shop."

"What did you do?" I asked.

"I opened the back window," Boo whispered, looking to the basement stairs as if Tara's parents—or Tomney—or a cop—or Deacon—would suddenly appear there. "Not opened it, opened it, but unlatched it, you know. So, all we have to do is climb up through that window and then drop down into his office and take the money from his desk. I'm talking the Brinks Job here. Quick and easy."

The room grew eerily quiet again, everyone waiting for someone else to speak. I wasn't all that surprised when Tara stood and, without a word, climbed the basement stairs. Even as I watched her go, I thought there was a chance she might reconsider, especially when she stopped halfway up the stairs. She looked back, as though she would say something. Then, apparently thinking better of it, she moved forward. I considered calling after her, asking her to stay, or even following her up the stairs, but I did nothing. The door closed behind her with a quiet click.

"What's happening to you?"

I said this not to hurt him, but out of genuine concern. Boo blanched nonetheless. Then, apparently emboldened by Tara's departure, he took the seat beside me on the sofa and we sat there for a minute, listening to Springsteen and waiting for the rest of the conversation to find us. When it did, Boo's voice was tired and hoarse.

"I ain't going to live like you, Sketch."

I turned sharply. "What, you don't like my life?"

"No, that's not what I mean," Boo answered, spitting into the bandana and pushing it back into his jeans pocket. "I mean I ain't going to live a nice long life like you are. You know, take a job, get married, buy the house with the picket fence and the kids and the dog and all that shit. That just ain't happening. Not for me. We always knew that."

As Boo spoke, I stared across at the basement's opposite wall, where a collage of family photographs hung on the pine paneling, snapshots in crooked frames, beaches and mountains and Thanksgiving dinners. I didn't really see the photographs. There was another image, distant and unclear. I couldn't determine what it was, I knew only that it was nothing good.

"Don't say that," I replied. "You'll live whatever life you want. The girl, the house, all that, you can get all of that."

Emphatic, Boo shook his head. "That's your life, man. Not mine."

"All right," I shrugged, even as a light approached, blue and misty, floating toward me like a slow threat, "so, do something else. We're young, man. We can do anything we want."

"You really believe that?" Boo asked, his voice tinged with hope.

"Yeah. Yeah, I do," I was surprised to hear myself answering. "Look, Boo, you can do anything, anything you want to do. Go buy a boat or join the circus or sign up for the freakin' army. See the world and get laid in every country. The bottom line is you got to stop all this bullshit and get the hell out of Phoenixville."

"Like my parents," Boo said, slumping back into the cushion.

A pause.

"Like a lot of people," I replied.

Another beat. Then, Boo squinted over at me.

"You going somewhere, Sketch?"

I reached for my soda and took an imaginary drink from the empty can.

"Maybe, someday. I don't know."

Boo nodded, like he understood more than he possibly could have. "All the more reason, then. All the more reason we should do this job, take the money. Listen to me. This isn't going to last forever. Right now, this is all we got."

The image brightened, the star revealed itself, and I saw it all now.

"Shut up," I said, anguish shredding the edges of my voice.

"Sketch."

"No, shut up. I don't want to talk about this."

Above us, Tara's footsteps moved across the living room floor, back and forth, then disappeared as she ascended to the second floor.

"You do know how sick I am, right?" Boo asked, after a time.

I only nodded, because this suddenly was all I could muster. Because I believed if I could just keep my reactions subdued, this would all go away. Burn up with the embers of the day.

"They say you can't live long with this," Boo continued, placing his hand over his chest and rubbing it lightly. "The doctors ... they say ... the doctors say nobody lives much past thirty with this. The breathing, it just takes over. It's like we all get a certain number of breaths and I got short-changed, you know? So I'm going to finish up all my breaths before you do. That's just the way it is."

We rarely talked about the illness any more. It had been with Boo for so long that I never thought too much about it. Maybe I did at one time, back when I first heard Boo's lungs exploding, but I don't really remember. It all just became a part of my friend, part of us both, and we never felt the need to talk about it all the time. Maybe we thought talking about the illness would only make it take hold more.

"So," Boo continued, seizing the opening when no more opportunity came, "I want to live now. Make the most of what time I got. What's that word you always say? You know, carpe diem, all that shit. That's what I want."

"Nothing wrong with that."

"Because living right now gives you the best chance at being, you know, being remembered later." Boo didn't stop to explain. "And being a Furnace Boy—"

"A Furnace Boy? Wait, what?"

"Yeah," Boo nodded, "a Furnace Boy. That's everything, Sketch, that's immortality. Our brothers, every Furnace Boy there's ever been, they get remembered. You can see that, right? Furnace Boys, that's the life we're supposed to be living, you and me."

"Boo, that's all gone now. Don't you—"

"The money, it's for Deacon," Boo said, finally seeing my confusion. "That's what it is. I don't want the money. I mean, what the hell would I do with it anyway, you know? But Deacon, I give him the money and show him what I can do and it makes everything right again. I know it ain't gonna be what he could have made off some guns or that stupid necklace, but it might be enough that he forgets everything else just the same. And then, me and you, we're back in Deacon's good graces. Just like Rusty and Billy, just like a Furnace Boy, and everything is right back where it was. Where it should be."

I could only stare back at Boo, my best friend, this skinny boy still raw and bruised from just two days before. At that angle, Boo's right eye appeared nearly shut, the still-swollen tissue an ugly smear of indigo and black and gold. Then, just as I was about to speak, I noticed the quiver of Boo's lower lip, and my own impatience broke.

"You can't buy your future, Boo."

Boo shook his head and smiled. "Grow up, man. The only future worth anything is a future that gets bought."

I could see there was no more argument and even then I couldn't say that Boo was wrong. A life as a Furnace Boy, a place to belong, a place to make a name, was it so wrong to want these things? Who didn't want to feel immortal, to live experiences that would leave something behind, memories to be treasured and relived?

I looked to Boo once more and this time I saw it, what had been there all along, what was there every time Boo and I spoke. History. Not a finite history, but a shared history still alive, added to each day with inside jokes and boneheaded pranks and arguments and laughter and fears and adventures. History. In every memory of those years I have ever replayed, Boo has been there. Sketch and Boo, side by side. We were as connected as two could be, already well on our way to immortality.

"We need more time," I pleaded, half-heartedly, because I knew it would make no difference.

"There is no more time," Boo insisted. "The money is there now. The whole town is over at the bonfire. Nobody's watching the closed-up stores, nobody's worried about anything. It's perfect, right now, but we can't just sit around here talking about things. Right now, Sketch. There is no more time."

Boo rose, then looked toward the window where the evening had grown dark.

"Look, I have to go, if I'm gonna do this. So, I gotta know," Boo asked, coughing into his cupped hands, "are you with me or not?"

And although I knew it was wrong, although I was frightened to my bones, I found myself standing beside my friend and saying simply, "I'm with you, Boo."

TWENTY

And so, it all came down to friendship, to shared history.

Beneath the back window of Tomney's store, it was too dark to read Boo's expression, but there was little doubt he and I shared the same anticipations and fears. We watched each other, trying to discern the smallest clues. Then, with effort that in any other time would have looked comical, Boo's hand jutted into his front pocket and struggled to retrieve something from his shrunken jeans. Eventually, an inhaler, the oft-forgotten accessory he'd miraculously remembered this time, appeared in his grip. He placed it to his lips and squeezed a burst of medicine, which he drew deeply into his lungs. Boo's eyes closed, his nostrils flared, and he held the breath for a small eternity. Finally, he shoved the aerosol back into his pocket and smiled. A broad smile, full at once of naiveté and daring.

"Help me up," Boo whispered.

Before I knew what I was doing, I was crouching low, my back supported by the brick wall, my hands braided and cupped open against my thigh. I received Boo's sneaker and the full weight of his meager frame and hefted him toward the window as easily as if I were tossing a kite into a summer wind. The ledge was deep and Boo was able to balance himself there, his forearm along the sill, his feet hanging down like curtain tassels, as he probed the sash with his thin fingertips for enough leverage. The paint seemed to have sealed the window shut and for an excruciating minute nothing

254

happened. Boo rapped his fist against the frame to loosen the seal, once, twice, until his effort gave way to desperation. One more smack. Then, the window opened. Just a little at first, but enough for Boo to edge his fingers inside. He finally managed to separate the sash completely and the window creaked open.

Boo dropped back to the ground. We stood beside one another again and waited, our backs against the brick, the quick breaths between us the night's only identifiable sound.

Nothing stirred inside the store. No alarm rang out.

No one noticed at all.

"OK," Boo said, in that same ridiculous stage whisper, "we're in."

If there was a moment to reconsider our actions, this was that moment. Not that either of us would ever express such a thing, of course. At that age, we would admit no fear, no second thoughts. We would do what we were expected to do, follow the course expected by the other, even if it made no sense.

We didn't belong here.

Not far behind us, just across the road, French Creek made its silent escape toward the Schuylkill, still swollen with the rains. The calming rush of the water was lost on me. I heard only my own shallow breathing, my heart racing, my pulse. I heard my fear. Everything was moving so quickly now—not just this night, but all the time—and I saw no immediate way to slow it down. I knew I was too young to want peace so strongly, but I did nonetheless. I yearned for it, the kind of peace I found when I drew. The peace I found at Wishing Manor. Boo should know this peace someday, I thought. We should go there, to Wishing Manor, now, right now, before the night swallowed us whole and it was all too late.

"Boo."

This was all I could say. I was not interrupted. I just stopped, the rest of my words evaporating, leaving me with only this, the name of my best friend.

Boo, who seemed lost in his own thoughts, gazed at me with a look of surprise and waited. Whether Boo suspected any further comment, any meaning behind this single-word plea, he didn't let on. Instead, after waiting a reasonable time for elaboration that didn't come, he just shook his head.

"I knew it," Boo said, looking away. "I knew you'd back out."

"I didn't say that."

Boo hung his head and muttered, "Chickenshit."

My irritation rose. "Boo, I didn't say I was backing out."

"It's right there on your face, man. Whatcha gonna do, go back to your girlfriend?"

"Screw you."

"Damn it, Sketch, this is important to me."

"I know," I answered. "I know it is."

We retreated to silent corners and waited for someone to tell us what to do. I tried to determine if Boo's indignation was in fact sincere or just carefully disguised agreement. His own quiet plea for a way out of this. This was not what we should be doing and we both knew it. We should be playing games or spying on girls or gorging ourselves on junk food and caffeine. We had no more business stealing from Tomney than we did running guns with the Furnace Boys. We were children.

"This is the whole future, right here," Boo finally said, without confrontation. "You see that, right? I mean, you do see it? We do this and we're golden, man, sitting pretty. We back out now and everything goes to hell."

"But," I said, "no one even knows we're here."

Boo sighed, heavily. "We know."

With that, Boo stepped away from me and headed into the alley. I could only watch him go. He darted in and out of the shadows like a neighborhood rat. For several minutes, he scoured the nooks of the alley, looking for God knows what, until he finally returned, his breathing labored, lugging a wooden sawhorse.

"Couldn't find no trashcans that weren't chained down," Boo said, "but this should do the trick."

I studied the sawhorse. "What do we need that for?"

Boo rolled his eyes. "Well, it's not like I'm gonna be able to pull you up there after me, once I'm inside. You'll need to boost yourself up through the window."

"Bullshit," I said, crossing my arms.

"No, this'll work," Boo said, "you're strong enough. I know I needed the boost, but you, you can just pull yourself up like in gym class or something. Just pull yourself up."

"No, Boo," I said, thrusting out my chin, "I mean, bullshit, I'm not going in there."

Boo laughed, nervously, like he was unsure of a punchline. "Yeah, right."

"No, I'm serious," I said. "I told you I'd come along for the ride and here I am. But this is it, this is as far as I go."

Boo looked incredulous. Confused, but incredulous. "You can't be serious."

"Like a heart attack."

Boo looked from me to the window and back again, as though he was determining just how necessary I was. We both knew Boo would go through with this at all costs. He was too far down the road. He'd been too far down that road for a very long time.

"Come on, man," Boo said, not arguing so much as whining, "you come this far. I'm not kidding around. I need your help in there."

"My help? What the hell for? This isn't some two-person job."

"I don't know," Boo answered, scrambling. "The money, maybe. I might need help carrying it all."

I laughed. "Shit, it's not that much money, Boo."

Boo lowered his eyes. "It ain't nothing to laugh at."

"No. I just mean," I said, still chuckling, "you're not gonna need any help carrying it. It's a bag of cash, that's all it is. What, you expecting gold bars or something?"

Even Boo smiled at this, although he looked like he would rather not. "Go to hell. Like you know what you're talking about. A minute ago, you're wetting your pants about this job. Now all the sudden you're an expert."

"All I'm sayin' is it ain't that big a deal—"

"Exactly."

"—and one guy should be able to do it himself, is all," I answered. "But then, maybe you bit off more than you can chew."

"Hell, no," Boo snapped.

So we went on like that, each of us stalling for time and each of us knowing it. Far in the distance, in the direction of Black Rock, a train rumbled by and sounded its whistle for three long bursts. The Saturday night regular. Ten o'clock. I absently checked my wrist for a watch I didn't wear. The Firebird Festival would be ending soon and Tomney would be returning home. If we were going to do this, we needed to do it now.

In the din of voices in my head, I suddenly recalled something my mother once told me. We were sitting on the front porch, not long after Rusty died, and I asked her if she would ever get married again. *I'm too selfish,* she said. This surprised me. My mother was the least selfish person I knew, and I told her. *Love is selflessness,* she answered, her blue eyes staring hard at our street. *It's about doing things for the other person, even when it's against your better judgment. Just because they want it. And I only have enough love left for you.*

I watched Boo wipe his mouth with his bandana after a small coughing fit. I knew then that he was on the edge, that with one word I could convince him to abandon this inane plan, to step back into the life he already had. I could talk him out of the whole damn thing.

"Come on," I said, "we going inside or what?"

Boo stared at me, questioning. Then, he grinned. "You serious?"

"Yeah," I nodded, "let's go."

"I owe you," Boo said, raising his palm for a high five. I slapped his hand and Boo held mine there, a bond in the air, for a moment. "Really, I owe you big time, Sketch."

I shrugged. "I'm only going so you don't screw it up again. We don't want another library job on our hands. I'll go in to make sure you don't fall asleep or break your leg or something."

I can give no reason for my decision to go forward, to urge him on. No reason, except friendship. And on that night, friendship seemed as fine a reason as any.

We moved the sawhorse into position and before I could change my mind Boo was scrambling through the window, a spastic Spiderman, his ass sticking out from the opening, his bony legs thrashing wildly against the bricks for some kind of foothold. I watched him struggle, then reached up for his sneakers and gave him a shove. In one graceful motion, a magic trick, Boo disappeared and a soft thud was heard from behind the wall.

"Jesus Christ," Boo hissed. "What the hell?" There was a commotion as Boo got to his feet and dusted himself off, checking for further bruises or injury. "What d'you do that for?"

I laughed and told him to shut up, then climbed onto the sawhorse and hauled myself into the window. As I wriggled through the opening, I got my first look at Tomney's storeroom, smaller than I'd expected and full of dark shapes and stacks. Before my eyes could adjust, Boo switched on the banker's lamp on a metal desk in the corner and the room was awash with green-tinted light. I scurried the rest of the way through the window and dropped to the floor. As soon as I'd landed, I was struck with a palpable sensation of violation, like visiting a church on a Tuesday. We should not be here. Fighting for some balance, I drew a long, steady breath and exhaled. I looked over at Boo, who seemed oblivious to any concerns and was already rummaging through the desk drawers.

"You sure that's a good idea?" I whispered.

"What?" Boo said, without looking up.

"The light. Somebody might see."

"There's nobody around, the town is deserted. Besides, probably nothing unusual about the old man working late.

People see the light, they'll just figure it's Tomney doing the books. That's why I didn't want no flashlight. That kind of light is too suspicious." He shot me a look. "You all right?"

"Yeah," I answered, but anyone could have heard the lie.

"So, come here and help me find the money."

"I thought you knew where it was."

"I do, I do," Boo answered. "It's in this office, I mean. I know that. That's what the old man told Gargoyle. I heard him—I told you this already."

"So, where is it?"

Boo had all the drawers hanging open, like pockets turned inside out. He riffled through papers and ledger books and old magazines. Jacob Tomney apparently was not an organized man and certainly hadn't found religion in his old age. It was one of the reasons he must have been grateful for Boo, who was surprisingly careful with inventory and kept a good stockroom.

The double doors leading to the store were propped open by soda-syrup canisters, to save Tomney and his employees the trouble of pushing them open and closed a dozen times a day. Beyond the doors, the pale bluish mix of moonlight and the streetlamps of Bridge Street staked its claim on the store, painting the displays and floor tiles and countertop with an otherworldly glow. In this light, the store looked smaller than I ever remembered. Smaller and more vulnerable.

"Go ahead," Boo said.

"What?"

"You want some comic books?" Boo said. "We got time. Go on and grab a few."

I didn't acknowledge this. I was too mesmerized by the store and its pools of blue light. The same light I'd seen in

Tara's basement. I looked at the front door leading out onto Bridge Street. Was someone there? Little more than shadow, a specter of light and darkness, passed across the room and the doorway and Tomney's private stairway to his second-floor apartment. No. No one was there.

Wait, yes, something was moving.

There, there it was again.

The walls.

The walls, expanding and contracting, closing in.

Suddenly, the store fell away from me and the stockroom collapsed inward and the walls, the walls, tightened around me. I was suffocating. I couldn't breathe, I couldn't think. Again, I felt eyes upon me. I managed to look toward the ceiling corners, but there were no cameras, no mirrors, no security. Still, I knew I was being watched. Every eye in the town was turned toward me.

Tara.

My mother.

Rusty.

Watching.

"We can't do this."

Boo looked up from the floor where he had just dumped the largest, most cluttered drawer, and stared at me.

"What are you talking about?"

"This isn't right," I replied. "It just isn't. You can say all you want to, Boo. Go ahead and tell me this is because you're sick. Spout your shit all night long if you want to, but nothing you can say is gonna change how I feel right now. This ain't right."

The walls were tight around me. I could feel them against my shoulders, my arms pinned to my sides. I heard nothing, not even my own breath, and I wasn't even sure I was breathing at all.

From the ether, I could just see Boo, smirking, a smile eerily like Deacon's condescension.

"You're a damn schizo," Boo said.

"This is Tomney's, for God's sake. It's not some nameless mark. Not that that would make any damn difference anyway, but there it is. This is Tomney's. We don't steal from here. We never have, we never will. Your rule. Remember that? That's what we say."

"It's not even his money," Boo said, like this mattered somehow. "Sketch, come on, listen to me—"

Air. I needed air.

"No, you listen, damn it, you listen! You do this, Boo, and I will rat you out. Swear to God, I will go right over to that bonfire and find one of those cops and I will rat you out. Don't think for a minute I won't do it."

Silence. A long, interminable silence. And the slowest, slightest leak of oxygen back into the room.

"Unbelievable," Boo finally said, as he replaced the drawer into the desk.

Our stalemate held for minutes. Boo slowly reassembled the room, but said nothing. He straightened the papers on the cluttered desk and chewed on his lip in that way he had when he was overwhelmed. But I noticed little of this. The room was still too tight around me. Sounds crept into the space, slowly at first, then gathering in intensity, until they overwhelmed it. Every sound seemed amplified—the buzzing exit sign was like a jet engine, the heater an ocean storm—as though my senses had gone horribly haywire. I needed to get out, to escape, to breathe. Before it all consumed me, consumed us both. Without another word, I walked toward the desk, plodding, like someone walking through water, and grabbed hold of Tomney's metal chair. I slowly made my way back to the spot beneath the window, jammed the chair against the wall, and began to climb out.

"Sketch ..."

I turned and looked down to find Boo just behind me, closer than I expected.

"Promise me something," Boo continued, not looking away.

"Yeah?"

Boo smiled. Impossibly, he smiled. "Promise me we'll laugh about this one day. You and me, when we tell people the story, we'll laugh."

It was the miracle of a fever suddenly breaking. Sunlight and air and the sweet smell of relief.

"Sure, Boo," I answered, allowing myself my own hint of a smile. "We'll laugh about it. Sure."

Then, starting toward the window again, I asked over my shoulder, "So, you want to come over? Watch some TV or read some comics or something?"

Boo made a big show out of thinking through his options. "Hanging out could be all right, if you can go without your girlfriend for a few hours."

"Shut up."

"You," Boo answered.

I laughed and lunged through the window opening. I was aware of my injuries again, the bruises persisting still, but I no longer cared. I was floating, I was invincible. Writhing and twisting through the window, I finally managed to get my legs around behind me. I was just about to drop when I heard Boo's voice again.

"Hold up a minute."

I looked back toward Boo just as he stepped through the double doors into the front of the store.

"C'mon, Boo," I said, stealing a glance down the empty alley behind me. "What the hell?"

"I'm starving," Boo called back as he sank into the streetlamp's misty glow, illuminated. "I need something to eat, or are you suddenly against lifting candy too? Just hang on a second."

Boo was always hungry. Something about his illness or his size. He constantly fed the machine. He would eat anything. The problem was, when faced with an abundance of choice, especially a glorious buffet of junk, it took him forever to decide. From my perch at the window, I agonized as Boo chose one bar then another, setting each reject back neatly into the display. I couldn't take it any longer and I was just about to bitch at him when Boo finally selected a regular old Hershey bar. We were out of there. But then, amazingly, Boo unwrapped the candy bar, right there in the middle of the store, and began to eat. His attention returned to me at the window, however, and Boo, his mouth full of chocolate, grunted something unintelligible and gestured toward the candy rack. You want something? he seemed to ask, with raised eyebrows. I shook my head emphatically and frowned.

"Come on," I hissed, too quietly for Boo to hear.

But Boo did not move. He just stood there, gnawing contentedly on his Hershey bar as though he had all the time in the world. My feet dangling just above the sawhorse, I was framed in the window like Kilroy, my hands on the sill, my face partially obscured. I was quite a sight and Boo smiled, a similar beaming smile as before, but even bigger, if that was possible. He was happy, as happy as I remembered seeing him in a long time. Maybe this was all Boo needed. One more shared adventure, albeit unconsummated. Enough of a thrill to get his heart racing again. Enough to create the legend, a story we would tell each other with embellishment for years to come. Immortality, at last. Yes, even I agreed, this was worth a smile.

Then, just like that, Boo's smile faded and he turned from the window once more and all the world slipped away.

The sound was not, no matter what people say, like a car backfiring or a thunderclap or a round of holiday firecrackers. It was a piercing shriek, a scream, a howl all its own, as unique as any voice.

The blast struck Boo in the chest and hurled him backward against the candy display. He hit the rack at full force, his limbs akimbo, the angles grotesque and unimaginable, and his impact sent the entire structure crashing to the floor. Candy and mints and chewing gum scattered like witnesses fleeing for cover. Magazines fluttered open, birds in brief flight, before plunging back to the ground.

It was over as quickly as it began, the scene suddenly motionless, captured as a still life, the only sound a perpetual echoing toll of a single gunshot. As centerpiece, the boy lay still upon it all, his arms out like a crucifix, his eyes open toward the ceiling, his face even in death that same expression of bewilderment and amusement he'd worn so frequently before. The only sign of life was on his chest, his white t-shirt alive with a crimson blossom seeping slowly over the fabric. The blast had torn open my friend's body, striking at his very core—the core of his illness, his soul, his fire—bringing a final and ironic relief.

From the darkness of the front stairway, Gargoyle appeared, a sobbing apparition, clutching a shotgun across his chest like a blanket. He shuffled forward toward the broken boy on the floor, his round face full of terror, his shoulders trembling with slow awakening. Gargoyle collapsed to his knees beside Boo's body and lowered the gun to the sliver of space between them. Reality and fantasy mingled, fact and fiction were confused. As though to test his understanding, Gargoyle reached over and clutched Boo's blood-stained shirt. If he recognized his victim, his face showed no sign. His clasp tightened over the red flower, its petals crushed beneath his fingers until the man, uncomprehending, raised his hand to his face and stared at his open palm, bloated and tender and red with blood.

In that moment, a dawn finally emerged, a new and wholly unprecedented dawn, and Gargoyle greeted it for all three present with a singular wail. Low and plaintive at first, then screeching and unceasing. The cries seemed to continue forever, long after the sirens arrived, and the ambulance pulled to the curb, and the young police officer led the slow man to his seat at the end of the coffeeshop counter.

By the time anyone looked toward the open back window, I was long gone.

HOMECOMING

Her Shane was coming for her. At last, he was coming home.

Waiting, Rebecca Wilton was once again an angel, aloft over the town of her father, looking down on it all.

From the air, Phoenixville looked little more than a garden of tiny parks, brown paths, and miniature rooftops. Puffs of smoke from the mill's chimneys and its furnace blossomed gray among the green of the dogwoods and elms. It was all so small and it would be so easy for one to think that nothing, not even the mighty smokestacks or the flaming forges or the Schuylkill River itself, was of any consequence. But Rebecca knew flight was deception, that the higher one flew the easier it was to think Phoenixville was no different from any other town. A town where nothing ever happened, where the future was as limited as the horizon. But for Rebecca, nothing could be further from the truth. She knew some differences could not be seen, some wonders were invisible, like railroads running underground, the scars of distant battles, the pains of heartache. Still, as Rebecca rose, she could not escape the sensation that everything else was shrinking away, receding into the shadows for fear of what they might see.

They knew. Everyone knew.

She flew, soaring ever higher until the clouds were at her shoulders, the wind light upon her back. Her wings were a graceful pair, their rhythm fluid and majestic, their feathers white as those of a dove.

But she was no dove.

And she was not certain she was an angel.

Rebecca squinted at the ground, the sun's glare piercing. From this vantage, she saw no boundaries below her. The cursed line of Mason and Dixon did not exist, not as far as she could see. It was an illusion, a trick of a pen, nothing more than a sketch on some person's map. And yet.

And yet.

The war continued, raging with renewed fury from the stillness of the winter. With it came the dead, like storms returning for the spring, arriving home in train cars stained with the blood of distant battlefields. Battlefields with names she did not know before all this: Gettysburg, Antietam, Fredericksburg, and Bull Run. Battlefields made from towns much like her own, small thriving concerns surrounded by green fields and open space. Not a boundary between them. The dead came from these places, when they came home at all. Most stayed where they fell, crops shorn in quick unison and replanted into red soil.

The whole of the town mourned the losses. The mill seemed to feel it deepest, as many of the furnace boys disappeared to those fields, never to return. At first, Father held their jobs for them, out of loyalty, out of patriotism, but the work needed to continue. The Negroes came to work the fires, working days at a time, building the machines and the cannons, but then they too followed the boys into the battlefields. Soon, with the coming conscription, there would be no young men left in town and those who did return would come in those boxes on the long trains, as Rebecca sat at graveyards with their mothers and sisters and widows with damp handkerchiefs and hollow words. She felt their loss. Like a knife in her bosom, she felt their loss.

But her Shane was coming home.

He no longer fought. His last letters declared as much. He was dispirited and exhausted, from the blood and futility and the insects and mud. He did not use these very words, but the emotion was there, within the lines. This was what Rebecca read. She knew he had already laid his rifle to the ground and turned away from it all and he was now making the journey back to her.

Coming home.

She knew this.

Her father would be so pleased. They were together again, she and Elijah, as they were before. Their work united them. Their work with the night visitors and the cellars and the railroad. It was good work, wonderfully rewarding. The railroad was a long line of miracles, Rebecca's own salvation, temporary or otherwise, not least among them. It rescued her and kept her sadness at bay. The sadness did not disappear, of course. It was there always, lying dormant except on the infrequent occasions when she allowed it to come forward from the shadows. Yet even in these moments, the sadness was more companion than master and she let it visit until she grew numb to its influence. Then, she returned to her work and the railroad.

There had been a hundred or more night visitors, arriving alone or in small groups, every person different, but each with the same look of fear in the eyes, as though they had seen the worst of this earth. They were men mostly, thin but strong, and scarred like animals upon their backs and shoulders.

They made their escapes on foot, or hidden in the wagons of others, Quakers usually, who brought them from the towns along the borders. Rebecca fed these men and clothed them with the uniforms of farmhands and furnace boys. The clothes of the free man. On occasion, she held them as well. She knew this was unseemly perhaps, her generosity and hospitality should extend only so far, but she did not care. She took their hands and held them, in prayer, in silence, in comfort, and they looked at her as no one else had ever looked at her, with gratitude that knew no depth, with tears spilling upon their cheeks, with words failing them as they tasted first freedom, however endangered.

Ever empathetic, Rebecca knew precisely how they felt. Yet even in her sadness, she could rise above it, for she had a purpose now, a name, a home.

And wings.

Rebecca soared back across the creek, its waters high and brown with mud, and up over the tall jagged cliff. For sport, she swooped along the treetops, the branches licking at her toes, the air thick with the scent of the pines, and then turned and headed for the house.

She had come to love the house, the enormous mansion, and the town it surveyed. They would make their home here, she and Shane, when he took the position in the superintendent's building upon his return. Here they would raise their family, mind their gardens, spend their evenings. They would take their walks again along the cliff, make their picnics on the rock, listen to the laughter of their children and the songs of the iron mill and the whippoorwills and cicadas.

Tracing a path around the house, once, twice, she climbed to the highest point, the cupola, and gripped the iron rail. She looked out along the roofline, the widow's walk, and scanned the open fields to the horizon, but she saw no one. No soldier on foot, no visitor hidden low in a carriage, no farmhands working the grains. Even the mill was quiet, the smokestacks dormant, the fires extinguished.

The world around her, all of Phoenixville, was still and Rebecca knew she was completely alone.

Alone.

With this house and this land and all this wealth, she was alone.

This awakening was all she needed. Suddenly and violently, a threat swept over Rebecca and she grew frightened, if only for a moment. This was nothing to fear, she told herself. This was only doubt. The same slippery villain that reared its head in the darkness of night and in the moments when Rebecca was off her guard.

As was her practice now, she surrendered to it, if only for a moment, let it soak into her, before it fell away like raindrops rolling from the slick leaves of the spring magnolia outside her bedroom window.

This time, however, it did not roll away.

She was falling, slipping from the railing, down through the slate itself, plunging through the roof and the ceilings until she was once again in her room, upon her bed.

The footsteps on the floorboards outside her bedroom door were heavy and slow. Then, silence.

He stood there on the other side, waiting, hesitating.

He was coming to her.

Rebecca sat up on the bed, arranging the pillows beside her, swinging her legs over the side and touching her bare toes to the cold floor. She adjusted the necklace at her throat, so that the black jewel laid just so.

A small knock, then the turn of the knob.

The tears in her father's eyes, tears she had not seen but on one prior occasion, told her all she needed to know. But then, she already knew. Before her father ever said a word, she knew.

Still, he told her.

Her first thought was to laugh. She felt so sorry for this man, this confused and mistaken man. Shane Ryan Hughes was not dead. Elijah and his letter and his newspaper and his government, the wretched government, they all had it wrong. She wanted to tell him, to reassure him, to laugh with him, but she took the news only in silence. Her Shane was returning to her. It was the promise he had made, the prayer

Rebecca whispered every evening, the sight she saw when she soared out over the hills and fields.

Her father stayed with her for quite some time, an hour, maybe more, until he had nothing else he could say to her. Rising, he placed a gentle but otherwise useless hand on his daughter's shoulder. With no words to hold it there, he soon took his leave, saying it was only for a little while, and Rebecca quietly turned the skeleton key in the lock behind him and returned to her bed. There, she waited. Waited for Shane to come for her and the night to take the dusk. Finally, when the house was quiet and she was certain her father was asleep, she slipped from her bedroom window, down the branches of the dogwood, and slowly out across the back lawn.

Her Shane was coming for her.

Rebecca ran her hands through the thick tresses she washed in such anticipation just that morning and smoothed the folds of her nightgown. Her robe was pulled tight, her bare skin hidden from the night air, though the sash loosened as she hurried across the grass. Her necklace bounced against her as she ran. When she reached the line of trees, their branches full with young leaves, she hunched her shoulders and slipped through them as easily as a raccoon. The moonlight was upon the rock, the granite sparkling like stars, and she took her seat there and she waited.

Everything was perfect.

Her soldier arrived not long after, when the moon was past its peak and all the world was quiet again. He was mere shadow at first, a shape along the path, tall and proud. He walked slowly, more tentatively than she expected, and her thoughts were instantly of an injury. But when he reached a particular clearing and the moonlight struck his face just so, she saw he was the same. Exactly the same.

At twenty paces, Shane smiled and Rebecca was on her feet, running to him. Crying with joy, she reached him and they kissed, wet and longing, his arms thick and strong around her. He held her like he was holding life itself, like he was desperate to never let it go. Rebecca let him hold her, her cheek pressed against his chest. His uniform was torn and filthy, and he smelled of gunpowder and campfires and blood, but none of this mattered to Rebecca. Shane was here, home again.

When he spoke, his voice was not quite the same as she remembered, though she had heard it every day and night for those three years. It was lower, weary and worn, the voice of a man. A furnace boy no longer.

"I have seen everything there is to see, Rebecca. I have crossed the rivers and the fields to battle brothers, boys not so much different from me. I have seen guns more powerful than steam engines and heard thunder like nothing imagined. I have endured weeks and months of waiting, interminable boredom, longing for a battle if only as interruption to the tedium. And death, I have seen enough to fill a thousand graveyards. It is all there in my memory, as real as this very moment, and I can never forget it. But through it all, I tell you now, I never feared for myself. I never felt the dread of the bullet or the cannons, nor feared the bayonets and knives of those rebels with their war cries and their wild eyes. Perhaps it was my time here in the mill, the hours at the fires, which made me this way. Perhaps this is so, but there was always something else. Within all this, this war and death, I never once believed they could bring me harm, for I was protected."

Shane paused. As he ran light fingers through Rebecca's hair, a chill swept through the girl like a first kiss. After a time, Shane spoke again.

"There is no certainty with which I can describe what was there, but there is no doubt I was under its care. An angel, she might be called, above me wherever my journey led. Protecting me, guiding me. I did not always see her, Rebecca, but I knew she was there. After a battle I would catch glimpses of her above, in the sky, racing the clouds. I would lie back in the grass, my rifle at my side, my bloody hands behind my head, and I would see her up there. She was a ghost, a gull, white as baker's flour, high and fleet and there, always there. Always."

Rebecca lifted her head and looked into Shane's eyes, but she could find no words with which to interrupt him. She knew now it had been the same vision they had shared, though she still searched for its meaning. She stared at this boy, this man, and waited.

"I know, Rebecca. Believe me, I know how this sounds. I have told myself as much in those quiet moments out there in the fields, when I felt myself within inches of insanity. I have to believe that war's greatest victim may very well be reason. But I have kept my wits, I promise you. Indeed, I have never been more certain of my thoughts. They came to me only hours ago, or perhaps days now, I no longer can tell. It was at the last battle, the horrors of which I see no purpose in recounting, that I knew."

Shane stopped and for quite some time Rebecca did not know if he would continue. In the subsequent silence, she felt something go out of him, some breath, some life. As the creek below lapped hungrily at the rocky shore, she could only listen to the world around them and wait.

"What?" she asked him when she could wait no longer. "What did you know?"

"I knew this angel was not watching over me, but rather calling to me. Showing me the way home."

With these words, Rebecca realized that all this time she had been mistaken. The traveler she had watched from above had not been her soldier at all. The journey home was not Shane's journey. The journey home was now her journey to make. Shane, her soldier, he was simply her guide, her angel.

They said nothing else that night, but remained in their spot for what felt like hours unfolding, until the hint of sunrise was on the horizon, until the birds united in morning chorus.

Everything has a destiny. Rebecca had known, from the moment their eyes met at the Harvest Festival, she had known they would be together, in a marriage everlasting.

With nothing left to say, Shane took her hand in his and they stepped up onto the rock, their rock, and embraced there, swaying like dancers, like willows in the breeze. When they kissed, it was with an urgency unmatched and Rebecca felt the world again receding. Just slightly at first, like an echo, returning and retreating again.

They kissed once more and breathed each other in and the rest of the world melted away. Their eyes met and the lovers smiled, like they were destined, like they were the only two on earth. Shane's fingers found the necklace, Rebecca's beloved necklace, hanging at her throat. He stroked the onyx, its glow pulsating beneath his thumb, until at last the fire seemed to expire. Then, her soldier, her angel, her boy from the roof, took Rebecca's hand and guided her out to the end of the rock and over the edge of the cliff. And as the ravenous waters of French Creek rose to greet her, Rebecca Wilton was weightless, floating, falling, leaving the rooftops and the smokestacks and the rest of the world so very far behind.

HALLOWEEN

Sleepwalking.

It felt like sleepwalking.

Like water, like clouds, like moving through a dream.

When I scaled the high chain-link fence and dropped with the graceful ease of an alley cat, I didn't feel the ground beneath my sneakers. I no longer felt the injuries from my brawl with the Furnace Boys. There were new wounds now, but even they were ignored. I felt nothing. I just kept moving forward, floating, disconnected. The way I'd been moving for the past week, as though none of it was really happening. As detached as the perfect autumn moon above me, that bright white witness.

The backpack heavy on my shoulders, I maneuvered through the shadows with unwavering purpose. Even in my trance, I sensed the steel mill around me was now different. The shapes appeared more ominous, the broken buildings taller and more forbidding, the shadows deeper and darker. It was to be expected. When someone you love dies, the entire landscape changes. A river shifts its course, a mountain range disappears, a forest turns to desert. People make you see the world one way and, when they are gone, you see it for what it is. Just yesterday, when the sun was high and the world was awake and alive, it was all right there. And then it's gone so suddenly that you begin to wonder whether it was ever really there at all.

I loved Boo, I knew this now, and I missed him beyond pain and tears. There had been enough of those, of course, for the past seven days and nights, but they paled in comparison to what I truly felt. I didn't talk about it. Not aloud. Not to my mother, not to the guidance counselor who called every afternoon, not to the minister who'd stopped by twice after the funeral. But late at night, in the moment before dreams when we tell ourselves the smallest secrets, I offered this confession: I died that night with Boo.

So I moved across the ghost town of Phoenix Iron & Steel with the peaceful resignation of a spirit finding his way home. The shadows served as my eager protectors and I sank into them with gratitude. I moved slowly along the machine shop, or what was left of it, with its broken walls long and narrow, stretching on forever. I remembered Boo's grandfather Henry had worked here, cutting the grooves into the parts the rest of the mill needed to do their jobs. Grinding, cutting, year after year. Each day, each shift, no different from the last.

Henry cried at the funeral, burying his face in his scarred hands when his grandson's casket was lowered into a plot seven rows down from Rusty's grave. Billy T, returned to Phoenixville to see his little brother buried, stood beside their parents, all three of them broken. Tomney was there too, shaking his head the whole time like he was trying to erase some thought or just stunned by the waste of it all. I paid little attention to any of it. I saw that funeral as nothing but an endless parade of hypocrites: adults who ignored Boo or frowned at his coughing interruptions, devastated classmates who pretended they knew him, and Deacon and the Furnace Boys, the most obvious hypocrites of all, standing at the edge of the cemetery like they owned the place. I just tried to block it out and stood without stirring beneath my mother's embrace, as my best friend was lowered into the cold ground.

Even there at the funeral, people wondered what Boo had been doing in the store that night. The gossip had started immediately, with voices whispering that the punk kid had been looking for money for drugs, or performing another absurd teenage prank, or simply retrieving something he'd left at work.

The rumors of my involvement had started the moment the police arrived at Tomney's that night. The height of the window being what it was, it seemed doubtful Boo had acted alone and his best friend was understandably his most likely accomplice. But there was no evidence, no witness, no proof at all. Gargoyle was a shattered mess of incoherence and I was pretty sure the man never saw me at the window. My mother must have heard the rumors and endured the questions, but she never asked. The police came by the house the next day, but I immediately knew from their questions that they had nothing. I chose silence as my best course of action. Rumors be damned.

I didn't go to school for a week. I thought maybe I should, that it might distract me or weaken the gossip, but my mother had told me to stay home and rest. She took off work to care for me. Even that morning, when she finally returned to the hospital, she seemed overly concerned about me and spent most of the morning asking if she could get me anything. I kept telling her I was fine, because I didn't want her to worry, but I knew I was far from fine. I suspected she knew this, too.

I wanted only to be left alone. To be anonymous.

Harley and the guys had stopped by several times to see me, but I didn't see anyone. Not even Tara. We spoke briefly at the funeral and then again on the telephone the other day after she got home from school, but I found I couldn't get out more than a few words. Guilt left me strangled. The same poison continued to lay in wait for me, usually at night, when the guilt would reveal itself in vomit and tears and laughter that bordered on maniacal.

I battled against it all, telling myself I had nothing to feel guilty about, but I lost ground every day. I knew I wouldn't be able to keep it buried forever. I also knew that when I was ready to talk about it, Tara would be there. For now, however, there was no talk. Only the overwhelming need to move forward.

Hunched over like a soldier ducking enemy fire, I scurried across the open section of the mill, where there were no shadows to hide me and the moon shone like a spotlight from a prison tower. I was exposed, nothing to protect me, and I sprinted. I flew. Twice, I nearly fell under the weight of my backpack before finally reaching the old lookout shed. I ducked into the structure and crouched behind a stack of wooden pallets, no more than twenty yards from the Furnace. My stumbles were enough to rattle me and, removing the backpack and placing it gingerly at my feet, I paused to collect myself.

I crouched there in the dark, until an electric jolt of paranoia shot through me and I rose just enough to peer from the shed toward the creek, where the cliff loomed from the shadows like a dark tidal wave. I knew my rock was somewhere up there, the line of trees, the mansion behind it all, and although I could see none of it in the darkness, this small knowledge gave me some confidence.

The millyard was deserted. No one was here.

I was sure of this. Halloween night, the trick-or-treaters all back home counting their loot, the mischief makers all out on the town.

No one was here.

But people just appear sometimes. Out of nowhere.

Gargoyle was not supposed to be at Tomney's that night. He no longer kept the room upstairs. This was what Boo had insisted, in any case. He was positive. But the guy was there, Gargoyle was there. As the entire town celebrated at the bonfire, the rest of Phoenixville was empty. I heard my mother tell someone on the phone that Gargoyle was simply too tired after the Duck Race to go back home and Tomney let him take a nap upstairs in his old room. I never gave much thought to what exactly brought Gargoyle down those stairs. It wasn't like it mattered.

I was trying to convince myself of this yet again, when my attention was suddenly diverted by the low rumble of a car and I squinted out into the darkness, across the empty property to the gate on the chain-link fence. I waited, breathless, but it was nothing. The car was moving too quickly to be a cop or a parent or anyone of concern. Just a car passing by. I checked the Casio tied to my backpack. Well after midnight. I wasn't tired. My energy surprised even me. I was running on adrenaline and fear and caffeine.

The car returned, much slower this time, easing its way on the road's shoulder along the fence. Sinking back behind the pallets, I drew a breath and held it like it was my last. I waited. Through the slats I could just see the gate and a single figure walking toward it. Soon, a flashlight swept across the property, but its beam was dull and impotent and I was safely beyond its limits. Still, I fell prone upon the ground and didn't dare to breathe. I waited, invisible. After a time, the car engine started again and I stood just as it slipped away. When it passed beneath a street lamp, I thought I saw the red light on its roof, but I wasn't entirely sure.

The Furnace was only steps away, wide open and glistening in the moonlight, but its windows were all mystery, impossible to determine what lay behind the glass. The building was empty, I told myself. It must be, it had to be. If Deacon and his boys had been there earlier, they were long gone by now. Even on summer nights, they rarely stayed past midnight. I wondered whether Harley or the others had been coming here this week and I told myself they hadn't. They likely were just as lost in their mourning as I was. No, not just as lost, but lost. Or maybe they had come here earlier, out of defiance, to send a message to Deacon that this place didn't belong to him. That would be Harley's position, to be sure, but I doubted even Harley had come here. No matter. The Furnace was empty now.

Inspired, I stepped from the shed and made the last stretch at a clip. Reaching the door, I adjusted the strap of my backpack on my shoulder and took a last look behind me.

I was alone. No one was here.

I was sure of this, despite all else, despite everything, I was sure of this. I didn't know where this confidence came from, but I knew it, as I knew the feel of a pencil in my hand or the sound of my mother's voice.

I opened the Furnace door and stepped inside.

I'd never imagined it would turn out like this.

The match did not belong in my hand.

I needed the feeble light of the match to get my bearings, as the old building was the same pitch black it had been when

Tara and I had rescued Boo. I took the measure of the lobby and the staircase at its end, just as the match burned to my fingertips and I dropped it to the floor. Deciding to reserve the rest of the matches, I stood motionless, steeling myself, when I was immediately struck by the smell of something vaguely familiar. An unusual scent, not chemical, not man-made. I couldn't place it. Drawing in a deep breath, filling myself with it, I waded cautiously into the darkness. I was no longer weightless. Every step was now heavy by thousands, a sea diver plodding along the ocean floor, and when a sentinel floorboard creaked under my weight, I froze at the noise, my breath caught, my limbs paralyzed.

This was not supposed to be happening. None of this.

I was moving on faith. I really had no way of knowing if the building was truly empty or if the Furnace Boys were hovering upstairs in the shadows. My mind played tricks, as it so often did, imagining scores of them huddled up there in the black, waiting for me with their weapons and confident grins. I tried to reassure myself, but each subsequent movement was made with increasingly false confidence.

I shouldn't be in this position. I should be home, anywhere but here, doing whatever it was that other kids my age did, but I no longer knew what those things were. My reference points had disintegrated. It had all happened so quickly, as if my entire childhood had been spent by someone else.

The steps reached up into the darkness, disappearing like a mirage into the shadows. The rail quivered with age, but stayed mercifully silent. I eased myself along it, keeping my feet to the sides of the stairs to avoid any other noise. Despite the adrenaline, the momentum pumping through me, I was thinking clearly and I was pleased by this. I wanted so desperately to be present, to be awake to each moment as it unfolded. I'd been lost for too long. But not tonight. Tonight, I would know just what I was doing.

I reached the top of the staircase and stepped out into the room. Deacon's recliner sat empty, the windowsills held no guards, the shadows appeared vacant. I was alone.

Fear. The building smelled of fear.

The office waited for me across the room and I moved to its door without hesitation. My heart was pounding, my breath was coming in rapid and shallow rhythm. I reached for the doorknob and turned.

Empty.

No Deacon.

No Furnace Boy.

Empty.

Except for the locked trunk of guns in the corner.

And the ghost of Boo crumpled there on the floor.

I closed the door and returned to Deacon's recliner back by the stairs. I took a seat, sinking into the broken cushions, picking at the battered vinyl, kicking my feet and laughing. Laughing. After a time, I stood again and retrieved one of the bottles from my backpack and, in a graceful yet careful motion, poured its contents all over that chair. That fucking throne. When the bottle was empty, I dropped it to the floor.

The building no longer smelled of fear.

When I was outside again, I slithered quickly to the rear of the Furnace, to the spot I'd planned earlier in the day. I pulled away the vines from the window and wiped my hand over the grime. Everything was as I remembered. A metal drum, rusted and muddy, was nearby and provided perfect cover. I set the backpack between my feet. Then, drawing a deep breath, I reached in and carefully, very carefully, extracted two more large bottles. The fluid sloshed violently and I waited for it to subside before unscrewing the cap. The stench was strong, the evidence as loud as any gunshot. I pushed away the tail of my jacket when I feared it got too close, then replaced the bottle cap, twisting it as tight as I could. The odor, an ally now, floated thick in the breeze around me.

I'd had no trouble scoring the gasoline. As soon as the sun had fallen, I'd taken to my alley and slipped over the fence down at the corner house. The mower, a power Lawn-Boy I'd always considered overkill for such a small patch of grass, was stored beneath the back porch behind a lattice screen. The gas can, full and tightly capped, waited beside it. I had snatched it in a flash and hurried with it back to my yard, where I filled the bottles I'd retrieved from my own trash the night before.

Boo would be pleased. Not only because I had fulfilled this part of the mission, but because I was finally doing something, anything. A plan of my own. So many people, they were all nothing but talk. They took no action. This was action. This was why I was here. It wasn't revenge, no matter how it may look later. This was a reclamation.

Restoration, resurrection.

Rebirth.

I crouched there below the window, protected by the brick wall against the wind now escalating, as though it suspected my intentions. I waited. I can't say now why I hesitated, except maybe to wait out the wind and to decipher the voices in my own head. I remained silent, wishing those voices would go away, wishing they would stay and offer some reassurance. The conversation continued until there, beneath the shadows of the Furnace, it was a kind of prayer, a boy kneeling, trembling, searching.

"Where are you?"

I said this right out loud, imploring the silence to respond. The first time I had spoken in hours.

"Talk to me."

I steadied the two bottles between my feet, then scoured the ground for another weapon. I was on my hands and knees, stiff and sore, crawling in the dirt behind the Furnace. At last I found something suitable, a chunk of brick the size of a softball. Just like the one I'd used to break that library window, a lifetime before. It would do. I rose, pressing my back into the wall as if I could have been absorbed. With a long look down the length of the building, I waited for someone to turn the corner. An animal, a cop, a Furnace Boy. Someone.

No one came. I was alone.

The brick broke through the window in one easy motion, the crash of the glass swallowed by the wind. No one heard, yet still I waited. Looking up, I checked my position one more time and I knew I was in the right place, directly below the dark corner on the second floor. Deacon's lair and that damn trunk of guns. Without hesitation, I poured the whole of one bottle's contents through the broken window.

I looked toward the building's corner again.

No one.

I emptied the other bottle. Then, thinking of fingerprints, I threw both of them in after the gasoline and listened to their endless hollow clatter onto the floor inside.

The wind reeked of it all now. I knew the smell would be in my hair, my skin, my clothes. It would be there forever.

My hand slipped into the inner pocket of my jacket and my fingers found the box of matches once more.

Forward. Ever forward.

I opened the box and chose a match, which I promptly dropped onto the ground. My hands shook. My breath came in short, harried bursts. Retrieving the match from the dirt, I wiped it against my jeans, then touched it to the side of the box. My hand didn't move.

I couldn't do it. I couldn't strike the match.

Defeated, I slid down the wall and closed my eyes. I can't say for how long I stayed like that, but when I finally opened my eyes again, I was only slightly startled to see someone turning the corner of the Furnace. A shadow at first, nothing more. Then a figure, moving as though he couldn't see more than a few steps in front of him. I waited, watching the phantom grow larger, a specter in the darkness. Finally, I could see the baggy coat, flowing out behind him like a superhero's cape.

"I can't do this!" I called out.

The phantom stepped closer.

Tears blurred my vision, my voice cracked. "I can't do it."

Boo held out his hand. I gave him the box of matches and watched as he slid open the cardboard drawer, selected a match, and struck it against the flint strip. Boo raised the burning match before him and smiled, reassuringly, at me over the flame. His hand betrayed not the slightest tremor.

"We can be heroes, Sketch. You and me, together."

Fire.

That was how it started.

ALL SAINTS' DAY

Tara was crying big, uninhibited tears.

Surprisingly at ease, I placed my arm behind her, my palm on the rock beneath us, and let her lean back into me. She rested her head on my shoulder as we gazed out over French Creek to the ashes of Phoenix Iron & Steel on the opposite bank.

The fire was out now, although the ruins of the Furnace still smoldered in the morning mist. It looked like the remains of a small campfire from up there, but only hours before, it had been a magnificent blaze, violent and voracious, and had taken ladders from four different area companies to control. I'd only stayed to watch the arrival of the first engines, their sirens waking half the town. The gate chain was cut open and the trucks pulled right up beside the Furnace for the fight, but by that point it was already too late. From time to time, the flames ebbed with the water and the shifts in the wind, but they always returned, with renewed vengeance. Satisfied that the foundry would eventually fall, I had crept along the back of the fence to the grove where I'd hidden my bike and escaped along a forgotten service road just as the horizon showed the slightest tinge of dawn.

"Lots of people 'round here thought they'd never see that again," I said.

"What?" Tara asked.

"The Furnace burning one more time."

I laughed, but Tara didn't join in. Instead, she drew the front of her t-shirt from her jeans and wiped her eyes with it. The smoke didn't bother me. I liked the smell of the ash, still heavy in the morning air, and I breathed it in like a drunk sucking on the last few ice cubes in an otherwise empty cocktail. I waited for her, unsure whether her tears were from the smoke or from something else entirely that neither of us was yet discussing. After a while, Tara let go of her shirt and leaned her head once more onto my shoulder. I stroked her hair, so soft.

"I used to think that nobody in this town could ever let go of anything, you know? Like people can't admit when something is gone," I started, tentatively, "but that isn't true. They know. They know that just because something isn't there anymore, well, that doesn't mean it's actually gone." Stealing a sideways glance, I checked for some reaction, but Tara's eyes were closed as she listened. "It's all like a phantom pain, a missing limb you still somehow feel. It's there and it isn't. That's what this place is now. All that clanging in the hearths, the smell of those furnaces, the trains and the lunch whistles and the trucks rolling across the bridges. It's all still here. You can hear it and see it and smell it right now, like it was yesterday. Every one of us who grew up in Phoenixville, we still hear those noises when we try to fall asleep, just like we did years ago. The men in town, they never seem to get that soot from under their nails or wash the gray from their faces, even though they've scrubbed themselves clean a thousand times since that mill closed down. Phantom pain. It's crazy, I know, but I see it. It's all gone, but it isn't." I pointed at the dark smoke hovering like a vulture over the Furnace skeleton. "Breathe it in, Tara. That fire, that's the whole town right there. That's everything you need to know."

Dangling her legs over Wishing Rock, Tara kicked her feet like a child, the soles of her boots brushing the tops of the weeds growing along the edge of the cliff. She stared out over the creek at the steel property. I couldn't even guess what she was thinking.

If Tara was surprised when I showed up that morning beneath her bedroom window, she hadn't shown it. With little convincing, she'd needed only a few minutes to change before she came out to the street, pushing that banana-seated Huffy of hers. She said she'd heard the sirens in the middle of the night and smelled the smoke, but she didn't yet know the site of the fire nor the damage. I had told her as we rode and she stayed remarkably quiet. She displayed little reaction at all, which was the reason I had been taken aback when we reached the rock and I realized she was crying.

"What time is it?" Tara asked through sniffles.

"I don't know," I answered, looking toward the haze of a sun still low in the east. "Eight, maybe. Maybe later."

"Probably."

I knew I had to tell her. I knew it wasn't enough to bring her here, to the cliff and the rock and the distant smoke. I needed to explain everything. I owed her as much.

"I have to tell you something," I finally said.

Tara lifted her head to look at me, her brow furrowed, her chin jutting forward. "There are a hundred reasons a place like that can burn," she said. "Bad wiring or ... or, something like that. I don't know. No one will care anyway. They're just dead old buildings. That's all, Sketch." She placed her hand gently over mine. "You don't have to tell me anything. Some things just happen. Some things are supposed to happen."

I started to answer, but the words caught in my throat. I felt the tears coming again and I wiped a quick hand over my face.

"Boo was supposed to die."

Despite its truth, this seemed an awful thing for Tara to say aloud and now it was my turn to react. I drew away, taking a long look at her, and then slid off the rock and paced along the cliff, the tall brambles grabbing at my jeans.

"It wasn't your fault," Tara called after me. "Boo asked you to go with him to Tomney's that night. He wanted you there with him, needed you maybe, but he was going to do it anyway. Make no mistake about that, Sketch. He was going to rob that store no matter what and that man was going to shoot him and that's what was going to happen. That's what was supposed to happen. Stop putting this on yourself. It wasn't your fault."

Tara said this like she believed it. Like it was fact.

I'd thought a lot about destiny that week, about how events happen and don't happen and how things all build on top of one another like some house of cards. I figured this was probably true, that everything was predetermined, but I still wasn't so sure.

"Do you really believe that?" I asked, walking back toward the rock. "That it was going to happen anyway?"

Tara opened her palms in front of her like she was checking for rain and answered, "Everything that happens is supposed to happen. That's what I think."

"I don't know," I muttered, running my hand through my hair, which badly needed washing. "Maybe. I mean, you might be right about it, but I just don't know. Everything happened so quick, like it was all just exploding right there in front of me. I can't believe it was already ... it was destiny, or whatever." My voice dissolved away. "I don't know anything anymore."

Tara took her time with an answer, like she was afraid of saying something wrong.

"You're going to be all right," she finally said, "but it's going to take some time."

I let out something like a laugh. "I know it is. When Rusty died ... when my brother ...." I stumbled, choking again on my words. "Maybe—despite all that shit I was just saying—maybe I'm the one who can't let go. Maybe it's me that doesn't know when something is gone. When it ain't coming back." I covered my face, my fingers still smelling of gasoline, and tried to keep from crying. "None of this is what I wanted to say to you. It isn't what I wanted to tell you." A long while passed before I was sure I could take my hands away. When I did, I shoved them deep into my back pockets. Then, I looked directly into Tara's eyes, liquid and blue and alive. "I'm leaving Phoenixville."

Tara recoiled, then immediately waved her hand at the smoldering Furnace. "Sketch, they'll never catch you, if they even look for you in the first place. That mill was dead already. You did the town a favor." Then, she covered her mouth with her palm. "Oh, God, Deacon. Deacon will ... Sketch, is that what you're saying? He'll come after you?"

I was already shaking my head. "I don't give a damn about Deacon. Not anymore. He's gonna have a hell of a lot more than me to worry about once the cops start digging up the guns in those ashes down there." I walked the final steps back to the rock and retrieved my backpack wrapped over my bike's handlebars. "No, that's not why I'm leaving."

Forward. Ever forward.

Tara took the sketchbook as I offered it, turned to the first page and laid open on her lap. Silently, as I kept watching her from the corner of my eye, she studied it, concentrating on each page as if she was seeing it all again for the first time. She ran her hands lightly over the drawings like Braille and didn't look up until she got to the end.

"There's this school—" I said.

Tara was crying again and I didn't know how much more of all this I could take. The wind shifted, carrying the smoky ghost of the Furnace back toward us, and Tara let out a sputtering cough and rubbed at her eyes.

"—I can work on this there," I told her. "My mother and me, we drove up there a couple days ago, after the funeral. They want to help me with the art—"

"Sketch—"

"I have to live there, but the school is only an hour away and I can get back here every chance—"

"You should go," Tara said, closing the book and clasping it to her chest. "You need to go."

"It's not here," I said, "where I'm supposed to be, I mean. Not in this town. I don't know where I'm supposed to be, but I know that much." My voice gave way. "Sometimes, it's like I'm living the wrong life, you know? I know that sounds like typical lame bullshit, but there's more to it than that. Everything's changed and I don't know what the hell happened. This used to be something, living here. Now it seems like the only life that makes any sense is the one I'm living in my own head. Crazy, I know, but that's the only way

I can explain it." I pointed toward the sketchbook. "When I'm there, when I'm drawing, I look at things and I don't see them the way they are, I see them the way they ought to be." I stopped for a moment. "Swear to God, Tara, I've been living in my own world for so long, I just might be cracking up. I need to … I should get out of here."

Tara sniffled and tried to smile with reassurance. "There's nothing wrong with looking for escape, Sketch, something to take you outside yourself. Look around here. That's what everyone is doing—they drink or they smoke dope or they start breaking the law—because they need some way to get out of their own heads. They throw themselves at anything that might do it for them. Help them escape."

"Like my mother, the way she works all the time—"

"Or Deacon, or anybody looking for the way out. But the thing is, you can't do that forever," Tara argued. "Not without destroying yourself." She held the book to me and let me take it from her. "But art, this talent, that's free. I can tell you one thing: if you give in to what you have here in this book, it will offer you such an escape, nothing else will ever come close."

I loved her. It wasn't just a word now. I knew it was too soon, I knew we were too young, I knew all of this. But I loved her nonetheless.

I slipped down from the rock and put out my hand. "Come here. Come with me."

Leaving our bikes resting on the dirt path, I guided Tara into the barrier of trees behind us. Neglected and overgrown, the branches overlapped in a thick tangle of leaves and limbs, which lashed at us as we plunged forward. For just a moment, the morning melted away and it was as though we'd been swallowed whole by another world. And then we were out, on the other side, standing at the edge of that enormous lawn, brown and dry as straw and overrun by weeds. The grounds were desolate and abandoned, conquered by the years, and all looked well beyond repair.

Alone at the top of the lawn sat the mansion, waiting.

Wishing Manor appeared as it was, ancient and forgotten. Like the lawn it surveyed, it too looked overtaken by time. The windows were covered in grime or shattered altogether, their shutters broken-slatted and rotted through, dangling more often than not by a single remaining hinge. The patio stones were upturned and disheveled. Like a reminder of some distant age, the walls of the house still rose tall and strong, but their plaster was cracked and covered in a mass of wet moss and vines. The clapboard appeared so badly weather-beaten, it was impossible to tell its original color. At the roofline above, the remains of a rusted iron railing clung to the edge, bent at its center and torn out over the eaves.

"I always thought I would live here someday," I told her, as we looked up at the house. "With you, maybe."

For the first time in days, I smiled, a wide honest grin. Then, attempting to diffuse the remark, I quickly laughed, a loud, raucous laugh that stirred a crow from a thicket of weeds behind us. For a long moment, Tara watched the bird fly away, until it slipped over the tops of the trees and dropped over the cliff and out of sight.

"You never know." Tara said, sounding uncertain whether I was teasing.

And that was enough. Just enough.

I smiled and took Tara's hand and found myself thinking once again of rebirth. I imagined a path ahead, green and lush and fragrant with all possibility. I was there again, on the resurrected grounds of Wishing Manor. The gardens around the patio and the perimeter of the estate, colorful and bursting with life. The birdsong a rich melody of high-pitched caws and whistles through the trees. And the house, gleaming new and waiting for me there on the hill.

I walked slowly toward it, gossamer curtains dancing through open windows, the smell of a warm fire wafting from the chimney. Then, I was running, my feet moving at an impossible clip. Boo stepped from the porch to greet me and then laughed as I rose suddenly from the ground, my feet dancing along the lawn like geese skimming a lake and then finally letting go. Waving and laughing too, I continued low to the ground, the house looming larger and larger, until just at the last possible moment I ascended toward the roof in the graceful, perfect arc of a well-wielded painter's brush. Then, I was over the roof and out above the trees and the creek and the town spread beneath me like a net waiting for me to fall. I smiled, and rose higher. Far behind, Boo and Tara waited patiently for my return. But I knew it would be a very long wait. I was flying now, reborn in the fires of a furnace that burned once more.

Higher I climbed.

Into the clouds, into my future, into my life.

Rising.

"Who would you like the book signed to?"

I look down at the woman, holding your new novel, her pen hovering over a pad of sticky notes.

"What's that?"

"Ms. Hart will personalize your book for you. I just want to write down your name for her, to help the line move faster."

The line is fifty deep, maybe more, wrapping back into the children's section of the old library. Even with the long wait I have ahead of me, I know I still won't have enough time to decide what I'm going to say to you.

"I don't think I'll have it personalized, thanks. I'm probably not staying."

The woman doesn't seem to like this answer, but she doesn't say anything and moves instead to the young couple behind me in line.

I was shocked to get your email, the invitation to this event. Maybe I considered myself a hard man to find or maybe I just assumed you had forgotten all about me. After all, we were nothing more than a first love. Children, really.

No, that's not right. We were far more. I know, Tara, I know. That time we shared, no matter how brief, that awful October seared a mark like a branding iron, red-hot and permanent.

As hard as it is for me to believe, my daughter is the same age we were then. And already she is straining against her childhood, making her own choices, wrestling her own demons, finding her own angels. Tomorrow, her fall break will draw to a close and she will return to boarding school. Her *path ahead is already unfolding—graduation in two more years, then college and career, perhaps marriage and even children of her own—as predetermined as mine was unpredicted. And sometimes the uncertainty of it all keeps me awake at night, like an illness.*

I wonder if you have children. Your biography never mentions a husband, a family. Even this new book jacket shares very little information beneath your photograph. Although I've often been curious, I've never allowed myself to search deeper. I figured you liked it that way, some remaining bits of mystery.

I've known of your books, of course. Someday maybe I'll tell you about the shock I felt when I saw your first novel in the window of a Baltimore bookstore, next to a poster promoting a book signing. I bought that book, and all the others that came after, but I didn't go to the signing. I can't explain my reasons. Just as I can't fully explain why I am going to step out of this line. But I think you'll understand. After all, you were the first to know that escape runs in my veins.

My own work has been a blessing, my life's calling, this life of renewal and rebirth. My business partner, a friend I met at The Blake School and then followed to college in New England, deserves much of the credit for our success, though maybe I brought a certain appetite for risk to the venture. Our architectural designs, office towers and public spaces and luxurious homes for the wealthy, were exceptional enough to win awards and recognition from Manhattan to Atlanta, but we made our names on the suburban renaissance that swept through the small towns over the last decade, bringing with it an influx of new money and an unprecedented need for new designs and plans for restoration. We were lucky. Although I know you would tell me that luck had nothing to do with it.

This work of renewal is what eventually led me away from the firm I helped build. My decision to resign from the partnership and take a different road was met by initial disbelief and skepticism, as might be expected. There must be something more to this, they said, a mid-life crisis or a delayed expression of grief brought on by my wife's premature passing. It was none of these, but my assurances always fell on deaf ears. Few seemed to understand that it simply was time.

Time to come home.

My current projects are rewarding and plentiful and any stress I may feel from deadlines is purely self-inflicted. Phoenixville is ripe with opportunities for the designs I can provide, blueprints for the renewal of prominent buildings at the center of town, schematics for the ambitions of planners and dreamers and social activists. Already, empty stores have been converted into bustling restaurants, overgrown fields into parks and playgrounds, a dilapidated movie theater into a lively arts venue. The old civic hall was refitted as a gymnasium and activity center for after-school youths, with the Police Athletic League watching over the proceedings. Although each of these projects has had its own rewards, I am most proud of my plans for the old foundry, an exacting replica of the Furnace, re-imagined as a tourist destination and museum saluting the industry that built this country.

Change has finally come to Phoenixville, Tara, and I find some peace in knowing my work plays a small role in the renewed spirit of optimism now drifting through the streets.

"Excuse me, sir?" The bubbly young woman behind me, clutching two copies of THE FURNACE BOY to her chest. Her boyfriend stands beside her, only slightly less anxious. "When we get up there, would you mind taking our picture with Tara? If she lets us?"

The line ahead of us is now half as deep, twenty people or so. I can see you at the table, offering each patron a warm smile and a handshake, signing your books with an enthusiastic flourish. As one fan steps away and another takes her place, you look toward the back of the line and our eyes meet—I'm sure of it this time. You immediately look away. But a different smile has appeared. The smile of a teenager. As you return to the next book set before you, you touch your white-tipped finger to your throat and your shirt collar opens, just slightly. Enough to reveal the necklace there, the same black necklace from so long ago.

"I'm sure she'll let you take a picture," I tell the girl behind me. "But I don't think I'll be able to stay much longer. We'll see."

Sometimes I worry that I am forgetting things. Not yet fifty and already my memory is fading. Entire segments of my life have disappeared, as though they never happened at all. My past is no longer moving images, but more like a slideshow of individual points in time, long gaps between them, snapshots without context. Still, my return to Phoenixville has revived more recollections, many arriving at unexpected moments. In front of shop windows along Bridge Street, on benches at the park, on the banks of French Creek. And on the roof of an old house.

The estate was owned by the town government, which showed interest in the property only when I expressed my own. Negotiations went on for quite some time, but I never wavered. The wealth I secured when I sold my share of the firm was more than enough to alleviate any concerns about price. I simply remained patient and allowed the lawyers to handle the process, knowing full well the house would end up in my possession. Just as it was predetermined.

After my daughter started at The Blake School last year, I decided to move back to Phoenixville. To be closer to her, yes, but you can imagine there were other reasons as well. I took an apartment on Main Street and checked frequently on our renovations to Wishing Manor. On breaks from school, my daughter and I explored the town I once couldn't wait to *escape. We took long walks through the neighborhood around the hospital, ate ice cream in the park, watched the kids play Wiffle ball in the street. Like you, she helped me see Phoenixville with new eyes. Finally, on a sun-soaked summer day just a few months ago, we moved into the old house on the hill, our new home.*

I selected the southwest corner of the house as my studio. There is the magnificent view of the back lawn and the cherished distraction of my daughter in her garden. There is the line of trees, grown impressively large over the years, and a great expanse of sky rich with colors born anew every hour. The tall windows let in the coveted natural light at most hours of the day. Best of all, the studio provides the solitude I need, my rock on which to sit, and for that I am grateful, if not astonished by the path my life has taken.

The original rock remains, of course, jutting over its cliff and buried beneath weeds I haven't bothered to clear away, but I rarely walk out there any more. I have a new favorite spot now.

Up on the roof of Wishing Manor, among the bats and the crows black against the twilight, I have found a new calm. The small town spread out before me still seems a thousand miles away sometimes, but the people there—those who live here now and those who came before—are as close as ever. High above everything, I can see it all, just as it was so long ago, just as we were.

There on the roof, I find myself thinking of you from time to time. I remember the usual promises to keep in touch, but these were promises broken easily and in short order as our lives found their own paths, one of us to boarding school and architecture and the other a victim of divorce and your mother's return to New York City. You faded into the mist, along with Harley and the twins, Romeo and Bigfoot, even Deacon and the boy in the Batman mask.

But that October, our October, is still there. Indelible.

Ten people ahead in line.

I am closer to you now than I've been in decades. You are still beautiful, as you smile up at a reader and hand her your signed novel, and still so clearly alive.

I didn't come for the book or to hear you read or to get your autograph, Tara. I came because you asked me, I came for you.

And to tell you that I'm sorry.

Six people in line.

Sorry that I left. That I chose Boo and robbery and fire and flight. Sorry that I abandoned you.

Three people.

We all live with permanent shames. Even you, I suspect. Betrayals, regrets, missteps from the path. And the way I see it now, we have two choices: bury them deeper and let them eat away at our souls like rats in the shadows, or work to overcome them, to rise above.

Two people now.

I open your book to its first pages and that's when I see the dedication and I know then that I have been wrong. I never abandoned you, just as you never left me. And Boo still lives. And this town, so full of history and legends, flows strong within us. And always will.

"For Sketch and Boo,
Furnace Boys, Forever"

I remember vivid details—the crackle of leaves that autumn long ago, the smell of fire, the sound of a certain girl's laughter, the color of my best friend's blood—even as other details are irretrievably buried. I remember young men, boys really, with dreams already smothered and ambitions undefined. And I remember this town, with soot-covered chimneys and a perpetual autumn, slumped between the mountains and a creek that still today runs high and deep.

From these details I will reconstruct our story the best I can. If only memory could be tamed. If everything we lived could be recalled in an instant, sure and definite and true. But memory is a slippery liar, a reckless child running free, concocting facts and fantasies with equal abandon. It lulls us into belief, even as it delights in deceit. But between truth and invention and the impossibility of distinguishing the two, what does it matter as long as the gist of the thing is accurate? Memory is all resurrection, a reliving, and there will be failures of recollection among the miracles. This won't matter. My daughter is old enough now to take the story in whole, to hear it for what it is: a lament, a warning, a humble history as much as it is a story. It is the best way I know to tell her of the choices I made at her age, the paths I took.

It would be a mistake to believe I am driven by the past, though my work is rooted so firmly in its clay. The past may be paradise to some, but for me it is merely foundation. Important, yes, but less so than what rises from it, the marvels and the wonders that reach and climb like smokestacks toward the clouds. I no longer think so much about the past. The present is my time now and the future and all it holds. I live for the moment, while looking forward, ever forward.

This is what I tell myself.

Still, in the middle of the night, when a train makes its way along the river from Black Rock or a truck rumbles through the borough not so very far away, a stirring comes to me like a visitor in the night and I remember. I do remember.

Like it was yesterday.

ACKNOWLEDGMENTS

I am indebted to everyone who helped me on the long and winding road to publication.

Special thanks to early readers and supporters Rich Peterec, Barbara Yost, Laura Gross, Peter Fey, Barry Fabius, Jason Hafer, and Jim Breslin. To Joseph R. Daughen, a fine journalist and an even better father-in-law. To authors and inspirations Anne Lamott, Dennis Lehane, Laura Lippman, Jael McHenry, George Pelecanos, Jodi Picoult, Scott Turow, and The Liars Club of Philadelphia (especially Jon McGoran and Dennis Tafoya), who each offered encouragement and wise counsel along the way. To Larry Geiger for his spectacular cover design. To Kristy Dempsey and Caroline Joy for their expert photography. And to all my friends on Facebook, Twitter, and www.robbcadigan.com.

Many thanks to the Historical Society of the Phoenixville Area, the Phoenixville Public Library, and the Schuylkill River Heritage Center for their help with research and access to their treasures. And to the many proud Phoenixville residents, especially Josh Gould, who shared recollections about their town.

The laser-focused editing by August Tarrier was instrumental in shaping this manuscript into the novel it is today. The talented Vu Tran provided vital editorial suggestions at the book's early stages, along with much-appreciated encouragement.

Very special thanks to Dan Hornberger, a gifted editor and teacher, who read this manuscript in several forms and offered advice that was at once insightful and invaluable.

My parents, Bob and Dorothy Cadigan, taught me hometown pride and a love of creativity in all its many forms. Thanks for letting me read comic books by the light of the moon, way past my bedtime.

From the day we met on a blind date at Bucknell University, my wife Joan has been my best friend, editor, sounding board, publicist, advisor, biggest fan, and the love of my life.

Finally, to Ryan and Caroline: I am so proud of the young adults you are. This is what Dad does all day. I made this for you.

AUTHOR'S NOTE

This novel is not a history of Phoenixville.

PHOENIXVILLE RISING is an imagination, inspired by the history of Phoenixville, Pennsylvania, and the many small American towns with similar stories and legends. I have tried to be faithful to the spirit of the place, even as I moved or invented landmarks, events, dates, and locales to suit the needs of this story. The proud history of the Phoenix Iron & Steel Company and its surrounding community is rich and vibrant. I encourage interested readers to visit the wonderful Historical Society of the Phoenixville Area, the Phoenixville Public Library, and the Schuylkill River Heritage Center (in the beautifully restored Foundry) for more accurate information about the true history of this remarkable area.

If you enjoyed this novel, please help spread the word.
Leave a review on amazon.com, Goodreads, and social media.
Suggest the story for your book club. Give the novel to others.
Thank you for supporting independent authors.

ABOUT THE AUTHOR

A former advertising copywriter and television executive,
Robb Cadigan lives with his wife and two children
in Chester County, Pennsylvania.
This is his first novel.

For more information about Robb and his writing,
visit www.robbcadigan.com and sign up for the mailing list.

8334061R00174

Made in the USA
San Bernardino, CA
07 February 2014